FAKED

SINNERS OF BOSTON #3

VANESSA WALTZ

Copyright © 2020 by Vanessa Waltz

All rights reserved.

No part of this book may be reproduced in any form or by any electronic or mechanical means, including information storage and retrieval systems, without written permission from the author, except for the use of brief quotations in a book review.

ISBN: 9798693825161

Imprint: Independently published

ABOUT THE BOOK

My feelings are forever...the engagement is not.

Vinn Costa used to hang the moon in my sky. He's my brother's brutally handsome best friend. He doesn't know I exist, but I've always loved him.

Until he did something unforgivable.

Vinn's not a sweet boy anymore. He's grown into a cold gangster. He's the most powerful man in Boston, a beautiful lost cause.

I cut him from my life. I moved on.

Or I would have, if he hadn't roped me into a lie so dangerous I had no choice to play along.

Now I have to pretend I'm his expecting fiancée, or we're both dead.

I need to walk away, but I have to see this through. I'm stuck...with the monster in the Vinn-suit.

PROLOGUE

Liana

D*EAD*.

The word made no sense. Sometimes I heard it in cartoons, but I could never understand what it meant. They'd said it over and over—*your parents are dead*.

Where was Mommy?

Why wasn't she back yet?

The quilted coverlet wrapped my body. My head pounded. I'd spent the day crying, dragging Charlotte, my stuffed rabbit, throughout the strange house with cold floors, chased from rooms by that boy—*Mike*. He was mean. He'd stolen Charlotte, and I couldn't go to sleep without her. I rubbed the crust of tears sealing my eyes shut.

The door creaked.

A boy stepped through in pajamas. I tried to disappear under the covers, and stopped. His hair brushed his shoulders. He seemed much younger than Mike. A shy grin tugged at his lips as he lowered something to me.

"Charlotte!" The wool scratched my face as I hugged the rabbit. "Thank you."

"You're welcome."

"Who are you?"

"Vinny. I'm Mike's cousin." He kneeled beside the bed. "What's your name?"

"Liana." A dim hope flickered in my chest. "Do you know where my mommy is?"

"Sorry." He pulled the comforter to my chin. Then he stroked my hair, from the side to the back, just like my mother. "Everything will be all right. You'll see."

"I miss her."

"You have us now. We'll be your family."

I wasn't sure about that, but I believed Vinny's smile. His gentleness had lulled me into safety. I slumped with exhaustion.

"It's time to sleep, Liana. Close your eyes."

"Okay."

He planted a kiss on my brow, and then he disappeared, closing the door softly. Heat flared across my cheeks and burrowed into my heart. Years later, I wondered why its warmth had never left me.

ONE
LIANA
TWO YEARS AGO

It took being trapped in a burning building to realize I was in love with Vinn Costa, my brother's best friend.

It was Christmas.

Vinn sat at the bar as my brother Michael danced with his seven-year-old daughter to a George Michael song. Tinsel and green decorated the walls of The Black Cat, a mob-owned lounge and restaurant where the boss of the Family liked to hold his annual holiday celebrations. A mountain of catered food was piled on tables, but the tantalizing scent failed to draw Vinn from his lonely corner. Twinkling lights cast a colorful pattern over him.

He had a broad hero's face, with a chiseled jaw. A shadow of stubble peppered his dimpled chin under a shapely mouth which beckoned a kiss. A strong nose led to eyes so dark and terrifying, staring into them gave me a thrill. A full-blooded Italian, Vinn sported the olive complexion I'd always envied.

He was gorgeous—I'd seen him shirtless—and he could've given Henry Cavill a run for his money.

A flood of heat engulfed my cheeks. The breath sucked from my lungs. I was a five on a good day, but Vinn was a perfect ten.

Since I was four, I'd crushed on Vinn Costa. He'd held my hand on trips to the beach. He'd saved me from running off and hurting myself. From the moment I met him, he'd protected me. But as we grew older, we drifted apart.

It'd been a while. School had kept me busy. The last text message we'd exchanged was back in April.

I stepped forward.

Rough fingers wrapped my arm, stopping me. I frowned at their owner, my oldest brother, Daniel. We looked nothing alike, because we weren't related by blood. His mom had adopted me. My birth parents were a mystery, present only in faded photographs and even more distant memories.

Daniel's skin was darker, his hair blacker, and his eyes two amber flames next to my blues. He was more than twice my age at forty-three, and my only father-figure. His hooded gaze narrowed as he followed my beeline to Vinn, his attitude drenched in disapproval.

"Liana. *Don't.*"

My stomach fell. "What?"

Michael detached from his daughter to stand beside Daniel, wearing an identical frown. They stood within an inch of each other's heights, but Michael was more fine-boned and lean. Though, as similar as they may have looked, they never agreed on anything.

Growing up with two older brothers hadn't been easy. Family dinners became an excuse for Michael and Daniel to try to assert dominance over the other. They'd left me out of their fights, but it was still a grim way to grow up.

"You know what I'm talking about." Daniel's frigidity gave no doubt on the subject. "Leave him alone."

"It's Christmas," I whispered. "I was just going to say hi."

"And you hoped he'd ask you out? Because you brought him a gift?" Daniel's smirk was a little too knowing. "Oh, Li. You need to give this up."

"I have no idea what you're talking about."

"Come on, Li. You're not that dumb."

"*Easy.*" Michael shot him a glare. "She's a kid."

"Not anymore," Daniel snapped, oblivious to the agony building in my chest. "I should've said something a long time ago, but I held off because you're so young. Watching you pine after him embarrasses me."

His caustic tone bit my cheeks. They'd *both* seen through me, and it stripped me emotionally naked.

"Who says I am?"

"It's obvious, hon. I thought you'd grow out of it." Michael's mouth twitched with a bleak smile. "I know you're crazy about him, but it'll never happen."

It was like he'd fisted my heart. "You don't think Vinny likes me?"

"Not the way you want him to, sweetheart."

My eyes burned before he finished the sentence. "Maybe—"

"It won't happen. *Ever*."

A violent flush claimed my face as my insides rebelled.

Michael took my shoulder. "You're such a nice girl. There *is* a guy out there for you, but he won't be Vinn."

"Why not?"

Daniel groaned, kneading his forehead. "Fuck's sake, Liana."

"He's too damaged," Mike cut in. "He'll hurt you. And, more importantly, he is not interested."

Michael's determination to stamp out my attraction to Vinn was nothing new. He always had a not-so-subtle jab ready whenever he caught me hanging around his cousin-turned-best-friend, but I'd never heard it so bluntly. Every word sawed into me.

"Did he say that?"

"He doesn't have to." Michael released a long sigh, his tone pitying. "Don't take it personally. Vinn's twenty-eight years old. You're *nineteen*. That's a big gap."

"You're both assholes."

Daniel patted my head. He left, abandoning me with this hateful bastard.

Michael and I had never gotten along.

He'd mellowed out once he had a baby, but I'd never forget the angry teenager who hated me for existing.

"Why couldn't you leave me be?"

"Trust me. This conversation is just as painful for me." Michael massaged his temples. "I'd rather jump into a wood chipper than discuss my sister's crush on my best friend."

"I wish you would. I can't stand you."

"*Nice*. That's real nice, Li."

"I don't care. I'm not one of your kids," I hissed. "You don't get to swoop in and be overprotective after a lifetime of being an ass."

"I'm trying to give you a fast track to happiness." Michael gestured at his wife, Serena. "Life's too short to waste it on someone who doesn't notice you."

Ganging up on me about Vinn was a bridge too far. All I'd wanted to do was talk. What gave Michael the right to police my business? Compared to him, I was halfway to sainthood.

I looked at Michael. "What does your loveless marriage have to do with me?"

Michael bristled. His grip whitened on his glass before he slammed it onto the bar.

"Fine. Don't come crying to me when he blows you off again."

Ouch.

A rush of heat claimed my cheeks, but he'd said worse.

Was I wasting my time? Vinn had a life. I'd spent mine wishing I could change the impossible.

If only I weren't Michael's kid sister.

If only Vinn felt a fraction of my longing.

If only he weren't trapped in the arms of a gorgeous redhead.

A girl of staggering beauty had materialized on Vinn's lap. She used Vinn's massive thigh like a bench. Her manicured fingers caressed his glossy black shirt and tie with an intimacy that clenched my guts. She plastered kisses over his jaw as I struggled to breathe, the pain at watching him with another woman so raw.

I wanted to disappear.

Vinn responded to her antics with lukewarm interest, sliding his hand under her thighs, riding up her dress, but his gaze wandered as though he searched for a replacement. His eyes found mine. He stared, probably wondering why I glared at him while a woman dry-humped his groin. Without breaking away, he uttered a dismissal.

"Get out of here."

She giggled. "Merry Christmas, baby."

"Yeah, whatever."

"See you." She seized his lapels and kissed his mouth. "I've got a gift waiting for you in my apartment. You should stop by."

"Maybe," he said, but rolled his eyes at her back. He beckoned at me. "Li, come here."

As I approached, violent words begged to purge from my lips. I could barely hold my tears from the vicious gut-punch.

"Who is she?"

Vinn shot me a peculiar look. "Some chick."

"Your girlfriend?"

"For the week, sure." Vinn's low, gravelly tone stirred my stomach, awakening the butterflies. "What are you up to?"

"Nothing much."

"Were you ever going to say hello?"

I crossed my arms. "'Course."

Looking at him pained me. His shirt and slacks were wrinkled where she had rubbed on him, and she'd mussed his beautiful hair. I could practically smell her on him.

Vinn peered at me. "You okay?"

"Why does something have to be wrong?"

"Well, you're not talking my ear off, which is a red flag."

I wanted to tell him the truth—he meant the world to me, and it killed me that I'd always be his best friend's baby sister. I understood why we couldn't be together. Michael and Vinn worked for the Family. The last thing the boss needed was a rift between his captains, and as Michael pointed out, Vinn wasn't interested in a nineteen-year-old.

I usually grimaced through the pain, but not tonight. I couldn't talk to him. I flourished the wrapped present—a stupid throwback to our youth—and shoved it onto the bar counter beside his hand.

"Merry Christmas, Vinn."

Then I grabbed a half-open bottle of Chianti and disappeared into the Employees Only area. I walked through three sets of doors before shutting myself in a closet-sized office. I lifted the wine to my lips as the party raged. Nobody would miss me, and at least I wouldn't have to float on a wave of sadness when Vinn summoned another girl to keep him company. I was sinking into a stupor when a loud explosion rocked the wall.

Drunken idiots.

Christmas parties frequently spiraled out of control. Everybody overindulged. They sometimes performed ridiculous stunts. Before Michael had kids, he was wild. He'd done the dumbest shit, like drunken races with his cousins with a lit cigarette in his mouth. For a while, they got into firecrackers. Not the cheap, kiddie ones—the sort that blew a hole through your eardrum from the blast. Michael's Audi used to blaze through the Pike as he threw fireworks at other people's cars. Explosions seemed par for the course, so I wasn't alarmed at the noise nor the scandalized shrieking that was probably my aunts yelling at some moron.

I drank, ignoring the commotion, and then alarms shrieked overhead.

Whoa. I should see what's going on.

I stood.

The world swam as I opened the door and inhaled acrid air. As I headed out, my skull pounded. Everything became a confusing swirl of blackness. The smoke thickened. Where was the exit? The air bit at my nostrils. My eyes stung. I coughed and doubled over, swooning.

"Liana!"

No, not *him*.

A deep burn scorched my cheeks at the idea of Vinn catching me in a vulnerable state.

He stood near the light, his male figure silhouetted against smoke. His head turned left and right.

"Li, where the fuck are you?"

I raced headlong into the black, toward the heat. *Go away*, I prayed as he tore through rooms. *Leave me alone.*

My head spun as I slumped down, close to tears, way too drunk.

"Liana!" His heavy footsteps shook the ground. "Jesus Christ, kid. Do you not hear the sirens? What are you doing on the floor?"

Kid.

The swell of pain was beyond tears.

I opened my mouth to tell him to go away and inhaled a lungful of smoke. My consciousness zipped out and snapped back into place.

He'd seized my upper arm and yanked me upright. He propelled me forward, dragging me across the floor and outside, where my exhausted lungs filled with oxygen. His powerful grip spun me around. He shoved me toward an EMT.

A mask smothered me as Vinn stood nearby. He had saved me—after heartbreak had almost killed me. His image melted as my vision misted. Then he patted my head the same way Daniel had.

The ache slammed into my chest.

Damn...I really loved him. But I would never be happy if he lingered in my life.

Vinn was an unhealthy addiction. Interacting with him gave me hits of dopamine. The false high always left me unsatisfied and craving more.

Michael was right.

I'd never have Vinn.

I had to find someone who loved me. I'd learn to exist in a world without him because, if this continued, I wouldn't live at all.

While his back was turned, I abandoned the sidewalk blinking with red lights.

I didn't crane my neck to check if he'd followed.

I was done with Vinn.

TWO

LIANA

TWO YEARS LATER

I moved on.

It wasn't the straightest of lines. Like all addicts, I relapsed, but after Daniel's murder, I deleted Vinn from my phone and strangled the part of me that loved him. That Vinn was long gone. I shoved him out of my life, but sometimes he dropped into my mind unbidden, like a pleasant summer rain tickling my skin. Then I'd remember my brother's closed-casket funeral, and heartache fisted my throat.

I didn't think he'd be here.

My insides froze as my gaze passed over a familiar frame. Awash in gold-red light, Vinn's carved features stood out among the plain-faced mafiosos. A pretty girl I'd seen once or twice kissed his granite-like mouth.

I wanted it not to hurt.

I spun from the infuriating sight, searching for

Michael in the smoke-filled bar. He sat beside a mafioso in his thirties, who shot me an ear-to-ear smile.

"Speak of the devil." Michael grinned as the man got up. "Li, join us."

"Hey, Liana. How are you?"

"I'm good. It's Leo, right?"

Leo beamed, as though his name falling from my lips had made his night. He offered me his chair. "I'll let you catch up with your brother."

"Thanks."

I took my seat, and he drifted away. My elbows upset the pile of cards, earning a hiss from Michael.

"Watch it."

"Sorry. What are you playing?"

"Hand and Foot. Not that it matters." Michael shoved the cards together and clicked his tongue. "Vinn can't sit still long enough to finish a round. Anyway, thank you for coming. I've been meaning to talk to you."

"What'd that guy want?"

"You." Michael chuckled, packing his Ziplock. "He asked for permission to date you."

"*Really?*"

"He's a bit old, though. Thirty-eight."

I spotted Leo nearby. He caught my eye and winked. "Someday, a man will ask me out instead of going to you."

"Not done in our world."

"A girl can dream."

He snorted. "You're thinking like an outsider, not a Costa."

Daniel's constant refrain.

My throat tightened. "He would've wanted me to follow my heart."

"Daniel would've sold you to the highest bidder."

That sank a stone in my gut. Daniel wasn't perfect, but he was like my dad. Michael felt the same way, but it had never stopped him from insulting Daniel.

"Sorry," Michael murmured, looking remorseful for once. "I'm trying."

I nodded.

He'd turned a one-eighty after marrying a kind woman named Carmela, whom he'd met after Serena died. I was happy for my brother, but a pang of jealousy hit my chest. I'd *kill* for a relationship like theirs.

"I just want what you have, Mike."

He raised a brow. "Carmela?"

I threw a straw at him. "You know what I mean, idiot."

"I didn't expect to love her," Michael conceded, smiling wistfully. "Though I'd hoped it would lead to something more."

"I can't have that, too?"

"Sure you can." Michael eyed the seashell hanging around my neck. "Where's the guy who gave you that?"

Dead.

A vision consumed my mind—navy dress pants with a red stripe, seagulls cawing, warm waves lapping my feet, and the soldier who folded my fingers over a jagged shell. Our love was never allowed to blossom, because it'd been one-sided. Unrequited.

When I finally realized he was gone, I smothered those feelings. I mourned and moved on. I shook my head, clearing my senses of the sea and his gentle touch.

"He's out of the picture."

Michael digested that, his brows creasing. "So you know, I've received offers demanding your hand in marriage. I've said no to them, but you have a very aggressive suitor. He's a biker in Legion."

My heart pounded as I pictured the man who'd terrorized Michael's wife.

"*A biker?* Who?"

"You've never met him, but he's seen you at events."

My chest tightened as the sounds in the bar seemed to magnify. "You're not considering this."

"It's not that simple—"

"After what happened to Carmela, you'd give me to *them?*"

"I'm stalling him," he ground out. "There's a difference."

"When did he propose?"

"A while ago." Michael tucked the cards into his

jacket, his hooded eyes narrowing. "You're my sister. You're more than a bargaining chip. That's why I want to set you up with someone who will treat you well. I don't care who you pick but do it fast. This guy is relentless."

"Can't you tell him no?"

"Unfortunately, we're in a bind. He's high up. I can't say no without a good reason, like if you're already engaged."

"Ah. *Engaged.* I get it."

"No, Li." His lips pulled into a taut smile. "None of my guys will settle for a fake engagement."

"But you just dumped this in my lap! How long do I have? Two weeks? *One?* You expect me to find a husband like that—and why am I even considering this? I'm not getting married. I'm barely legal to drink."

"It's not what I wanted, either."

"I have my own life, Michael—separate from this mafia shit."

"Mafia shit," he repeated, his tone cooling. "You wouldn't have a sick-ass apartment in Allston-Brighton if it weren't for *mafia shit.* You wouldn't be able to afford the tuition at your ridiculously expensive Ivy League school or have any money for shopping, food, and *clothes,* if not for me."

"I need those things."

"I know you do, but show some respect for the Family." Michael leaned over the table, pinning me with his intense glare. "You've had it easy, baby girl. You have no idea what it's like to grow up hungry. You've had a cushy upbringing, and I've never asked you for a goddamned thing. All I want from you is your part."

I followed his gaze to Leo. "Which is?"

"I'm not saying you have to marry him, but give Leo a chance."

Fuck. "What if I hate him?"

"You won't. He's nice."

Whatever.

It wasn't a big deal to talk to a man for a few minutes. I'd entertain Michael, make my excuses, and split, but my brother was high if he thought I'd elope with a stranger. No, I'd get out of marrying the Legion biker on my own. I stood and headed toward the bar, forcing a smile as I approached Leo.

He was handsome in the traditional sense, but he wasn't drop-dead gorgeous. Crow's feet wrinkled his skin, and gray peppered his brown mane. He stepped aside, giving me his stool.

"Hey, there."

I liked his voice. It was smooth and thick, and as tempting as a warm bath. I sat beside him, which unfortunately gave me a front-row seat to Vinn making out with the flavor of the week.

"*So.*" Leo stared at me shrewdly. "You old enough to be here?"

"I'm twenty-one."

Relief rippled across his brow. "What's your poison?"

"I'm still figuring that out."

"Then I'll have to guess." He flagged the bartender. "Two Moscow mules."

Leo passed the copper drink and bumped his mug against mine.

I sipped, my nose wrinkling at the harsh taste. "So, what do you do?"

"I deal with construction. I'm a project manager. Lots of meetings with architects and city hall officials." He waved it off and leaned into his hand. "What about you? College student?"

"Yeah. Bourton."

He whistled. "Wow."

"Don't be impressed. I have no clue what I'm doing."

"They don't let just *anyone* into Bourton."

"Sure they do. You just need deep pockets or a family member who was an alumnus." I motioned him closer, whispering. "Have you heard of Alessio Salvatore?"

"Of course."

"He paid off the board to admit his wife. She didn't even take the SATs." The injustice of it burned every time I glimpsed her on campus.

"Sounds like my line of work. Bureaucracy gets

waived with enough cash. Do you know what you want to do?"

"Not yet."

"Well, a girl like you has a lot of options. Especially for dating."

"Because I'm Michael's sister?"

"Because you're beautiful."

"Thank you." The compliment stroked my body like warm feathers. It was a little cheesy, but I liked the attention.

"I saw you here a couple of days ago. All by yourself." He clicked his tongue. "No bodyguards, either."

I grabbed his wrist. "Tell Michael, and I'll kill you."

"Do I get any last requests?"

"None."

He laughed, his rich voice smoothing to a decadent silkiness. "I won't say a word, but I insist on walking you home."

"If you must."

My brother's promotion to consigliere came with its consequences, like an increased risk of being shot. Michael often complained that Vinn refused his security.

I hated him, but still hoped he was safe.

My gaze darted to Vinn.

Leo's finger slid along my jaw, pulling me toward him. My skin tingled as he released me.

"Your hand looks heavy. Can I hold that for you?"

My cheeks burned, but I nodded.

Leo's rough calluses glided over my palm, and then he balled me in his fist. Warmth buzzed inside me as he stroked me, right there on the bar counter.

I chanced a look at Vinn, who'd stopped reacting to the girl on his lap. His stare struck me through the smoky lighting. Seconds ticked by, and Vinn stood, a fortress of power.

He muttered something that made his date flinch. Abandoning her, he stormed across the room. He was like a dark cloud, gaining energy, siphoning attention.

What the hell?

Men in suits gathered behind him like predators sensing a kill.

This would not end well.

Vinn was tall and packed with enough muscle to fuel a football team, and he seemed to despise Leo, who greeted him warmly.

"Mr. Costa. Can I help you?"

"Who are you?"

Vinn's graveyard voice was like a magic spell, infecting the atmosphere with fear. A deathly quiet interrupted the clinking of pool balls, the laughter, and the clattering of flatware. Everybody watched us.

Leo cleared his throat. "Leo DiMaggio."

Vinn didn't seem soothed by the information. He

stared at Leo as though he'd just admitted to fucking me without a condom. His lip curled, taking in our closeness with apparent disgust. His accusatory gaze landed on me.

My stomach clenched.

What did I do?

Leo squeezed my hand. It felt nice, like lukewarm tap water, but Vinn's presence made it off-putting.

Vinn glared at our linked hands. "DiMaggio, a word in private."

"Be back soon." Leo sighed heavily, following Vinn to a deserted corner.

Chatter broke out as they walked away. I fiddled with my jewelry until their animated discussion pushed my curiosity and overwhelmed my common sense.

I approached them, Vinn's baritone railroading Leo's softer, insistent words.

"This isn't happening. You're not dating that girl."

Unexpected warmth shot through me. Since when did Vinn take a vested interest in who I dated?

"You can't be serious," Leo croaked, gaping at Vinn. "What's your problem with me?"

"I don't have to explain myself."

"So it has nothing to do with *you* wanting to add her to your Rolodex of flings?"

"Nobody uses a Rolodex anymore, but you wouldn't know that because you're too *fucking* old." Vinn's sneer rose to a shout as he cornered the increasingly rattled Leo. "I can make a scene and hurt you, or you can walk out of here. Those are your options. *No.* Don't look at Michael. He can't help you."

"He gave me permission!"

Vinn's black eyes flickered in the direction of Michael, whose stare burned with an air of a ravenous wolf waiting for the other to kill his struggling prey. "Doesn't matter. You didn't ask for mine."

"I wasn't aware I *had* to."

"Not everybody knows how close I am to Michael's family, so I'll give you a pass. One fucking pass. I don't approve, and it stops now."

"Based on what?"

"She is a catch." Vinn's glare could've melted paint from the walls. "*You* are not."

I winced, the pain from that vicious comment nailing me in the gut. "Vinn, stop. You're way out of line."

Vinn kept his focus on Leo, pointing at the door. "Go."

Leo's dejected gaze flicked to my shoes before he murmured a goodbye. Then he turned and disappeared into the crowd of smirking men.

Mortified, I went after him.

Vinn grabbed my arm, pulling me into his orbit. "You're not seeing him again."

"What is wrong with you?"

Vinn's grip tightened. "*Me?* What are you doing with a loser like DiMaggio?"

"We were getting along fine." I shrugged, irritated. "You didn't have to run him off. I *liked* him."

"Unless you're into changing adult diapers in a few decades when he turns geriatric, I suggest you move on."

The bastard was probably right.

That didn't mean I'd thank him for ruining my night. Annoyance darted my heart as he winked, apparently taking my silence as submission. Then the arrogant fuckhead dragged his fingers through my hair, patting my back as though he'd done me a huge solid.

Rage festered inside me like an infected wound, boiling to the surface. He was such a condescending asshole.

I couldn't take it anymore.

"Fuck off, Vinn."

Michael's groan cut through the male, scandalized jeers, but I ignored his chastising *Li-ah-na* and stared Vinn down.

"What did you say to me?"

I squared my shoulders. "Fuck off."

Michael shot upright. "Li, that's enough."

No.

I'd never been so rude to Vinn. I'd always been a tongue-tied, stammering mess, throwing myself at the nearly-ten-years-older man with an embarrassing lack of self-control, but I was finished with being nice. I didn't care how bad it looked.

"Everybody here might scrape and bow to this *asshole*, but I won't." I tore my gaze from Vinn and glared at a horrified Michael. "I'm not a sycophant. If you don't like it, my middle finger salutes you."

I flashed it at them and strolled for the exit, elbowing past grinning men. A couple of them cheered as I burst outside into the streets clinging with a warm mist. I headed toward the subway, heart hammering.

"Li, wait!"

I kept walking.

"*Hey*." Vinn jogged to my side. "You're ignoring me now?"

"You're not worth it."

"Says the girl who used to be all up in my shit."

"Yeah, well." My face burned at the reminder. "Those days are over."

"You're telling me. I don't tolerate—"

"Go nurse your wounded pride with someone else."

He laughed. "When did you become so difficult?"

"About the same time I stopped giving a damn about you."

"*Liana*." He gripped my elbow, stopping me. "I'm not messing around. You can't talk to me like that."

"I'll insult you however I want when you mess with my personal life."

"You won't—"

"And whenever you're with another woman, I'll be there to make a big stink about how their vagina isn't the right fit for your cock and run them off."

Vinn raised his brow so high that it was in danger of joining his hairline. I'd never said the word *cock* in front of him. If anything, he seemed amused.

"Have at it. I'd pay good money to see that."

I snorted. "You might change your mind when you can't get hookers to line up for you anymore."

"You have a filthy mouth."

"I've grown up, in case you haven't noticed."

Judging by his bobbing throat, he hadn't. "Leo's not your type."

"How would you know?"

His mouth thinned. "What were you doing in there?"

"Looking for a one-night stand."

A flash of warmth passed through his stony expression, like a match igniting kindling. "What was the plan? Leave with the first guy who paid you attention?"

"Yeah. So?"

I smirked when that seemed to infuriate Vinn.

"I should've let you take off with DiMaggio," he said acidly. "He would've lasted about five seconds."

"I doubt it. I've dated older men." I hadn't, but Vinn's outrage tickled my stomach. "I think he would've been quite the ride. Handsome. Confident. Nice. A *great* flirt. Gosh, the things he said."

"He's lucky I didn't hear them."

"Would you have hurt him?"

"Of course." He ground the word out. "That's sick."

He still saw me as a little girl.

A ripple of anger went through me. "I'm not a China doll. I won't break if I go out with Leo DiMaggio."

"No, but *he* will."

I shot him a penetrating glare. "Not up to you."

A shadow flickered over his face. "Liana, I'm trying to protect you."

"All you did was massage your ego." My gaze dragged down his body and flicked to his slanted eyes. "Makes a girl wonder why you feel the need to flex your muscles. Are you not measuring up in another way?"

"I'd tell you to go fuck yourself, but I'm sure you'll be disappointed."

"Hilarious." I stepped around him, and he uttered a frustrated noise.

"How are you getting home?"

"The same way I arrived," I threw over my shoulder, surprised that he still followed. "What are you doing?"

"You can't take the subway."

"*Yes, I can.*"

"Martial law. Mandated curfew." He gestured at the

walled-up businesses. "There's a biker war tearing apart this city. Michael would lose his shit."

"Leave me alone."

He grabbed my elbow and yanked me into his chest. "Stop blowing me off."

"It's annoying, isn't it?"

"*Enough.*"

He clutched my neck, startling me. Then he pushed. My back struck the wall, but the hand didn't pin me there.

His eyes.

Fathomless, black, and fiery.

They wouldn't let me go.

Vinn's frosty demeanor rarely thawed. He was a beautiful, giant block of ice suspended in outer space. I used to think he was unbreakable, but I was mistaken—he was *unreachable*. It seemed that I'd provoked him into an unreasonable rage. The freezer burn spread where his touch lingered, and, as he closed the distance between us, heat consumed me.

"I'm the boss of this family." He steamed with an anger never before directed at me. "Not your childhood friend."

"Yeah. That's been clear for a while."

"I won't hesitate to make an example of you."

Whenever Vinn made an example of someone, they ended up in a funeral parlor.

I despised him.

I hated the thin chill clinging to his words, his instincts for brutality, the way he looked at me, his *infuriating* arrogance. Most of all, I loathed the heat spinning in my belly as he held me. When he was close, he bathed me in his fresh scent that recalled those summers at Salisbury Beach when I was too young for him.

My memories of Vinn were sweet. Reality was bitter.

He'd finally noticed me, but I *hated* him.

I had to finish this before he destroyed me, so I rattled off what I'd spend the week regretting.

"Vinn, go fuck yourself with the fat end of a pineapple."

THREE

LIANA

I'D PUSHED him too far.

The set of his chin suggested I was in trouble. His tall figure stiffened, his stony features kindling with rage. His pupils had dissolved into the black pools that'd watched the end of so many lives, and his fingers tightened on my neck.

The gold chain cut into my skin, which struck me as morbidly ironic. I'd die wearing this stupid necklace, strangled by the very thing that had shoved me into Vinn's path.

Hope.

"Perhaps you're under the impression that you're special," he rasped in the dead voice I hated. "You can talk to me however you want. You're Michael's little sister. I'd *never* put my hands on you."

"I don't believe that anymore. You're nothing but a huge disappointment."

His mouth curved with a cynical twist. "What part of me isn't living up to your expectations?"

My hand grazed his muscled chest and rested over his heart.

Vinn's head jerked as though startled by the touch. He frowned, cold dignity carving into his face. He scooped up my hand and pinned it on the wall behind me. Our eyes clashed, and my stomach flipped.

"If I'm harsh, it's because I have to be."

What a pitiful excuse.

"Nobody makes Vinn Costa do anything."

"For now," he agreed. "That won't last if I allow you to disrespect me."

"So what's your plan? Beat me until I cry?"

I smoldered when he rolled his eyes. He shot me a look that flickered with heat.

"Something like that."

His threat hung in the air, darkening the atmosphere.

"If Michael were here, he'd stop you." My words tumbled out in a broken whisper. "You wouldn't dare."

"You're right," he drawled. "Let's go somewhere private."

Fear jangled in my insides as he grabbed me, but I couldn't deny the spark in my chest. His embrace still wrapped me in all-encompassing warmth, and his appeal was devastating. I shut out my awareness of him and shoved his biceps, fighting his viselike hold.

"Stop! Let me go!"

He pulled me violently toward him, locking his arm around my waist. I choked back a scream as he cinched tight. My breathing hitched as he kicked open a random service door, yanking me through a darkened restaurant. His loud footsteps drowned the thudding of my heart.

Stainless steel gleamed from the moonlight that filtered inside, but Vinn manhandled me past the kitchen and thrust me toward an eating area with vinyl booths.

"Get off, Vinn." I swallowed the tight knot begging for release. "You don't want to do this."

His lean body molded into my curves. "What am I doing?"

My stomach churned. "No idea."

"*Guess.*"

I flinched at his whiplike tone.

Vinn wasn't a man of impulse. He weighed every action against its rewards and consequences. He took nothing lightly, which meant I'd soon be writhing in pain. His hand was buried in my thick hair, his grip punishing. Hard.

My struggle ended in a few breathless seconds. He rendered me immobile with a vicious yank of my arms. He'd twisted them behind my back, balling my wrists in his powerful fingers. He shoved me over a table. His hard body was on top, pinning me.

"Vinn, stop!"

"Stop *what*?" he taunted.

"I don't know," I growled into the wood, desperate for a wall between us. "But going any further is a huge mistake!"

"I doubt my life will be impacted in the slightest." He teased the hem of my dress, gently stroking a growing fire. "And maybe you'll learn to shut up."

"I won't be silent if you hurt me!"

"Let me count all the fucks I give." His quiet voice seethed with cold contempt. "None."

My startled hurt turned to white-hot anger. "What the hell are you doing?"

My pulse skittered as he grabbed my thighs and casually moved upward. The brazenness lodged a golf ball in my throat, the roaring in my head drowning the panic.

He'd never fondled me. An alarming amount of heat dipped into my belly as he took my hips, close enough to thrust my legs apart and—

No.

"Vinn, this is crazy." I turned, catching his feral gaze. "What would Michael say?"

"I'm not thinking about your brother." He slapped my cheek. "But he'd agree that you need a firm hand to tame that out of control mouth."

"I'm pretty sure he'd kill you."

"What about my wrath?" His grip tightened, and blood rushed where his fingers branded me. "You should worry about what I'll do to you."

"Get off me!"

"No."

I stamped on his boot, grinding my heel where his toes should've been. It broke off on the hard surface, causing me to stumble. His soft laughter grated at me as he slid closer, wedging me between his knees.

"Congratulations," I snarled. "You've overpowered a woman a quarter of your size. I'll buy you a fucking medal. Can I go home now?"

"Not yet."

I gritted my teeth. "But I did nothing wrong."

"*Liar.* You've been rude, obnoxious, and petulant. You told me to fuck off in front of everyone. If you think I'll let that slide, you're delusional." He bent, his body folding over mine. "I am not letting you go until I believe you're sorry."

I wouldn't be. *He* would.

My chest pulsed against the wood as his weight crushed me. Somehow, I found enough air to snap at him. "I'm sorry I'm not a braindead idiot like everyone else."

My heart somersaulted as he yanked at something on his waist. There was a metallic jingle, followed by the slapping of leather. A sensual thrill stroked my body as he fisted my dress to my middle back.

Too fast.

"Wait," I begged, licking my lips. "Let's—let's talk."

A deep note rumbled from his throat. "An improvement already."

I had no idea what he intended with the belt, and I didn't want to find out. "Look. I was having a bad day."

"Liar."

"What do you want me to say?" I burst, fed up with his bullshit. "That I misspoke? I meant every fucking word. I should've kept it to myself. I should never be honest with you."

"Don't turn this on me. You screwed up."

"I told the truth!"

"You keep saying that, like honesty gets you far in life. It fucking doesn't, Li. Look at where you are. Bent over, humiliated, about to be punished. Just because you couldn't smile and kiss my cheek." His featherlight touch became a swift burn as the leather swatted me. "I'm the boss. You are an unmarried woman. We aren't equal. You belong to nobody."

"Michael—"

"Michael isn't here, and you can't hide behind him forever."

This was spiraling out of control.

Since Vinn took over as boss, his arrogance had soared to dangerous heights.

He thought he could get away with this?

I struggled to free myself, but he shoved my back.

"You're good right there."

"Vinn, *please*. You've made your point."

"I have yet to make an impression on you." He palmed my ass, giving it a rough squeeze.

A hot ache grew in my throat. "Vinny!"

"Don't *Vinny* me. That hasn't worked for a while."

A surge of heat consumed my body as though I'd been shoved into a furnace. "I'll go to Michael!"

"I'm not afraid of your brother."

Vinn wound the belt around my wrists, cinching the knot. Then he pulled the excess leather like a leash, forcing me to hover.

My heart pounded as he explored my curves, his hands soft. A sheer black fright kept me riveted. I ignored the strange pang ensnaring my limbs as Vinn played with my thong. He hooked his finger, snapping it. The sound was like a gunshot to my heart.

When did my childhood crush become a nightmare?

"Stop now, Vinn. I won't mention this to Michael. Any of it." My voice broke as I bargained for control. "Go any further, and that's off the table."

"I'll pass."

I bucked forward. "You're a fucking lunatic!"

"You were doing so well with the pleading and negotiating." He tutted, tracing my lips with his forefinger.

"Vinn, take a breath. Think about what you're doing!"

"Oh, I am." He yanked my arms, pinning me against his chest. "You'll remember me whenever you sit. When you step out of the shower. When you meet my gaze at a social function and I smile."

A spanking?

Oh my God, he couldn't be serious. Shame flooded my cheeks as I pictured my flayed body underneath Vinn's. My pulse throbbed so hard that he probably felt my fear.

"Fuck you," I growled, hating myself for trembling. "I will get you for this, Vinn Costa. I swear to God, I will ruin you."

He smiled a rare grin that would've made me melt like butter if he weren't such a monster.

"We both know I run this town. I'm untouchable. You, however..." Vinn palmed my back, bending me. "You're begging to be slapped, groped, and *fucked*."

He gave my ass a condescending tap. Then his palm lifted.

WHACK!

Agony burst across my skin. He landed another blow. The force knocked the protest from my mouth.

Vinn's big hand struck me. Pain returned with a

flash. I jumped forward, gasping with the fierce sting. Agony spread from cheek to cheek as his palm rained hellfire. He *hit* me—I couldn't believe it. Humiliation flushed my neck and face as he unleashed his rage. The more I struggled, the harder he smacked. He alternated between open-palmed blows and sharper swipes, hitting me so hard that tears slammed into my eyes. I bit my lip to keep from crying. It hurt, but the shame of a man I'd held a torch for beating me into submission was a thousand times worse.

Vinn stopped. He stroked the raw skin as I clung to the table, shaking. A thrill knotted in my stomach as his fingers scraped my thong, pulling it to my knees.

"What are you doing?"

Vinn answered with a brush of his fingers on my inner thigh, the sensual touch lighting me on fire. He continued to spank me. With each strike, he was a little bolder, following my curves to intimate places.

Oh my God.

"Vinn, *please*. Please let me go."

"Tell me you're sorry and that you'll be a good girl."

"I'm sorry. I'll be..." I trailed off, swept in the heat blooming in my body. "Jesus."

He pinched me. "Say it."

I gritted my teeth. "I'm sorry I told the fucking truth!"

"Li, I can give it to you much harder."

I bit my lip against the delightful shiver of *wanting*. *Do it.*

The challenge almost tumbled from my mouth. Graphic images flooded my head, my pulse racing. I *enjoyed* this. I'd never known that I liked it rough. Waves of shock slapped me. I could've laughed at the irony, but he would get more forceful and then...it'd be obvious that he'd affected me.

I couldn't let him find out. "Enough. S*top*."

"You know what to say."

"I-I'm sorry." I licked my dry lips. "I'll be a good girl."

"And you won't tell Michael." He tweaked the burning muscle, his voice smoldering. "Because if you do, my retribution will be a lot worse than a sore ass."

My stomach dropped.

I couldn't believe what I heard. "Are you threatening me?"

"Yes," he said, grinning. "I am."

He squeezed.

I gasped.

The pain sharpened from the dull ache, and then his palm lingered below my ass. A small noise rumbled from his chest, an appreciative groan that charged the atmosphere.

This felt different.

Dirty.

He swept the curvature of my hip, his grip tightening

and loosening. He cupped my cheeks, stroking my curves. The burn from my wound spread inward, seeping through me, diving between my legs.

What the hell?

A delicious shudder heated my body, and then he yanked me upright. My bound wrists bumped into his groin. He hooked his neck over my shoulder, his closeness tingling my belly.

"Next time, I'll take it further."

My breathing hitched.

He wouldn't *dare*.

Shock zinged up and down my spine as Vinn slid from my thighs. He shifted the fabric over my flaming skin, but his hard body stayed glued to mine.

I splayed my hand over a rigid muscle. As I touched him, he inhaled sharply. I moved over the thick bulge and traced the mushroom head—*holy fuck*—and I rubbed his cock.

I released him.

"Keep going." His velvety command slicked my body with liquid heat. "Since you're so concerned about my size."

Now he was inviting me to *touch* him?

"Vinn, this isn't right," I stammered, suspended in a freefall. "You don't talk to me like this."

"I do now."

I opened and closed my mouth, unable to string a

sentence together. My shattered thoughts lay in pieces. I couldn't pick them up fast enough.

"I-I didn't mean—I wasn't coming on to you."

Vinn pressed his mouth into my ear. "Now you're acting like the blushing virgin?"

I am a virgin.

My cheeks flamed. "*Vinn.*"

"Touch me."

It was a command, not a plea.

I shouldn't have played along with his twisted game, but he left me little choice, with my hands confined and his pelvis grinding into my ass. I drifted from across his slacks to the hardness. Somehow, his warmth smoldered here. I wrapped my fingers around him.

Vinn's grip bit into my arm.

Tension loosened my muscles. My palm moistened as it followed his length. He was so big that he made laying pipe an accurate visual. I couldn't imagine that monster fitting *anywhere*. I tightened my grip, moving up and down, warmth chasing the ice in my limbs. My body ached with the need to be touched, a need that grew as Vinn's cock thickened. He was so hard it made me feel powerful. The fact I'd done that to him was intoxicating.

He grabbed my hand, stilling my movements. "*Touch me*, not jerk me off."

His judgmental tone should've annoyed me, but I couldn't stop shaking. Vinn wasn't supposed to be attracted to me. His heart hammered my back. His breathing slowed, as though he struggled to regain his composure. He uttered a soft curse, but he didn't immediately let me go. Vinn clenched my fist.

"Well, now you know who you're dealing with." His silky voice boomed through me. "Next time, it goes in your mouth."

"*What?*"

"You heard me."

I didn't believe him.

Maybe I'd wake up to find this was a bizarre wet dream. I touched my seashell necklace after he ripped at my restraints, freeing me. Vinn whirled me around, fingers biting into my shoulders.

I tried to throttle the dizzying current racing through my body as he closed the distance between us. Red stained his neck and face. I'd never seen him so agitated.

"I don't want you dating Leo. Understand?"

Vinn grabbed my chin, frying the oxygen in my lungs. His black pools danced over me before settling in one place.

My mouth.

"You so much as bat your eyes in Leo's direction, and I will make you dig his grave before I kill him."

FOUR

VINN

Damn her.

That sweet temptation would be my undoing. The mental image of Liana in her revealing dress taunted me. My reaction to her ass hanging out hadn't been disgust.

Far from it.

What I felt—apart from a murderous rage toward Leo for touching her—was pure lust.

Which made the fact I'd almost fucked Liana problematic, considering Michael was my consigliere, best friend, and pretty much my *only* family.

After she left in a taxi, I jerked off in a bathroom. Then I circled the block a few times to cool off. I couldn't stroll through the bar looking all hot and bothered, advertising that I'd crossed the line with Michael's sister.

Jesus. If he'd seen what I'd done.

Michael's little sister.

What a hell-raiser.

She used to be the picture of innocence. I could never raise my voice around her, even when she badgered me with questions. I met her when I was thirteen. She was four. She'd always hovered in my life. She'd written when I was deployed to Iraq. I'd kept the letters folded in my pocket. When I was shot last year, she'd visited me in the hospital. She'd kissed my cheek while I basked in a fentanyl haze, and the warmth blazing across my face made me smile. Sure, she turned heads.

But it wasn't like I'd wanted to *fuck* her.

That's changed.

I used to squeeze the cute dimple in her chin, charmed by her doll-like face. I didn't like kids, but she was different. Maybe because I'd been abandoned by my piece of shit parents and hers were dead. So I'd picked her up, held her hand, kept her safe, and smacked Michael around when he was too rough with his sister.

She grew up.

She filled out.

Little Liana had grown more beautiful by the year.

It'd been way too easy to get her alone. In a blink, I had her tied up, bent over, and her thong to her knees. I could've gone further. I imagined rubbing my thumb along the shadow of her pussy. She didn't put up a strong fight, which gave me ideas. My filthy thoughts revolved around Liana, kneeling and choking on my cock.

I'd never look at her the same.

I didn't bother wiping my grin until I returned to The Sunset Tavern, a dive whose orange lights cast everybody in sepia tones. Uncle Nico, the *don* of the family, owned the bar. He was serving a five-year prison sentence.

I maintained things in his absence. I oversaw Nico's investments in condo developments and was partner to several construction firms. Later, I had a meeting with Larry Spada, a municipal politician, who would help me with zoning if I took care of Skunk, a crazy street boss who'd named himself after the bold white streak in his hair.

Michael sat at the same table, staring at his phone. He frowned as I approached. "What the fuck did you do to her?"

Shit. I didn't think she'd squeal that fast. "Nothing."

"She's pissed, man. Check it out."

He showed me his cell.

Liana: I never want to see V again.

Me: Why?

Liana: He's a PSYCHO.

Liana: Don't ever put me in the same room as him.

Me: What did he do?

She never replied.

Good girl.

Zero remorse plagued my conscience, but there was no sense in pissing off my most loyal associate. If Michael saw my hands all over his sister, he'd fly into a fucking rage that'd end with one of us beating the other into a coma.

We were total opposites.

Michael was the life of the party. I couldn't charm a potted plant. He wore tailored suits. I'd rather be in shorts and a T-shirt. He loved children. I'd never wanted them. He was easily provoked. I barely felt anything these days.

And I'd let her get to me.

A lethal calmness settled in Michael's gaze. "Did you threaten her?"

In a manner of speaking. "I was harsh."

"What does that mean?"

I waved, indicating it was nothing. "I gave her a stern talk."

"You should've left that to me."

"It doesn't work coming from you. You never follow through." I needed to steer the conversation away from these dangerous waters. "She knows better than to mouth off to me."

"What's going on between you two?"

I wiped images of Liana from my mind. "No idea. I only see her when you're around."

"She's stressed." Michael sighed in the same way he did when his kids misbehaved. "I need her to pick a husband, but she's dragging her feet. I'll have to decide for her, and our relationship is already strained."

A *husband*?

That shot a bolt into my chest.

"Oh. I didn't tell you." He swept his brown hair. "Alessio came back from New York. Nico wants us to make peace with Legion MC, but the president is demanding Liana's hand in marriage."

The vision of Liana in a wedding dress next to an MC member shoved a white-hot poker of rage into my heart.

"Are they fucking crazy?"

"I know," he groaned. "It's *insane*. They've never even met, but I guess he thinks she'll be good collateral."

She would be.

I didn't have a lot of people in my life, but she was one of them. If I ever had to choose between Liana and the family's interest, I'd take her.

No question.

I'd destroy every Harley dealership from here to California before giving her to a biker.

"No." I balled my fists. "Hell no."

"Preaching to the choir. You should hear what my

wife has to say about it. Anyway, that's why I'm trying to find her a husband."

"You should've told me."

"Doing that right now. You asked me to handle Legion," Michael reminded me in a sharp voice.

Yes, we needed to end the biker wars.

Since Boston had spiraled into complete chaos, the mayor had contacted me weekly, threatening to call in the National Guard if the car bombings didn't stop. They'd already imposed martial law and mandated curfews, slamming all business to a screeching halt and tanking the local economy. I had enough on my plate with Legion and Rage Machine turning Boston into a war zone.

Ending Crash's trafficking ring was supposed to cut Rage Machine at the knees, but they seemed to have an endless supply of guns and cash to bribe judges. They'd also been stealing dynamite from our construction sites to terrorize the city. Helping Legion defeat them made sense, but I'd had no idea the president of the club wanted Liana.

The possibility of Michael setting Liana up triggered an avalanche of *no*. How could he do that? You didn't give a prize to a decrepit *soldier* like DiMaggio.

I could've reached across the table, grabbed his tie, and bashed his skull into the wood.

"So that's the reason behind the DiMaggio disaster."

"Funny you mention him." Michael tensed, his amber gaze lighting with fire. "I wondered why you ran off the harmless guy I set up for her."

"He would've slid his disgusting hands under her dress as soon as he got her alone."

"No." Michael shook his head. "He's old school. He wouldn't have touched her before marriage."

"Yeah. Right."

"You know, I thought maybe you noticed something I didn't." His mouth took on an unpleasant twist. "Now I'm ninety-nine percent sure it was jack shit."

"I saw a pathetic waste of space." My throat burned as Michael gave me a searching look. "He's a soldier at thirty-eight, which means he lacks ambition or he's incompetent. He's chasing a twenty-one-year-old who's way out of his league."

"I decide that. Not you."

"Mike, you're out of your mind. She won't be happy with him."

"I'm getting a distinct jealous vibe from you."

I wasn't jealous—I was fucking *annoyed*. "I'm amazed you'd hand over your sister to a guy who doesn't make six figures."

"If you think Liana cares about money, you don't know her at all."

"That's not the point," I shouted, fed up with this argument. "He's a nobody. Unworthy."

"And you are?"

Yes. "It's not about me."

"*Good*," he boomed, his voice heavy with sarcasm. "I'm glad we agree on that."

I could've hit the son of a bitch. "If you have such a hard-on for DiMaggio, why did you let me kick him out?"

"Like I said, I thought you saw something. I also wanted to see if he'd stand up to you, but he didn't, so..." Michael clicked his tongue, shrugging. "No matter. I'll find someone else."

"What do you mean?"

"Nico's hounding me about this deal. I can't stall any longer. I shouldn't go behind Nico's back, but I won't give my sister to those animals. So I'm bringing her to the gala at the Institute of Contemporary Art. She'll pick from the pool of guys there."

Irritation burned a hole in my chest. "What a desperate, *stupid* idea."

"You have a better suggestion, smartass?"

"Give her to me."

The command ripped from my mouth before I could bury it under a layer of denial. Michael jerked back, knocking over a glass of water, but he paid it no mind.

"I'm acting-boss. I'll tell Nico we're dating, and that'll be that. No need to marry her off."

"Except you're *not* dating her."

"Who the fuck cares? It's what he believes that matters."

Michael's tone cooled. "I appreciate it, but no."

He was unbelievable.

"You'd rather force a stranger on Liana than let her fake-date me?"

"I'm not an idiot. I know where this is going, and the answer is *hell no*." He pulled an ankle over his knee, his voice rising. "You've shown no interest in Liana. But now that she might be off the market, you're breaking my balls."

He was right, and I hated it.

I also didn't need his permission.

"There's something else I could use your help with." Michael's gaze flicked at me, his eyes burning. "Liana keeps ditching her bodyguards to go out alone."

A thrill of heat seared my spine.

"She's pulling an Anthony." Michael rubbed his forehead. "This girl. I swear to God. I hope my daughter's not this much trouble when she gets older."

"What do you want from me?"

"Talk to her. Make her see sense."

All I wanted was an excuse to be near her again.

Michael clawed the arm of his chair. He looked on the verge of giving me a warning. He hated asking me for help.

I smiled. "Leave it to me."

"Cool," he said, suddenly stony. "And Vinn?"
"Yeah?"
"Hands off my goddamned sister."
I wiped the smile off my face.
Too late, buddy.

FIVE

LIANA

It was a trick of the light.

Vinn couldn't be standing in the middle of a rowdy college bar. He hated crowds. And people. He was allergic to fun, too. Pink and blue lights flashed across a wide jaw and full mouth that pulled into a kingly frown. Vinn scanned the crowd with a laser-like focus until his gaze stopped on me.

Gotcha.

I glared at him, convinced the Vinn-lookalike would vanish into smoke. He didn't hang out in places other than Italian cafés and the bars and restaurants he owned. Of course, he'd also never dragged me into dark rooms, bared my ass, and spanked me.

The whole incident made me burn with an unwelcome blush. Was he trying to punish me? Did he want me turned on and flustered? What was his angle?

Vinn's over-the-top behavior had to be a fluke. He'd been angry. The power had gone to his head. He got carried away. We both did.

It meant nothing.

I pushed it from my mind, but that was hard, considering I woke to bruises on my ass. In the days that followed, they burned with the acute sensation of Vinn's handprint.

I'd ignored Michael's probing texts. As much as I'd have loved to see Vinn get his due justice, Michael would go overboard and kill him. I hated Vinn, but I didn't want him dead.

Vinn's blank stare hardened as it fell on the man beside me. His menace seemed to pour into James, a boat-shoe-wearing moron who'd gained admission into Bourton with a resumé of bullshit jobs like Wellness Advocate.

"What's with that dude?" James grumbled, sipping his beer. "He's, like, staring at me."

"Who knows what's wrong with him."

"Come at me, you little bitch," James muttered at Vinn, who made his way toward us. "You want some?"

"I'd love to watch you fight him."

James grinned, not catching on.

Watching James and Vinn club each other to death would be nice, but I knew better. The former Marine wouldn't break a sweat subduing James. The fight would end swiftly, or Vinn would drag it out to be cruel. Vinn's merciless expression suggested he was down for torture.

I needed to head this off.

"Holy shit. Is that—is that your Vinny?" Queenie's face broke into an ecstatic grin as he stomped in our direction. "You weren't kidding. He's a freaking babe."

"Keep that to yourself," I whispered. "His head's so swollen it might explode."

"Which one?" she slurred. "He has a big dick, right? I'm right. I can't even see you through his blinding Big Dick Energy."

That reminded me of the thigh I'd grabbed, which actually was his long, impossibly thick cock. I'd traced the mushroom shape before making the connection.

My toes curled. I said nothing, but Queenie seemed to guess the truth from my flushed cheeks.

She knocked her glass against mine. "Awesome." Then she slugged my arm. "I'm so mad at you. You're seeing him, and you didn't tell me? Bitch."

"We're not dating."

"Bullshit! He's here for you." Queenie launched from the couch and headed off Vinn before I caught her. "Hi, Vincent!"

"Vinn," he barked. "Never Vincent."

She took his hands, forgetting everything I'd told her about his personality. "This is like meeting a celebrity. It's so nice to meet you."

Vinn yanked from her grip, scowling. "Who the hell are you?"

"Queenie! Liana's ride-or-die girl." Queenie whirled, glaring at me. "You haven't mentioned me?"

"We're not dating! Jesus H."

Vinn beckoned me with a finger. "We need to talk."

"What part of *I never want to see you again* do you not understand?"

"I'm not done with you."

Queenie's drunk ass still hadn't put it together that we weren't a couple. She beamed at me. "He's feisty."

I pointed at the exit, ignoring her. "Door's there."

"I know where the fucking door is," he barked, my sarcasm flying over his head. "I just walked through it."

"Good for you. You've mastered the basics of entering and exiting a building. Now turn around and do it again."

"Careful, Li. I'm in a mood."

"I'll write down the name of Michael's therapist. He'll give you a discount for all the sessions you'll need."

Daniel had raised me to be a killer. He didn't back down until someone was on the floor, bleeding. He'd lacked an instinct for self-preservation.

Apparently, so did I.

"You're very brave tonight, considering I had you begging for mercy on Saturday." His eyes narrowed into black slits as he grasped my jaw. "Remember?"

His thumb brushed my bottom lip, echoing his promise to take it further.

Fine. I'll stop.

My nerves tingled when he didn't budge. "What?"

"You're here without bodyguards." His voice pulsed with disapproval. "Get up."

"My apartment is four blocks from here."

"I don't care. We're going."

He grabbed me, but I twisted out of his grip.

Vinn fumed. "You're driving me up the wall."

Sorry, not sorry. "This might be tough for you to understand, but I don't need your approval."

"You need a lot more than my approval."

Like your big dick?

I almost rattled off the saucy response before I remembered this man wasn't the brotherly figure who'd stopped Michael from committing countless pranks. He'd threatened to shove his cock into my mouth two days ago, which should've bottomed my stomach. Heat pricked the skin around my lips as I imagined his hands slamming into my shoulders, making me kneel, forcing me to take him.

The hell was wrong with me?

I pulled from him, overwhelmed. "I'm not leaving."

"I swear to God, Li. If you weren't my best friend's sister, I'd throw you over my goddamned shoulder.

Twenty minutes, and then your little ass is out that door."

"*Fine.*"

"Fine." Vinn sat beside me, shooting James a pointed glare. "The fuck you looking at?"

James snapped his head to the side, cowed. My other friends had noticed nothing strange. Luckily, they'd been distracted by pickleback shots.

Vinn sank into the couch, his back ramrod straight, unaware of the dark spell he'd cast on the group. He had a menacing presence and intimidated everyone I knew.

The overprivileged, pampered, indulged kids at Bourton could never understand the criminal underworld that'd made him ruthless. Most people wouldn't recognize him unless they stayed up to date with local news, but some had probably seen or heard his name mentioned in connection with gangland shootings or thrown in with the Commission of Public Inquiry.

"Everyone, this is Vinn Costa." I searched for the words to describe him. "He's a family friend."

"Just a friend, huh?" James's round face trembled with a good-natured grin. "I thought you wanted to kill me."

Vinn was supposed to laugh and apologize. He did neither. He stared, his expression blank.

I grimaced at James. "Sorry. He's a bit extra."

"You're him," Queenie blurted, shattering the tense silence. "You're the guy!"

Vinn gaped at her, ignoring James.

"Yeah," she gushed. "You're the one she talks about! Vinny!"

His mouth fell open. Then he turned, his eyes raking my burning face. "I'm the guy? You talk about me?"

Cat's out of the bag.

Fuck.

"No, I don't." I dismissed Queenie with a wave, and she snickered into her drink. "She's drunk."

Vinn leaned toward Queenie. "What does she say?"

"A lot. Most of it's too inappropriate to repeat."

He laughed, the loudness stunning me. "I've got to hear this."

I waved my hands behind Vinn, mouthing a silent plea. *Queenie, stop.*

"You're dating him. What's the big deal?" She huffed, turning her attention to Vinn. "If you guys aren't married and pregnant by the end of the year, I'll be shocked."

I would kill her. "Queenie!"

"Huh. Imagine that."

"Oh, she has. Many times, buddy." Queenie giggled, offering him a glass that he declined. "You sure you don't want a drink?"

I winced hard, very conscious of Vinn's stare. "Queenie, please shut the hell up."

She grimaced. "Sorry. I'm pretty lit."

I'd take care of her later.

I had a more significant concern—Vinn.

He'd corner me afterward and mock me about this revelation. Worse, he might think I still felt the same, but I didn't. I'd stopped obsessing over Vinn a while ago, but, of course, Queenie wouldn't forget the years I'd spent moping in our shared dorm.

I clenched my fists because it was preferable to wrapping them around Queenie's throat. The twenty minutes were up, and then Vinn tapped his watch and dragged me upright.

"This was fun." Queenie beamed at a smirking Vinn. "I totally get why she likes you. We must have brunch!"

"Thanks. It's been...illuminating." He shook Queenie's hand, ignoring everyone else. "Have a good night."

Vinn palmed my hip.

I obeyed the pressure, my heart galloping ahead. A growing awareness pulsed behind my ribcage, clawing at me like a frightened animal as we crossed Boston's deserted streets. Somehow, I preferred his outrage to the unpredictable silence that hummed between us. I climbed the staircase to my brownstone, refusing to acknowledge him, clinging to a desperate hope that he'd disappear.

I searched for my keys, and then dropped them twice. "You can go."

The heat of his body warmed my back. His head hooked over my shoulder. "I'm coming inside."

"Do I need a condom or a gun?"

His soft laughter tingled every nerve, and regret sunk into my stomach at the joke.

Vinn's voice smoothed into a purr. "Well, I've got both."

I fumbled with my purse, dropping it.

He stooped, picking it up. He'd taken control in the guise of helping me, and now he had my key. He slid it into the lock, opened the door, and strolled in. A fiendish expression lit up his face.

Terror stirred in my belly.

"Vinn, you need to leav—"

He grabbed my arm, yanked me into the apartment, and locked the door. Vinn cradled me, and a shudder heated my body. Darkness carved a vulgar smile between his cheeks.

My alarms blazed red as Vinn's six-foot-something frame pushed me deeper into my home. I bumped into a wall and rolled into the kitchen. The expression in his eyes made me wish I were closer to the door. Vinn gripped the counter, caging me in his arms.

"You've given me an interesting night."

"H-how so?"

"I came here to punish you. Again. Now I'm rethinking that. Spanking you didn't work because you liked it," he whispered, awed. "You enjoy my hands on you. Don't you?"

I jerked my head in the negative. "There's nothing pleasant about being tied up and beaten."

"Don't exaggerate."

"You hit me. It hurt."

"Good." Vinn grabbed my chin, staring me down. "Some lessons hurt worse than others. Especially when they're given by someone you like."

"I don't like you. I find you revolting."

"Really?" He passed a thumb over my bottom lip, showering my skin with sparks. "Is that what you tell your friend when you talk about me?"

The only thing more infuriating about being outed by Queenie was the fact I'd been completely off his radar. He'd needed someone to tell him about my feelings.

Pathetic.

And now he was throwing them in my face, humiliating me like a monster.

Heat lashed my mouth. "Get out of my house."

"Oh, come on."

"I mean it. You're not welcome here."

Vinn wasn't in the listening mood. His touch fluttered across my waist, sending off a chain of electrical impulses that begged me to march us to bed.

"I haven't gone to Michael," I said, shoving his chest. "That doesn't mean I never will."

Vinn's smile and raised eyebrows suggested he didn't believe me, but he allowed me to retreat. I left the kitchen. He followed like a giant shadow, barging into my bedroom like he belonged there.

It wasn't much. A queen bed and desk covered with trinkets from my youth. Blasts from the past decorated the walls in the form of posters, things I'd never outgrow, the most important one standing in front of me.

Amusement flickered over his face as I stumbled into my desk. My ass hit the corner, and I hissed in pain.

His self-satisfied smirk seemed to mock me. "Did you bruise?"

"Yes," I murmured, hating him. "I took photos."

"I'd love to see them."

I ignored the thrill shooting down my belly. "I plan to send them to Michael after I tell him what you did."

"Just what every brother wants—pictures of his sister's ass."

"Maybe I'll put them on Tinder."

"Do that, and I'll bend you over. You'll get another reason to hate me."

I sat on my bed, arms crossed. "Why are you here?"

An unfathomable look smoothed his face. "I want you."

I forced myself to settle down. I'd worked hard to cut Vinn from my life, and I couldn't afford to be distracted by a fantasy. I wouldn't fall under his spell.

"Well, I don't want you, so it's time for you t—"

"Li, I can't go back to treating you like Michael's little sister."

His flat eyes prolonged the moment, my skin prickling as I gazed into their infinite depths.

"Put it behind you, and I'll do the same."

"That's not an option."

"Why not?" I clenched my jaw to kill the waver in my voice. "Why the fuck did you spank me?"

"Why did you grab my cock?"

I met his accusing eyes. "To mess with you."

Vinn's lips parted. He ripped open the first button of his shirt and glared as though I'd made him too hot. His possessive gaze bored into me.

"Well, it worked."

Blood pounded in my temples. "Vinn, I'm not one of your goddamned floozies."

He blinked. "My *what*?"

"The girls you see for a week and discard."

Vinn smirked, reminding me that while he might've been a sweet boy, he hadn't grown into a tender-hearted man. "You're way above them, Li."

"I thought I wasn't special," I sparred.

"I let you get away with a lot."

"Well, you're nothing to me."

"Yeah, I'm not worth a damn." Vinn's tone sparkled with sarcasm. "Otherwise your friend would know my name."

Screw you, Queenie. "She didn't mean you."

"Vinny is what you've called me since you were four."

"Now it's a nickname for someone else."

That sucked the joy from his face.

The life drained out of him. He gave me a black look layered with bitterness.

I'd shot an arrow through his maddening arrogance, but it felt less like a victory when his features clouded over, transforming him back into the block of ice.

"Queenie mistook you for another man. That's all." My hand anchored on my hip as Vinn cleared his throat. "You share the same name, but that's about it."

His gaze bolted me to the floor as he lapsed into a stony silence. "Why haven't I met him?"

"Because he left me a while ago."

Not quite a lie. The old Vinn died. He'd abandoned me for war, and he'd never returned. His body had survived.

Everything I'd loved about him hadn't.

"This *Vincent*," he drawled. "Is he Italian?"

"I won't talk about him to you."

A hardness replaced the twinkle in his eyes. Apparently eager to change the subject, Vinn headed toward the desk. He picked up a photo of us as children. A shirtless, teenage Michael stood in board shorts beside Vinn, who'd slung his arm over eight-year-old me. I'd never grinned so hard, but I'd also never been plastered to his bare chest.

I fidgeted with my dress. "Do you remember those summers at Salisbury Beach?"

"A little."

Disappointing. "I think about them often. You, me, Mom, and my brothers. All of us hanging out at the beach. The heat baking my feet. The waves."

"Only you would reminisce about that place."

"I like remembering a time when I was happy, and my family was whole."

Vinn's gaze locked on Daniel's portrait. "It never gets easier. You learn to deal with the pain."

The pain of losing Daniel—or killing him?

A crushing sadness squeezed my lungs. The seashell necklace burned my throat, like it contained a piece of Vinn's black soul. Maybe wearing it every day, having the constant reminder, was less of a token of hope and more a torture device.

"I want you to leave. Now."

My voice throbbed with agony.

Thankfully, Vinn must've decided he'd tortured me enough. He stepped past me, his fingertips brushing my waist, as though to remind me what he'd done.

"I'm your date for the gala." He paused, halfway out. "I'll pick you up at eight."

My stomach clenched. "Why are you messing with my life?"

He offered no answer as he strolled toward the exit. Michael had probably filled him in on the dumb plan, and Vinn took it upon himself to save me.

"Vinn, I'm not going with you!"

"You are. Everyone will think we're an item." He curved his hand over the edge of the wood. "You'll hang on my arm. You'll smile. It'll confirm rumors that we're dating, which will get back to Nico."

"Like a stupid game of telephone."

"Exactly. He can't give you away if you're already mine."

I crossed my arms and leaned against the wall, wishing I could tell him what an arrogant dickhead he'd turned out to be.

"You're not the boss of me."

"I am, and I don't care how many summers we spent on that shitty beach. I'll make you submit, and not in the way you hope, darling."

Asshole.

"Do as you're told, Liana."

SIX
VINN

Why was she blowing me off?

Why did I care?

I cycled through my phone, swiping past Girl A through Girl E to banish Liana from my mind. I banged a handful of girls on a semi-regular basis, never giving anyone too much attention because I had no use for a clingy mistress. My tolerance for company dried up long before the cum on my cock. Luckily, Boston didn't lack hot girls with low expectations.

Girl B had sent a nude photo, a mouthwatering shot of tits beading with moisture. It generally would've dragged me to her place. Instead I put her on read and paused at *Liana*.

I didn't chase women.

That required effort, which was beneath me. And yet, I'd spent hours checking my cell, wondering why I didn't have her wrapped around my thumb, annoyed that I'd ignored my mistresses because I'd assumed Liana would take up my time.

On paper, Liana and I made little sense.

She *was* too good for me. The girl never went outside without looking perfect. She'd never touched a drug. Unblemished, inside and out. Until recently, she'd acted like a teddy bear stuffed with cotton candy.

I'd climbed a mountain of bones to get where I was. I wanted nothing to do with marriage. I didn't like people, so having one chained to my side for eternity seemed like a horrible idea. If I walked down the aisle, it'd be for political gain.

Never love.

We couldn't be together. Liana would *not* like being a mistress, and I couldn't do that to her. Michael would have a big problem if I fucked his sister, and I had nothing she'd want. The reasons to leave her alone outweighed getting involved, but I couldn't stomach leaving her future to *Michael*. The idiot wanted to give her to a stranger like DiMaggio.

I wouldn't let that happen.

Liana should've fallen in line, but she'd returned zero of my messages. I showed up at her doorstep as planned, only to have to field a call from Michael. She'd taken a taxi. And she'd come with another man.

I parked my armored car next to the waterfront

museum and stormed inside, almost blowing off the mayor on my way to find Liana.

Michael waved from a balcony strung with lights. Beside him stood Alessio, a tight-lipped, broody asshole. He'd been acting-boss before I ousted him. I'd fucked him over, and he paid me back by disappearing from Boston, leaving us without his wealthy contacts for months. We were even, but Alessio still stared at me like he'd love to have my head on his wall.

I ignored them, looking for a brunette among the red, white, and blue decorations until I found her lurking near the catered food.

Liana wore a backless, sparkling, wine-red dress, the shiny bauble of this boring party. Her hair was pulled into a braid, and she'd put on dark eye makeup, her eyes popping like icicles against the black, her porcelain innocence transformed into savage beauty. A dimple shadowed her chin, but I couldn't believe this was the same woman.

I tuned out a man who called my name, lost in a daydream that involved Liana hanging on my arm, her face tipping to mine. My hands clenched and released.

I wanted her.

Want was too subtle a word for the warmth that grabbed my balls. I needed to be inside her, my hands tangled in her hair as she moaned my name.

A man in a suit approached, embracing her from

behind. My jaw clenched as he linked his arm with hers. His shaven baby face filled my stomach with fire.

The college boy. She'd brought *him* to the gala.

The possibility that kid had seen her naked infuriated me. My abs tensed as his palm roved all her skin. Suddenly, her going home with him was intolerable, like inhaling smoke. My throat tightened. Air was scarce.

I headed for them.

A body slid in front of me.

Convinced he was yet another politician with a grievance, I raised my head and schooled my tone, but my best friend blocked my path. His hawk-like stare narrowed as he followed my gaze to his sister.

"Vinn. What are you doing?"

I could've thrown him aside. "Getting my date back."

"About that," he snapped, setting his wine glass down. "You never asked my permission."

"No, I didn't."

A muscle flicked in his jaw, and his lips flattened. His chest puffed out.

I held my ground, resenting the line in the sand he'd drawn. It shouldn't have been such a big fucking deal to go out with his sister. Michael was being unreasonable.

"I'm interested in her. Why is that a problem?"

Michael said nothing for the longest time. Then he spoke in a tight, angry voice. "You're my best friend, but I don't want you dating Liana."

I saw that coming, but it burned.

"Why not?"

"You're an addict," he explained, as though he wasn't one. "You were kicked out of the military."

"What the fuck does that have to do with anything?"

His body tensed. "You don't *do* relationships. If I look in your phone, I'll see Girl A because you can't be bothered to use your mistresses' names. You have no interest in kids, marriage, or a relationship beyond sex. Of course I don't want you involved with Liana."

"You think I'd do that to Li?"

"I never know what you're thinking. All I can do is make a judgment based on the facts."

"Who looked after her when she was little? Who slapped you around when you were too rough? You think I'm not good enough. *You*." I spat the word like it'd poisoned my stomach. "The man who snorted everything in sight and knocked up a stripper."

"Fuck you."

If he dug up my past, I'd do the same with his. "Remember when you strangled a made guy to death?"

It happened during one of his coke binges when the hotheaded idiot reacted to insults by dialing everything to eleven.

'Course, I wasn't much better.

"Lower your goddamned voice," Michael hissed. "They're still looking for him."

"Let's take a walk down memory lane to last year. You and Alessio murdered Anthony's kidnapper and lied about it." I smiled as a spasm of panic crossed Michael's face. "Yeah, I'm aware of that."

Anthony was Nico's silver-spooned, pain-in-the-ass son who'd never shouldered any real responsibility. He'd been a constant liability, so I didn't give a fuck when he disappeared.

Unfortunately, his father cared. He threatened me daily for "losing" Anthony. The risk of my uncle's wrath hung over my head every waking moment. The fear wafted from Michael as I talked. He'd gotten rid of the only guy with information on Anthony's whereabouts. If Nico ever found out, he'd kill Michael.

"Honestly, Mike. If we hadn't grown up together, you'd be dead, many times over."

Michael's foot tapped an erratic beat. He glanced over his shoulder, eyeing the exit. Motherfucker should've been worried. He'd made a severe error in judgment.

"I was protecting my wife!"

"Carmela was safe. You killed him because you *felt* like it. Now I have to deal with the consequences."

Michael stiffened as though I'd struck him.

"You need to make this right."

"How do I do that?"

Give me your sister.

It was on the tip of my tongue, but I didn't want to be *given* Liana. If I wanted her, I'd have her.

"You'll stop setting up Liana with other men. And you'll step aside when I take her."

"No. She won't be Girl H on your fucking phone!"

I fisted Michael's collar and dragged him out of sight, hurling him into the wall. My arm flattened his throat, a show of dominance more than anything. He wasn't stupid enough to raise a hand against me.

"She's not walking down the aisle with a biker." I leaned in, increasing the pressure on his larynx. "And the next time you feel the urge to share your holier-than-thou bullshit, *don't*."

"I'm no pushover, Vinn."

"Neither am I."

I threw him into a table, which he caught and shoved. Glasses toppled, shattering over the marble. Michael balled his fists as though to stave off a violent impulse. Part of me wanted to let loose.

I'd love an excuse to beat his ass. My heart throbbed, anger pulsing through me in sickening waves. I'd never been so angry with him. I couldn't figure out which bothered me more: his assessment of me or that I agreed with him.

His mouth twisted, and he straightened his suit. A staff member approached him with a broom. Michael moved away as they swept the broken glass. The action seemed to defuse the tension, but when Michael looked at me, his eyes filled with fire.

"Fine. I apologize."

He'd said the words, but the lie burned in my chest. He wasn't sorry, so I wouldn't be.

I had things to do.

His sister.

SEVEN

LIANA

"Want to get out of here?"

James's voice echoed as though from an empty grave. His hollow words rang with a slight suggestion, but they stirred nothing inside me but contempt. Barely thirty minutes into this black-tie gala that cost thousands to attend, and the high-maintenance jerk wanted to leave. To fuck me, no less. As though he even had a shot.

Did he think this date was going *well*?

He'd worn enough cologne to knock out an elephant, and he'd annoyed me all night, jerking my arm, pointing at people like a toddler at the zoo. *Look, Li, there's the mayor!*

We stood next to the window wall overlooking the harbor outside the museum, which lit up like the Fourth of July despite the violence rocking the city. Red, white, and blue dominated the décor in a patriotic display that fooled nobody. This was a networking event for my gangster brother and his friends.

"Li, I've had my fill of this party. It's nice, but not my thing."

"You'd rather have cheap beer and chips? I'm not leaving this food." I shoved a spoon into the bowl of chocolate-covered strawberries to heap them into a plate. "Aren't you an athlete? Eat."

"I'll put *you* in my mouth."

Not a chance in hell.

I smiled at him as though mildly tempted by the idea, but his husky voice made me want to barf.

"Oh my God," he moaned, abandoning his Lothario vibe as he tugged my hand. "It's the running back for the Hurricanes, DeShaun Brown. I'm going to ask for his autograph."

I grabbed him. "No, you're not."

"I just want a selfie."

"Do I have to call security?"

"It's a party. What's the big deal?" A faint line settled over his brow as he downed his drink. "And why is your bro rubbing elbows with politicians and labor union officials? He owns restaurants."

"He's a rich guy who invests in his community."

"How did that happen?" James seized the strawberry from my fingers. "I know someone who opened a roasted chicken place in the heart of downtown. Rent costs a fortune. It took him years to turn a profit."

"He owns a lot of them."

"Huh. Does he have a fairy godmother?"

I glared at James, annoyed that he'd guessed correctly that something was amiss, but wasn't smart enough to Google my last name.

"Can we not discuss my brother?"

He shrugged, his lip forming a pout.

I deserved this for taking an outsider to the gala, which was more about securing the Family's interests than a fundraiser. I couldn't walk without stumbling into a Costa or a Ricci.

Depressing.

Hating the mafia wasn't that easy, because everybody I loved was involved. I'd been orphaned by mob violence and adopted by Costas, but I wasn't one of them. Blood was everything, so I'd always felt like a pariah.

I resented Michael's world. More than anything, I craved an identity outside of *Costa*. No matter what I did or where I went, I'd be Michael's sister, forever trapped in a gilded cage, unable to get a coffee without a bodyguard hounding me, reporting to Michael, my comings and goings monitored. Anybody who dated me would defer to my brother.

An arranged marriage was the price I paid for having this name—*Costa*—the albatross around my neck. I wouldn't trade my family, but sometimes I fantasized about a saner upbringing.

That's why I liked my Bourton friends and teachers. Nobody sucked up to me there because they had no idea who I was.

Bringing James to this was like taking a stripper to a tech conference—inappropriate as hell. I'd only invited him to thumb my nose at Vinn and Michael. I thought he'd be easy to control, but I'd spent the evening fending off his hands, pretending to care as he waxed about growing up in Ridgefield, Connecticut, and fantasizing about stabbing my ears so I couldn't listen to him speak.

"You'd think they'd have oysters." James frowned at the banquet of seafood. "Not all this fried garbage."

Ungrateful jerk.

He stuffed his mouth with shrimp, chewing loudly, and then he wiped his chin with the back of his hand. Crumbs clung to his cheek. College boys were so disgusting.

I should fake a crisis.

"You ready to go, babe?" he asked, patting my butt.

I exhaled a sharp breath. "A—don't call me that ever again, and B—don't touch my ass."

"God, you're such a priss. You act like we've never fooled around." He shot me a wounded look. "You were all over me at the Sigma Fi party."

"I was unconscious for most of our *fooling around*, so I'm not sure why you're surprised."

I'd never brought up the incident, because it embarrassed me to death. Part of me wanted to pretend it never happened.

James reacted like I'd taken a dump on the floor. His eyes widened, and he shook his head. "You weren't asleep."

My nails bit my palms. "We both made mistakes, but *you* put your hand down my pants while I was out of it."

A muscle jumped in his mouth before he went on the offense. "So you're one of *those* girls. Everything's all good until you sober up, huh? Suddenly, it's a mistake. Fuck you, Liana. I didn't—I did nothing wrong."

"Then why are you freaking out?"

"Accusing me of this could get me expelled!"

"*This?* What do you mean?"

He shot me look. "You know."

"Say it," I taunted sweetly, watching the tan drain from his face. "What is that called, James?"

"You're crazy." He chewed on his lower lip, looking away. "I mean—just—*wow*."

Your gaslighting is on point tonight.

Behind James, a man's silhouette carved through the crowd. He walked with a nonchalant grace, towering over the other men. The rich outline of his powerful shoulders strained against his jacket. Vinn's square jaw tensed as he spotted me. Just the man who'd beat James into a puddle of crimson if I felt so inclined. It wasn't like me to crave vengeance, but inviting James had been like lighting a match to a powder keg.

Luckily, Vinn paid James as much attention as the dirt under his shoes. He approached me, beautiful with his hair tamed to a smooth wave, his well-groomed appearance incongruous with our last exchange.

Do as you're told, Liana.

I hadn't.

His fingers, tapered and strong, brushed my collarbone before his palm rolled over my shoulder and held me. His biting grip sent a chill through my body.

"You were supposed to wait at your apartment," he admonished, squeezing hard. "What am I going to do with you?"

Danger throbbed behind those words. The warmth of his smile wasn't echoed in his tone. It said I'd suffer a worse fate than a bruised ass if I defied him.

"What the fuck, Liana?" James snapped, reminding me of his presence. "You still with the Neanderthal?"

Vinn's eyes lit up in vague amusement. "Get lost, kid."

"I'm her date, Mr. Cockblock," James snarled. "Sorry, I mean, *Costa*."

Vinn's firm mouth curled as though on the edge of

laughter, but when he slid his gaze from mine to James, a cold fury radiated from him.

"I'm feeling charitable tonight, so I'll allow you ten seconds to leave. Mouth off to me, and I'll stop being amused at the man-child throwing a tantrum. I'll drag you outside and hurt you."

James flinched and stepped backward.

My stomach knotted. "James, just go."

"How can you blow me off?" He shot a terrified glance at Vinn. "That dead-eyed creep needs to be locked up."

I groaned. "James, go home."

"Why the hell did you even invite me?"

"Because she's pissed at me." Vinn caught a loose tendril on my cheek. "My girlfriend likes to act out, but she knows who she belongs to."

Girlfriend.

My hands found the seashell necklace, and I stroked the ribbed edges, pressing my thumb into the sharp corners as though the pain might distract me from my most desperate ache. I imagined the old Vinn saying that, my insides somersaulting with butterflies. The same heated rush from all those years ago, when he'd kissed my head, stained my cheeks. Then his stare drifted to two men hanging in our peripherals. He nodded.

They grabbed James, who protested with a loud, *"What the fuck?"*

"Take him outside." Vinn dismissed the security with a wave. "I'll be there in a few minutes."

"Let me go," James roared, struggling. "*Stop!* I want to speak to your manager!"

The lump in my throat sank.

I hadn't meant to *harm* James. I'd pictured a public humiliation—my way of teaching the fucker that there were consequences to treating women like garbage. Vinn delivering a beatdown was over the top.

"Don't hurt him." I studied his clenched jaw. "We're in the same social circles. Queenie will never forgive me if I let you beat him up."

"Let me? You have no pull over me."

"She's not going to care!"

His hawk-like gaze swung to me. "You should've thought of that first."

"Vinn, this is ridiculous. James is just a friend."

"Not when you ask him out and wear a fuck-me dress."

A sliver of heat rippled through his words, lashing my face.

His black eyes burned with a strange intensity. It was an insolent, possessive stare, like he had every right to look at me and gape down my neckline. He plucked the drink from my hand and slammed it on a table.

"What's your problem?"

"We were supposed to go together. Coming here with that fucking kid messed everything up."

"I didn't feel like hanging on your arm all night."

"You'd rather be on his?"

"Yeah." The lie heated my cheeks. "It might surprise you, but some women like to be treated like they're more than flesh wrapping your cock."

"Or you just did it to piss me off." Vinn wheeled us away from the open bar, his fingers gouging my waist. "For someone who hates me, you sure have a lot to say about me."

I gritted my teeth, annoyed at Queenie. She had planted this seed in his brain, and it'd grown out of control, taking root in places it had no business. He was getting all sorts of wrong ideas. They needed to be killed with fire.

Now.

"Vinn, I am not interested in you. *At all.*"

"The more you say that, the less I believe you."

"Well, you need to," I blurted. "I can't stand you."

"You're not my favorite person, either."

I grabbed his tie and yanked. "I'm serious."

"So am I." Vinn's roaming gaze lingered on my mouth as he stole the tie from my fist. "I like my women submissive and easy. You're a pain in the ass."

"Cut your losses and leave."

"Not happening."

I held out my hand. "Give me your phone."

He lifted a brow. "Why would I do that?"

"I'll block your mistresses since you're so hell-bent on controlling my life. Or maybe I'll tell them humiliating stories, like the time I caught you and my cousins watching porn in the living room."

"That story is only embarrassing because you were nine."

"No, it was weird because we'd just returned from a *funeral*." I still remembered tottering downstairs after the wake, captivated by the moving limbs on the television. "What kind of kid watches porn after seeing a dead person?"

"Blame your brother. His idea."

"Oh, it's all Michael's fault?"

"He was in charge," said Vinn, not looking remotely abashed. "We visited the video store after the funeral to rent something. We were trying to cheer up our cousin. He'd just lost his mom."

"Nothing says *I'm sorry for your loss* more than a porno."

"Teenage boys." Vinn shrugged. "We didn't know any better."

I shook my head. "Did it work?"

"Well, no. You barged in and ruined everything."

Waves of heat bounced from me to him as the light overhead dimmed, throwing us into shadows. Candlelight softened Vinn's stony features, making him less a predator, more Prince Charming.

"Mom was so mad," I whispered, alarmed by the electricity pinging my skin. "I remember you springing from the couch to cover my eyes."

"Like this?"

Vinn slid his palm over my gaze.

Warmth bloomed inside me.

A slender thread of attraction slowly formed between us.

His hand weighed as heavy as it had back then, and the arm hooking my shoulders echoed his gentleness. Suddenly I was a breathless girl, disarmed by his undivided attention.

He pressed his mouth into the shell of my ear, sending a jolt through me. "Close them, Little Li. I'll know if you cheat."

"I hate this game."

"Do as I say, and I'll make it worth your while."

Twelve years ago, he'd lured me from the living room with those words to the attic. My reward was half an hour of board games, which for a nine-year-old was huge. We'd played while the floor rumbled with my mother's scandalized voice. My mind swam with the image of Vinn hunched in the cramped space.

Until his lips grazed my neck.

The sensation made my head spin. Still blind, I sank

into his arms. He kissed a line from my ear downward, every touch striking a vibrant chord inside me. He slid against my palm, hot and dry. Then he led me by the shoulder, steering me across the room. My heart pounded an erratic rhythm, his magnetism so potent that I obeyed.

A door groaned.

He crowded my back, his impatience making me stumble. The noise from the party dropped as the door slammed. A lock latched. We stood in an empty gallery. White walls and concrete surrounded me.

Vinn grabbed me, dropping the pretense.

My smile dissolved.

Reality set in.

This wasn't Vinn, my protector. He was a *predator* who'd lured me away from safety, locked the door, and immobilized me. His arms wrapped me like a straitjacket, freeing my vision but binding me everywhere else.

It'd all been an act—the banter and his gentleness.

He'd put on a show to get me alone.

Fuck.

EIGHT

LIANA

I bucked against his strength, but it was like pushing rock slabs. My breath hitched as he wheeled me toward a blank wall. I was too aware of his brutal power. He could strangle me by squeezing me too hard, but Vinn had other ideas.

"Put your hands on the wall. Bend over."

The impersonal words lashed my mouth with unbidden heat.

"Too soon, don't you think?" I rattled off, my nerves haywire. "Usually guys start with dinner and drinks before jumping into foreplay."

"You're just like your goddamned brother." Vinn plastered my wrists above my head, his weight buckling my knees. "Impulsive. Hotheaded. No sense."

"You're the one ordering me to bend over."

I should shut up.

But I relished his punishing grip. Vinn never lost his temper. He seethed. I still remembered the flare of indignation across his brow those few times I'd disobeyed him, but this was something else.

Vinn had no reason to grind against me. His thigh brushed my hip, and a jolt seared me.

"You push me to the brink." His words blasted my ear. "I should rip off this dress and parade you outside. Leave no doubt who you belong to."

"My brother would have a problem with that."

"He can go fuck himself."

His palm slipped through the side slit and stroked me. My senses leaped to life at the hands roaming my curves, though I could've thrown myself off a cliff for my body's response. His touch hardened as he groped my bruised skin.

His roughened voice interrupted my gasp. "Did you think I'd overlook that little shit? I'll kill him for touching you."

"He didn't."

"Liar. I saw his arms around you."

I twisted, intending to slip from his loosening grasp, but his glare riveted me to the spot. The jealousy caught me off guard. Vinn and I were barely friends.

My heart pounded. "Why the hell do you care?"

"Because I've marked you as mine." Vinn pulled the fabric off my thigh, continuing his leisurely caress. "And, petulant brat that you are, you mean something to me. You're decent most of the time. You've done things for me that nobody else has." He paused for a moment, as though to dwell on them. "I don't know what happened to the sweet girl who doted on me, but I want her back."

Now he wanted me?

He'd never *known* me. He didn't want the messy, complicated version of me. The girl who exploded when she didn't get her way. I'd always been difficult, but I'd toned it down in front of Vinn. He missed the girl who worshipped him, never questioned him, who did *anything* for his attention. I'd immersed myself in distractions, hoping the routine would camouflage the deep ache of loneliness.

Pathetic.

I choked out a laugh. "The Liana who waited on you hand and foot is gone, and good riddance."

"Bring her back to me."

The torment of his presence ate at me. A terrible bitterness crushed my heart. "*No.*"

"Yes." His sensual touch slid to my waist, igniting sparks. "If I'm faking a relationship with somebody, it'll be with a girl who plays nice in public. Not a vindictive woman who brings her exes to the party."

He'd said some infuriating shit, but *that* bothered me the most.

"James is not my damned ex."

He paused, his breath tickling my neck. "Bringing him here was a big mistake, Li."

His painfully light fingers teased me, as though he knew how much I'd suffered, and he intended to make me beg.

I won't. "What will you do about it?"

"I have some ideas."

The taunt sent a thrill down my spine.

Slick flames wrapped my stomach as his hands cascaded down my shoulders, rippling over my curves. He seized my dress and pushed it over my hips, dragging a hiss from my teeth.

"No underwear," he purred. "Was this for James, or for me? Did you want to be *prepared*?"

"I hate to pop your overinflated head like a bubble, but that has nothing to do with either of you. A thong would show under this dress."

"You wanted to look hot for me."

My jaw dropped. "You are so delusional."

He gathered the flesh under my ass and pinched brutally.

"Fuck—ow!"

"Can't help it," he murmured, his thumb drifting close to my pussy. "You're so inviting, with your tight ass shining with my handprint. I never in a million years pictured myself doing this." He traced the fullest area of my butt, sighing. "Now it's all I think about."

His hand unstuck from my cheek, and my skin prickled in anticipation.

SMACK!

Heat bloomed over my skin with the loud crack. Just as before, the shock of it ran through me. An indignant part of me demanded justice. He should pay for the humiliation, but the shame stinging my cheeks was not because Vinn spanked me.

It was because I liked it.

I enjoyed the pain, his possession, this demeaning position, even his unhinged violence. He'd transformed from an ice giant to a red-blooded man. His blows radiated inside me as though he claimed my soul, too.

Warmth shot to my pussy as he cracked his palm on me, his movements less brutal and more playful. He seized handfuls of me, squeezing, swatting. He made delicious groans that dipped in my throat. He stopped, soothing the burn with a caress.

Vinn's hips jammed into mine. A growing hardness pushed against my sore ass. My senses short-circuited. I breathed hard as his hands seemed to search for pleasure points—ass, thighs, hips, stomach. He touched me everywhere, stroking a path so sinful I couldn't breathe.

I staggered through a fog of ecstasy, palms slipping.

"I didn't say you could move."

He shoved them where they belonged, and then he eased my bra aside to tease me. The rough pads of his fingertips were surprisingly tender as he followed the swell of my breasts, playing with my swollen nipples. He seared a line down my abdomen and into my thigh.

Oh my God.

He groped my hip, reaching into an intimate space. The shock doused me in liquid heat as two fingers traced my clit. They were barely there. He brushed me. Then he danced about in a slow stroke.

I slacked against the wall, panting.

He slapped my clit, tearing a groan from me.

"You knew what you were doing when you wore this fucking thing. You flaunted that asshole in front of me, knowing I'd fly into a rage." His growl darkened as his hold bit into my hips. "You've blown the lid off my self-restraint."

His hands were harsh, but they gave me a sense of protection. His raking gaze made me clench everywhere. I struggled to stay calm. My determination collapsed like a crumbling rock inside me.

I couldn't take this anymore.

I lurched toward the door.

He yanked me back. "You're not going anywhere."

I'd dreamed of being trapped in his arms. It didn't help that I fit perfectly in the crook of his head and shoulder. A thrill shot into my battered heart as I scrambled for an exit strategy.

"Vinn, you're not doing yourself any favors." I forced

my lips into a stiff grin, cobbling together words that'd stop him. "Michael's outside."

"We've already talked. He won't be a problem."

"You told him we were together?"

"I said what I needed to get him out of my way."

He turned me around and thrust me against the wall. Vinn's mouth brushed the pulsing hollow at the base of my throat. It triggered a wild swirl in the pit of my stomach.

"Vinn, I want you to let me go." I raised my voice to a shout. "Vinny!"

"Thought that was the other guy's name."

My whirlwind thoughts couldn't make sense of anything.

Oh, yes...I'd taunted him with that, days ago.

"Wonder where he's from," Vinn mused as he leaned in, smiling. "Allston. Hyde Park. *Dorchester.*"

The neighborhood he grew up in.

"*He's not you.*"

He patted my cheek. "Sure he's not, honey."

"I feel nothing for you."

"Liar. You went out with that *jamook* just to piss me off." He jerked toward the door. "The college boy with a major crush on you."

"What right do you have to be jealous?"

A war of emotions raged within me as he dragged my hair behind an ear.

"The fact that you want me means I own a piece of you."

"Vinn, that's not true." The words were weak, even to my ears. "Please leave me alone."

"Not a chance in hell."

He moved in, angling his head. His full mouth molded to mine. He was like crushed velvet, so soft and sensual that my skin burst into flames. It was tentative, a kiss worthy of a Hallmark romance, and my mind *reeled*.

Heat fanned my cheeks. This was like a daydream, so euphoric it couldn't be real. I swam through a haze of desire and confusion.

Would I kiss him back?

I hesitated, my insides tearing apart.

Then I slid my hands up his chest. I anchored on his shoulders, lifted on my toes, and pressed my lips into his. It was like dipping into a spa after a long, cold night. Sweet and clean, like mint. Hot. Dangerously silken. My nerves buzzed with need. It was so right to be held by him. I wanted to offer him all of me, my neck, my hardening nipples. He indulged, nipping under my jaw before a wet heat soothed the sting.

The stars had aligned.

Vinn Costa was kissing me.

His mouth returned, crushing me with harder strokes. He cupped my face as I released tortured sighs. Perfect. Better than my imagination.

I couldn't believe it.

The teenage-girl crush I'd buried alive clawed to the surface, bursting forth like champagne bubbles. We exchanged slow, drugging kisses, and then Vinn's forehead rolled over mine. His luminous eyes flicked open. A burn settled into his tan, spreading to his chest.

I'd seen him make out with countless models, but none of them had seemed to give him pleasure. I thought he was dead inside—the fact he wasn't sent a shockwave through me.

We separated as though struck by the same lightning.

He definitely wasn't dead. The proof thudded against my hand and slicked my palm where I held his neck. He stared at me with a silent question. He was a man who'd finally noticed me.

He grasped my chin. Then he fused his lips with mine. He seized my hips, shoving me backward.

A wall hit my back.

I gasped at the impact, forgetting the shock as he crushed me over and over. He smothered the sounds I made, even the pathetic, small moans when his tongue dove in. He slipped down my waist and cupped my bare ass. A groan broke from his lips.

Jesus.

This wasn't the tender stroke I'd imagined, complete with a confession that he'd always loved me. Vinn's feelings were anything but loving. The kiss deepened into something carnal. Biting. He sucked me like I was candy.

There was no angst.

No second-guessing.

I was on fire. My pussy throbbed. I clutched his collar and met him, stroke for stroke, bound to this savage harmony. I kissed every inch of him in case this never happened again. I sucked his bottom lip, and he gripped the backs of my thighs and slid up, cupping my ass. He hoisted me up the wall. He gyrated into me, rolling his very hard cock against me.

He bit me, soothing the hurt with his tongue.

I groaned.

The sound seemed to snap him out of our frenzy. He backed away with a low hiss, looking half-mad with lust. A bright flare sprang into his eyes. He blew a stream of air.

My heart exploded with need and anguish. I couldn't disguise my body's reaction to him, and now he'd have more ammunition against me. I ran toward the door and seized the handle.

Vinn slammed it shut with his foot. "Where are you going?"

"Home."

"After we mauled each other like that?"

"I don't want to see you again."

His gravelly laughter made me flush. "You sure as hell pick an odd way of showing it."

I had to shove my confused thoughts in order, and I couldn't do it if he touched me. The stitching of my life had unraveled. It was his fault.

I needed him to stop touching me.

I headed out, but he caught my waist. "Vinn, please."

His finger curled under my chin, and an electric shock scorched my body. "Come home with me, and you'll get anything you want."

My pulse skittered. "I'm not going anywhere with you."

"Why not?" The electricity of his touch became a lightning storm as he traced the fullness of my mouth. "I think we'll work out our differences better in bed. So you might as well come over."

This was too much.

I wouldn't say yes, but my heart squeezed at the *what-if*.

I'd pictured losing my virginity to Vinn. Even now, I liked imagining him shattering the last of my innocence. It dangled in front of me like a rope. If I dared reach out...

"I can't." I swallowed hard, stepping back. "This is too sudden, and I'm not—I don't—we're not a thing."

"We are as of now." Vinn scooped my hand and

kissed it, making me feel like a rose blowing apart in the wind. "Fake. Real. It doesn't matter."

It mattered to me.

My throat tightened. "No."

His voice raised sharply. "Why?"

I slid away from him and strolled to the door, trembling. "I don't owe you an explanation."

"What's the harm in taking it further if I'm already dating you?"

"We're not dating," I seethed. "Fake or otherwise."

"Yes, we are," he snapped, blocking my way out. "It's not up for negotiation. This isn't about me."

I gave his boner a pointed look. "Really?"

"Liana, you'd hate being with a biker. You think I'm harsh? Just wait until you're a sweetbutt."

"Come again?"

Vinn hesitated before answering. "A girl that's passed around by club members. *Yeah*. They have a name for their whores."

"And you don't with your *comares*?"

"That's not the same. I don't like my women fucking other men. I tolerate it, but I don't invite guys to touch what's mine."

"It doesn't matter. I'm not marrying him."

"He'll take the decision from you. You don't understand what they're like."

"You hate them. They hate you. Werewolves hate

vampires and vice versa. I get it." I sighed, bored with the conversation. "I read *Twilight*."

"I don't know what the fuck that is."

"It's a joke. I've listened to Daniel and Michael complain about bikers my whole life. I'm sure they do the same with us."

"Their culture is sick. We cross the line here and there, but we don't traffic women and kids. We're not involved in anything so fucked up."

"Yeah, you're an angel. Right up there with Mother Teresa, canonized for your huge cock. *Saint Dick*."

He stood over me, hands on his hips. "Liana, don't start with the smart mouth."

"You won't scare me into a relationship with you, fake or otherwise." I crossed my arms, the warmth from his kiss gone. "I'll take my chances with the biker."

Vinn could barely contain his rage. He jerked his shoulder in an irritated shrug. "You're just trying to piss me off."

"No, I'm not," I snapped. "If I have to marry someone, why not him?"

"*Are you crazy?*" The force of his yell blasted my ears as he rounded on me, snarling. "Are you out of your fucking mind?"

I flinched from every syllable. "Don't talk to me like that."

"I'll do whatever I damn well pleased, you *annoying*

brat. Is there one thing you can do without aggravating me? What is wrong with you?"

I lunged for the door, and he kept tossing me back like a rag doll. "Get out of my way!"

"Not until you start making sense."

"I see no difference between my *choices*. He's a gangster. You're a gangster. And also—I don't want your help!" I screamed brokenly. "I'm sick of you. I'd rather marry him than *pretend* to be with you."

Vinn's eyes flashed and dulled over. He seemed to stare through me, but I knew I'd hurt him.

He'd hurt me, too.

I'd spent every waking moment trying to heal from what he'd done.

"Li, I will only say this once." His graveyard voice spread ice through my stomach, his dark face set in a vicious expression. "You are mine."

NINE
VINN

Michael would kill me.

He'd eviscerate me for locking her in a room. Then he'd boil my balls in motor oil for making out with his sister because I'd done it under his nose. Fondling her pussy at the charity gala wasn't part of the plan, but how could I resist?

She'd given me the perfect opportunity. She had a sentimental side that I'd picked up on after visiting her apartment. Stepping in that bedroom was like looking into a time capsule of my youth. I'd been surrounded by photos of us, warm memories, things I'd forgotten. Luring her away from Michael had been easy.

I traced my lips, replaying how she'd kissed me so eagerly. If only I'd dragged that gorgeous fuck doll to her knees, I could've fed her my cock. As amazing as that would've felt, it was good that she rejected me. Hooking up with Michael's sister would've been the scandal of the century.

That didn't stop me from imagining. For days, I marveled at her reaction. I'd barely touched her, and she'd thrown herself at me. Liana was hot for me, and clearly in deep denial.

I'd rather marry him than pretend to be with you.

A feeble lie. Her tongue had been in my mouth only minutes before. She knew she wouldn't last a second as Killian's wife. The hell was wrong with *her*?

I kept tabs on her with the bodyguards I'd hired to replace Michael's. It took everything not to *drop in* her neighborhood. I had to figure out what I'd do with Little Liana.

I couldn't just fuck her.

Michael would murder me. He'd have to ask permission, but Nico would give him the go-ahead. Knowing Michael, he wouldn't bother dealing with our boss. He was never the rational type. He'd just shoot me—and I'd deserve it.

I owed him the truth.

Confessing my sins wasn't an option. I needed a well-crafted story that'd satisfy Michael and my aunt, the only people in my life who mattered. Lying would be easy enough. Getting her to agree would be difficult.

I thought about her way too much. Obsessing. Stalking. Poring over photos. I'd made a social media profile just to follow hers. Then I combed her online presence for *information* to answer a burning question.

How could I make her want to be with me?

"*Hey*. Are you listening?"

A baritone cleaved through my half-baked idea.

I dragged my gaze from the floor to Sergeant O'Flaherty, a police officer in his fifties with bags under his eyes, who was having another meltdown. His use as an insight into the Organized Crime Task Force hadn't dried up, but I hated the *coward*.

We stood at the construction site of Nico's next condominium development.

"I wasn't. Go again."

"Rage Machine told me they'd break into my house, tie me up, and make me watch as they rape my wife if I didn't release their member," he babbled. "I'm not the only one, Mr. Costa. Anyone who doesn't take bribes gets a death threat or their car torched!"

"Then accept a fucking bribe. What do you expect me to do? They're animals." I shrugged, watching a forklift shower dirt onto a pile. "I'm staying out of their war."

"Help Legion crush Rage Machine."

Fuck you, pay me. "I'm not sure that's worth my time."

"Well, you have to do something."

Or what?

I wasn't in the habit of throwing my soldiers into

unnecessary conflicts. I had enough of that shit with other men in charge. "Aren't you a cop? Arrest someone."

"No judge is willing to sentence a one-percenter. Nobody is standing up to the MCs. People are dying." Pete wiped his brow, leaning against his beat-up Chevrolet.

"How sad."

He stilled. Loathing marked his face. "You're a callous prick."

"Might surprise you, but I dislike not being able to walk around my city without a bomb going off. However, I won't get involved until it makes sense for the Family."

"You don't care about anyone."

Correct.

"Look, you want to stop Rage Machine? Follow their money. Find it. Choke it. Cut it off. Do whatever it takes to kill their finances. Everything will calm down when they can't finance their fucking war."

What could I do?

I wasn't a detective. I had no clue how a brand new MC group had the means to out-finance the much larger Legion with chapters in several states. I didn't feel like solving the mystery. It didn't concern me.

"Tell them to stop threatening us!"

Unbelievable. *Tell them*—like I could pick up the phone and boss a guy I'd never met.

"Okay. I'll ask if I can fuck their wives, too."

"This is serious!" He banged my car hood, and I shot him a glare. "The local economy is dead in the water. If you don't give a shit about citizens, maybe you care about *your* business drying up when everybody leaves Boston."

"Jesus, fine." I was sick of his mewling. "I'll keep my ears open. If I hear anything, I'll let you know."

I leaned in the driver's seat as Pete drove off. I viewed the biker wars like a cold. It'd worsen before the power struggle shook out its kinks, and then we'd be back to normal. Inserting myself into the conflict was unnecessary. I didn't understand why Nico kept harping on making peace with Legion. Who cared which MC emerged the victor? If they destroyed each other, perfect. My money was on Rage Machine. I hated Legion on account of the president demanding Liana's hand.

My thoughts went haywire. I'd offered to save her from them. What more did she need? I scanned our conversation—why had she been so pissed?

Vincent.

My stomach clenched.

I'd assumed Vincent was a dumb lie, but she'd practically thrown me from her house. Then she'd shown up at the gala with that college boy. She mouthed off to me constantly. Perhaps she resented me for taking her from the other guy.

My knuckles whitened. Heat pricked my chest.

Maybe she wanted to get with the other *Vincent*—or that prick who'd made my skin crawl.

What was his name?

James.

I let him off way too easy. My lip curled as I pictured them cozying up in some diner. I shoved my keys into the ignition, stopping as a shadow rippled the ground.

Fucking Pete.

I rolled down the window and stuck out my head, but the angry retort lodged in my throat.

Because I stared into the barrel of a gun.

TEN

VINN

Nico got out of prison.

Two years early.

Nothing could've prepared me for being jumped by my bodyguards, forced at gunpoint into a car, and driven to my boss's mansion. He'd materialized in Boston like a rabbit out of a magician's hat. Nobody told me he'd been released. Not the lawyers I kept on retainer or my informants inside his jail. He'd blindsided me.

I stood with Michael in Nico's living room, which doubled as a museum for my cousin Anthony. His athletic trophies filled the china cabinet. Pictures of the shithead smiled at me from every direction.

My father gave me his stupid name—Vincent—shortly before running out on my mom after I was born. I had no family except Michael's, and they were a hot mess.

Anthony had it all—money, great schools, sports, parents who loved him. I'd always felt like a peasant when I visited here. My clothes were too dirty for their furniture. I taught myself not to eat everything in sight because my mother couldn't pull it together enough to make me a sandwich.

I'd envied Anthony.

I'd resented his privilege. I'd stewed in jealousy at the mountain of gifts under the tree every Christmas. As I grew older, my contempt for him deepened into disgust. He'd wasted his potential. Thrown away all that education to become a waste of space. He'd been a junkie and liability.

But as I watched my heavyset uncle pace the living room, gun in hand, I wondered who was the real disaster.

"How did prison treat you, *zio*? They feed you well?" I pretended not to notice the thirty pounds of weight he'd added, smiling. "Should've told me you were back. I could've stopped at Lucchese's."

"Alessio did already." He motioned to a pile of meat on butcher paper. "Got me it as soon as he heard. Good kid."

That fucking asshole.

I ground my teeth. "He knew?"

"No. I called him a couple hours ago." Nico grabbed the bottle of wine, his hands trembling. "I wanted to get the full story. He said a lot of things that concerned me."

Great. "So he's underboss now?"

"I offered, but he doesn't want the job anymore—"

"Which he made clear when he left town!"

"You ruined what I built." His voice leapt from the low baritone to a thundering roar. "You destroyed our leadership, compromised our position in Boston, and you lost my son!"

Jesus. "I didn't lose your dipshit son!"

Nico seized the handle of his Glock and pointed it at me. "What did you call Anthony?"

Was he drunk?

It wouldn't be the first time Nico had one too many and shot someone. But I wasn't in the mood to lie down and die.

"Nico, put it down. You've had too much to drink."

"I'm not drunk." He stabbed it in the air like a toddler. "You have a lot to answer for. *Both* of you."

I rolled my eyes, meeting Michael's slanted gaze.

He stood beside me, fists clenched. He looked ready to blow, and the sight of his lips pressed together winded me like a gut-punch.

"You fucking maniac. You *bastard*." Michael's words blazed like a wave of fire as he screamed at Nico. "You took me in front of my kids! While I was picking them up at *daycare*."

A shock rippled through my limbs. Even I wasn't that crazy.

I stared at Nico. "Seriously?"

Nico seemed unconcerned. "I needed a conversation with you both."

"Where's Alessio, then?"

"I've already dealt with him," he snapped, wearing a sneer that reminded me of his douchey son. "You're next."

I opened my mouth to snarl an insult, and changed my mind. I bit the inside of my cheek. I fought the ribbon of anger working through my muscles.

Michael seized my arm, his grip biting. His pleading stare dug into my chest. He didn't deserve to have his brain dashed out in Nico's dated living room. People depended on him. Unlike me, he had a family who'd miss him.

So be it.

"Send Michael away," I muttered, my stomach hardening. "You've made it clear you can get him wherever he is. If you need to put a bullet in my head, fine, but leave him alone. Anthony was my responsibility."

Nico didn't budge. "He stays."

I had to save him.

I licked my dry lips. "Michael shouldn't be here."

"He. Stays."

Let him go, damn it. "This is fucked up, Nico."

"You know what's fucked up? Sitting in a cell while your nephews destroy everything you've built. You're a goddamned parasite, Vinn, and you." He faced Michael, who went rigid. "What the hell were you thinking? You murdered the asshole who knew where Anthony was!"

"I gave the order," I blurted. "Michael was just following orders. It's my fault—not Michael's."

A total lie, but whatever.

Michael buried his head in his hand. The other clawed his leg. It probably killed him to say nothing. The idiot better stay quiet and let me take the fall.

"How could you do something so stupid?" Nico screamed, the sound blasting my ear. "You should've kept him alive for questioning."

"No point. Crash was out of his mind. He didn't want to negotiate. He wanted to torture, so I made a decision."

"Yeah, a reckless one," he replied in a low voice. "Alessio would've never pulled this shit. He would've run it by me."

"How was I supposed to do that with you in jail?"

Nico pointed the gun at my face.

I waited for his judgment.

Images streamed in my head—waves lapping ashore, preening seagulls, gloomy skies and cold nights, tall glasses of beer and stacks of fried cod. A flicker of warmth shot into my chest.

The sting of metal on my cheek chased it away.

"You're lucky I'm in a forgiving mood," Nico sneered. "I'll give you *one* last chance."

Michael blew a sigh, but my insides roiled.

"Toe the line, because if I pull this trigger, you're headed straight for hell." He dipped his head, teeth flashing. "You cold *snake*."

Nico backed off, stowing the piece in his robe. "We're repairing the alliance you broke. The Legion president knows where my boy is, and all he wants is the girl."

The president didn't have Anthony. He was dangling him in front of Nico, hoping he'd bite.

"The girl is Michael's sister, and it's a scam." I jigged my knee restlessly, eye-fucking him. "They're playing you."

"No, they're not," he muttered. "He's on Leda, but I can't get to him without their connections."

"Well, that's convenient."

Leda was an island off the Caribbean owned by several billionaires. White-collar criminals, arms dealers, drug traffickers, and all manner of rich and corrupt flew in at invitation-only to network and make multibillion-dollar business deals. It was also a major human trafficking hub.

I hadn't bothered investigating because a mafia boss from Boston didn't pull any weight on Leda, and I'd assumed Anthony had been sold to a local rival syndicate and murdered.

"They sent me a proof-of-life video. He's there. I'm getting him back," Nico said, his fat face melting with a smile. "All I have to do is give him the girl. Liana."

A tide of nausea crawled up my throat.

Michael exhaled a ragged breath. "Again, we are not giving Liana away because it's up to me, her brother, not you."

"It's not up for debate."

"You might be boss, but there are rules." Michael's voice strained like a piano string, his growl darkening. "Break them, and you better be ready for the consequences."

Nico closed his eyes as though to shut out everything. "You'd understand if it was your son."

Michael shot upright, upsetting his chair. "I'm supposed to stand by and watch one of those animals marry my sister? *No fucking way.*"

"Michele," Nico warned. "Remember who you're talking to."

I couldn't believe Nico would sink so low.

This was the man who'd harped on the importance of family at every get-together. *Blood is thicker than water* was his constant refrain. Never mind that he'd picked an outsider to succeed him. And now, he was willing to sacrifice his niece for his impotent son.

The hypocrisy stabbed me in the brain, provoking a white-hot response in my body. Pain spiked into my head from my clenched teeth. I wanted to rip him apart.

"She'll be raped, Nico."

Nico jerked his head. "The president gave me his word he won't mistreat the girl."

"Do you know what this will do to my mother?" Michael exploded, his nostrils flaring. "You're forcing her to be a hostage."

"We are making this deal," Nico fired back. "I forgive you for screwing up with Crash, but you need to meet me halfway."

No.

My hands shook as I fought to keep them from wrapping Nico's throat. Michael met my gaze. Bloodlust glazed his red eyes. He would attack Nico. If I didn't defuse the situation, he'd beat the shit out of Nico, and it would end with him dead. We couldn't kill a boss and escape untouched. The hired guns outside would make sure of that.

"It's done," Nico said, interpreting our silence as mute acceptance. "Killian's picking her up right now."

My stomach knotted as I pictured the president throwing Liana over his shoulder.

I had to do something.

"Nico, I'm dating Liana." I licked my lips, grasping.

"I actually...I just asked her to marry me, and she said yes. We're *engaged*."

Nico set down the bottle, a ring of burgundy staining the tablecloth. "Bullshit."

I needed to sell this.

If I didn't, I had no idea what I'd do. "I swear to God, I'm marrying her."

He fisted my hair, digging the barrel into my temple. "I'll put my gun up your ass for lying to me, boy."

"Nico, come on. We've known each other since we were kids." He'd have to confirm the news at least, and that'd buy me time to talk to Liana. "I never told you, but I've been seeing her for a few months."

Michael stared at me before he had the sense to wipe his expression. "He's telling the truth."

I met Nico's pitiless gaze. It wouldn't be good enough. He was desperate. He'd do anything to save his son, even order me to break my fucking engagement.

"There are other women, Vincenzo."

His bitter voice bottomed out my stomach.

I blurted the first thing that came to mind—"Nico, she's pregnant."

ELEVEN
LIANA

Three days passed, but the memory of Vinn's mouth ghosted mine in the shower, pressed into me at work, and swirled my head with doubt. The intimacy of those kisses burned me. As did the ache when I pulled away. Whenever I replayed his flicking tongue and that initial jolt of surprise, sparks flooded my cheeks and spread *everywhere.*

He'd kissed me like he'd waited his entire life for a taste, and that poked a splinter of hope into my pessimism. Maybe he had feelings for me. People's opinions changed, didn't they? Michael had clashed with Carmela before falling for her.

I needed to stop thinking about Vinn.

I had to reorient myself and find the level-headedness that had severed him from my life, but I couldn't think about dating without wondering if I'd recapture the dreamlike intensity of that kiss.

I clocked in from my lunch break, returning to the glass-walled cafe. It faced Bourton University's limestone buildings, the grandness a harsh reminder that I'd never afford the tuition. Luckily, Michael footed the bill, but I used as little of his money as possible.

Working as a barista was all right. Occasionally, I dealt with frazzled grad students crying over their thesis papers between wiping tables, steaming milk, and drowning shots of espresso in flavored syrups. The summer job distracted me from my brother's death, Mom's chain-smoking, and the danger on the streets. Without it, I spent too much time cooped up in my apartment.

Staying busy was the antidote to a troubled mind. I only wanted to worry about whether I should take Chemistry or Physics to satisfy my physical science requirement.

Someone rapped on the counter.

I beamed at the customer, a lithe man in his thirties who carried himself in a way that said that he'd made it. My gaze slipped over his Adam's apple to a wide jaw and full lips, which pulled into a thick smirk when I met his sparkling blue eyes.

I studied his tattooed, muscled arms and leather cut.

My heart thundered as I read the small white patch —*president* and *Legion MC*. A ball throbbed low in my throat.

Not a coincidence.

"Mister President."

"I don't know about mister. Seems overly formal." He leaned over and offered me a hand. "Killian."

"Liana." I shook it, my eyes dry from not blinking. "Nice to meet you."

His powerful grip swallowed mine. Everything about Killian was too much, starting from the sensual flame in his smile, to his friendly touch. I gave him a pointed look, and he released me.

I stopped myself from wiping my hands on the nearest towel.

"You're cute in the apron," he murmured. "But I would've thought Michael treated his sister better."

My chest tightened. "I chose this job."

"So you *want* to earn minimum wage?" Killian's lips twitched as his voice took on an oily quality. "Boy, your brother should get a refund on that pricey Ivy League tuition. What are they teaching you?"

Ice touched my spine. "How do you know that?"

"I'm familiar with everybody, Liana. Especially you. I've watched you for a while. You run the treadmill every morning at eight in your Allston-Brighton flat. Your favorite pizza joint is around the block. You like hanging out with your friend Queenie. You're single, and, rumor has it, *untouched*."

My creep radar shot to the stratosphere. His hungry stare landed on intimate places. I shivered as though stripped naked.

"I was going to kill you," he confessed, stunning me. "You were supposed to be retribution for the six guys your brother killed a year ago. I had you in my sights. Almost pulled the trigger."

I snapped to attention.

All that registered in my brain was the jaunty French music breezing from the speakers, which dissolved into a saxophone cover of "La Vie En Rose."

"What stopped you?" I said.

"That's an excellent question. I'm still figuring that out."

He'd scared me with the dossier of information, the stalking, and watching me through windows. I needed to buy curtains—*fuck curtains*—I'd move to a high rise like Vinn's.

This had to be a joke.

"Did you get it out of your system?"

His eyebrows knitted and he pulled back his head.

"Scaring the shit out of me," I added for clarification. "Order a coffee, or I'm calling the police."

Not like they'd do anything.

He glanced at the menu and lowered his voice. "I'll have a steamy twelve-ounce of Italian roast. Don't need any sugar, but you can kiss the cup for me."

"*Buddy*, ask for her number and leave," a heavyset customer hollered. "Let's go!"

Killian's eyes flashed with a deadly arrogance as he glanced at the growing line behind him. His lips yanked over a wolfish smile as he flipped off the man, who cringed, turned tail, and jogged toward the exit.

When Killian swiveled back, his jacket drifted over his waist, revealing a gun.

Shit.

A lump swelled in my throat. My thoughts staggered in a thousand different directions. "Look. I don't want any trouble."

"Well, that makes two of us. Meet me there and bring me something sweet." He slid away, winking. "Besides yourself, I mean."

The fuck?

He strolled to the tables where he sat, his leather and jeans looking out of place among the students tapping on laptops. Nobody paid him any attention as he lounged there, bumping his knee to the happy music.

What should I do?

Vinn's warning pitted my gut with dread, because

this guy was nuts, and not leaving without me. Beyond the glass walls, chrome winked on the sidewalk. My bodyguard was gone—probably held at gunpoint—*crap*. I reached for the panic button, hesitating. Calling the police would create more problems than it'd solve.

Maybe I could smooth this over.

We'd done nothing but banter, and he had a calm presence. The president watched me with a small smile. His gaze never left me as I drifted to the espresso machine.

I made a drink with whipped cream and stepped around the counter. His expression lit up as I approached. He pulled out the chair next to him and patted the seat. I sank in the chair, pushing the cup toward him to bring this situation to sane ground.

"It's an iced mocha."

"Looks nice. Would you mind?" He nudged it. "You don't look bloodthirsty, but I can't be too careful. Nico Costa might force a pretty girl to poison me."

Whatever.

I rolled my eyes, grabbed it, and drank. Then I sucked the contents from the bottom of the straw.

"Satisfied?"

"Very. You're not what I expected." He took it back, rubbing at the spot where my lips touched. "I thought you'd be high maintenance, but here you are, slaving away at a cafe. Wiping tables. Picking up chairs. Is this what you really want?"

He'd spent way too much time thinking about me, and his unwelcome frankness gritted my teeth. I didn't need a stalker, especially a biker who was supposed to kill me before deciding to bulldoze my life and tell me what to do.

"Killian, you seem...decent," I settled on, skipping *crazy*, *creepy*, and *odd*. "But the truth is I'm just a college student. My brother's world has nothing to do with me. I have no interest in playing mafia politics. I'd like to take my classes and my internships in peace, so I'd appreciate it if you left me alone."

His smile grew, and my insides squirmed. "Like it or not, you're involved."

My nostrils flared. "But—"

"You're just what I need. Too good to be wasted as a sweetbutt."

Whoa.

The heaviness in my gut sank further. What would make him leave?

I stood. "I have to get back to work."

He caught my arm, locking me in the chair. "Sweetheart, you're not working here anymore."

"Says who?"

"Your future husband."

A violent throbbing began in my throat. "And who the hell is that?"

He lifted an eyebrow. "Me."

This guy was off his rocker, and I wasn't dealing with it.

"I don't have time for this. You're obviously drunk or high, and you thought coming in here and harassing Michael's sister would be hilarious."

"Your uncle gave you away," he growled, fingers digging into my flesh. "You're part of a trade."

I tried to keep my heart cold, but the idea that I'd been used for a transaction dipped me in lava. "My uncle wouldn't do that!"

Killian's voice smoothed to a velvet caress. "I won't hurt you. I just want you to be my wife."

Fear knotted inside me.

What disturbed me more—his words or the earnest hush in which he said them? I shrank from him, shaken by his intensity.

"You're crazy."

I shouldn't have said that.

Killian waved me off. "An arranged marriage isn't crazy. It's par for the course for people like us."

"*I'm not marrying you.*"

"You'll get to know me, and you'll realize I'm not horrible." He took my hand, but I wrenched from his grip.

"No. I found out what you did to Carmela."

"That wasn't me," he responded coolly. "And I wouldn't judge us all on one bad actor. Let's go."

"*No.*"

His lips thinned, and he frowned as though I behaved in a way that disappointed him. "I don't want to have to strap you to my bike."

"My brother would never, *ever approve of you*."

"You're not listening. It's not up to him."

He grabbed me, dragging me past the students gaping at us over laptop screens. We burst outside, and he marched me to a row of chrome.

A black fright swept through me.

"No." I yanked my elbow back. "I—I don't want this."

"Too bad." He engulfed me in his steel embrace, restricting my movement. "It's a done deal—"

My chest strained against a bottled scream, killed by my clamped lips. A fist wrapped my guts as he shoved me toward his motorcycle.

"Killian. S*top*."

My joy soared at the graveyard voice. It boomed from a Mustang rolling to the curb. Vinn stepped out, positioning himself behind the vehicle. He draped his arm over the door, his hair mussed, and his clothes wrinkled. He seemed off-kilter, not himself.

"Take another step toward those bikes, and I'll blow up every Harley dealership in this city."

Killian laughed, and so did the bikers lined on the street. "What do you want, Costa?"

"To chop off your hands for touching Liana." Vinn's slanted gaze shifted, warning me not to interrupt. "There's been a major miscommunication. She's *my* fiancée."

A horrible thrill shot through me.

"Really?" Killian's amusement grew as he faced me. "Where's your ring?"

I wet my lips. "I-I don't have one yet."

"How does someone propose without a ring?" Killian quipped.

"Not all women need a diamond, but I guess you wouldn't know that." Vinn leaned against the car, arms crossed. "You people buy your wives."

Killian beamed at him. "You have got to teach me how you nailed this girl down."

"Persistence," he said silkily. "We're childhood sweethearts, and I haven't had the chance to go shopping with the doctor appointments. She's pregnant." His words just about gave me a heart attack. "Nico was just released. He had no idea. Nobody did."

What the hell is he doing?

Lying through his teeth. He expected me to back

him, and I would, but then what? I wasn't pregnant and wouldn't be for years.

"Y-yeah," I stammered, recovering. "I'm a few weeks along."

Killian huffed. "I'm not buying it."

Vinn stepped forward, his eyes gleaming like volcanic rock. "I have two police cruisers on standby to raid your cocaine smuggling operation. Let her go, and I'll call them off."

Killian's mouth twisted. None of them would get jail time, but losing all that product would hurt. His pocket chimed a second later, and he laughed at the screen. "Oh, he's fucking good."

"Answer it." Vinn waved. "I'll wait."

Killian stabbed the button and held the phone to his ear. "What's up?" He sighed as a woman's voice blasted from the speaker. "Really?"

After a few moments, he ended the conversation. A heavy silence dropped between them before Killian broke it. "You won—this time. Shithead."

I wrenched free of Killian, walking stiffly. The walk became a run as I whirled around the car and flung into Vinn's embrace. I burst with a relieved gasp and threw my arms over his massive shoulders, squeezing.

Vinn soothed me without words as he drew me close, bathing me in his scent. He cupped my face, and my heart lurched madly. Blood rushed where he touched me. He smelled like the sea, fresh and weightless, like suntan lotion and the countless summers when I played with my brother and his best friend. The images washed over me like a wave lapping my feet.

Vinn's lips brushed my ear before trailing to my cheek, where he kissed me. Foolishly, I let the heat from it warm me.

"Do exactly as I say. You're mine now."

TWELVE
VINN

Nico had put a gun to my goddamned head.

After everything I'd done for the Family.

The countless pep talks with his son, sending him to rehab, visiting Nico in jail...all of it had added up to a big, fat zero. I'd killed men I barely knew. I'd fiercely defended our interests because, without my uncle, I'd still be a jobless felon.

I had nothing but this.

I would've gladly died on a Costa hill.

For *what*?

He'd been ready to blow out my brains a few hours ago. Nothing mattered to him but that jackass, Anthony. He'd only spared me because Liana's "pregnancy" made her a worthless bargaining chip. I would've jumped in front of a speeding train to save her life. *He* was in a hurry to dispose of her.

The betrayal sat like a rock in my throat.

Fuck up again, and your kid won't have a father.

He'd said it right before I drove to Liana. I didn't feel the impact until Liana was safe. Now, I burned with a corrosive hatred.

I charged into the kitchen. Drawers slammed as I searched for something to drown the rage. I tore through cupboards, finding a half-filled fifth that some chick had brought over. The tinted liquid poured like oil.

I pressed the cup to my mouth and drank. The floral syrup hit my tongue, pitting my stomach with nausea. Like death in a bottle. Specifically, like the purple flowers that had sprouted all over Iraq. Bitterness chased away my short-lived relief.

Tentative footsteps tapped the floor.

Shit. I wasn't alone. Suddenly, resentment over all those times she'd shown up at the hospital and rehab washed into my gut with my next gulp. Liana was always there to witness my weakest moments.

"Vinn, you're stronger than this."

I closed my eyes. "Leave."

"No."

Of course she wouldn't. "I'm not asking."

Judging by her approach, she didn't give a shit. "What do you really want, Vinn?"

To be numb.

It was no use. I couldn't wall myself in ice. Liana had

blown back into my life, and, ever since, I'd been a fucking mess. Distracted. Angry. Impulsive.

Jealous.

Killian's face materialized in my head.

I hurled my drink.

A small gasp echoed behind me as glass shattered over tiles, the shards slipping into the gas range. My vision fogged over with the image of Killian all over Liana. It'd been so much worse than James, because the biker had the means to steal her from me.

Over my rotting corpse.

Liana bumped into my back. Her hands slid across my midsection and anchored over my arms.

My pulse skittered from the unexpected touch. I didn't do well with being restrained, even if it was by a pint-sized girl I could toss a hundred yards. I tugged her wrists.

She cinched harder.

"Li, I don't like being held."

"That's because you're not used to it." Liana stroked my abdomen, and discomfort swooped into my gut. "Get over it. If you're this uncomfortable about a hug, we're screwed. You'll never convince anyone we're a real couple."

She had a point.

I clutched her forearm as my heartbeat galloped ahead. "I'm not in the mood for whatever this is."

"You need a hug, Vinn."

I need to kill everyone.

Annoyance stabbed at me as she inhaled deeply, tightening like a belt. The last thing I wanted to be was violent, especially to her, but a dangerous impulse stirred in my body. I ached to throw her on the bed and fuck away some of this frustration.

"I can't be nice to you right now."

"You don't have to be."

"Liana." I gritted my teeth, fighting to keep my rage under control. "Leave me the hell alone."

I seized the vodka, breaking from her hold.

"No." She latched onto me like a barnacle. "Vinny, don't do this to yourself."

That soft tone beckoned too many bad memories.

A knot sank in my throat as she shoved herself between me and the counter. Something in her voice had stolen all desire for drinking, and I let her take the bottle. She tipped the booze, emptying it into the sink. As the purple liquid circled the drain, she leaned into me.

"It'll be okay," she murmured. "We don't have to jump into anything."

She was dead wrong.

If you're not pregnant in a few weeks, he'll know I lied.

I couldn't pile that on top of everything else.

I tensed as she rubbed my back, the warmth a shock

to my system. Pink stained her cheeks as she stepped away, transferring her grip as she led me from the kitchen.

Watery sunlight filtered through the clouds, filling my living room with washed-out tones. We sat on my couch, facing the Boston skyline. She untied the green apron and slipped it from her neck, shaking out her hair that'd glided through my hands like goose down. A black tank was all she wore underneath, and the seashell necklace dipped in her cleavage.

The sight of it encased my chest in ice.

I wished the man who gave it to her a slow, painful death.

"Let's figure this out," she said mildly, as though we faced a tricky problem on an exam. "What can we do to change Nico's mind?"

"Nothing."

"I can't accept that, Vinn."

I clenched my jaw so hard, pain shot into my teeth. "Well, too bad. It is what it is."

"He can't do this to us," she burst. "There are *rules*."

"They don't apply to him."

"Of course they do. Nico's the boss of the Family."

"He cares more about his son. Our *baby* is the only thing in the way of getting Anthony back." I rubbed my forehead. "Nico will come after me."

"Not if you kill him first."

Apparently, we were on the same page.

Disturbing.

My back stiffened. "Don't talk like that."

"Why not?"

Her brows flickered as she met my gaze, her beautiful face shining with a naive optimism that clashed with her words. She was supposed to be all sweetness and light.

"I'd hate it if you lost the part of you I like the most."

Liana rolled her eyes, but her blush spread to her chest. "Says the guy who threatened to fuck my mouth."

Maybe she was right.

I was a goddamned hypocrite, and Liana had changed from the mousy girl who'd doted on me. She talked a lot more. Most of what she said, I *resented*, but she had a steel spine like her brother. She didn't seem to give a damn about my approval.

I respected that.

But it was inconvenient as hell.

Giving up on placating her, I shook my head. "I'll handle Nico, but it'll take a while. I can't just snap my fingers and—"

Kill him.

I couldn't say it.

"How, then?"

"Don't worry about it." I breathed deeply, sinking

into the cushions. "Real question is, how will we make it until then?"

Liana crossed her legs. "No idea."

"We'll have to fake ultrasounds, doctor appointments, blood tests, baby showers, *everything*. Nico will be hanging over my fucking shoulder, waiting for me to make a mistake to shoot me, so he can hand you over to Killian. You'll be here all day."

I hated this.

It wasn't in my nature to *bluff*. When threatened, I hit back.

I hit *hard*.

However, I couldn't murder Nico without the Family backing me, plus I'd risk pissing off every greaseball from here to Montreal. Nico had powerful friends who'd hunt me down. I could strike him down and die, or I could bide my time. And if I chose to wait, I needed to buy a ring. Book a venue for our party. Move her in the house. I had to tell Michael I really did knock up his sister.

Liana's hopeful face filled me with dread. The words stuck in my throat. She would *not* be okay with this.

"Li, he needs to think I got you pregnant."

A strained laugh burst from her clamped lips. "This is so insane."

"I know."

"A pregnancy can't be *faked*. You fudge all the tests

you want. My flat stomach gives it away." Liana's incredulity slashed through my calm. "What about my mom, my friends, the coworkers who've seen me drinking, and God, what about *Michael*?"

"You'll have a miscarriage."

"Then we're right where we started, and I'm not fabricating a goddamned miscarriage." She groaned, rubbing her eyes. "I'll leave town."

"Then he'll figure out I lied and kill me. And he'll force you into Killian's arms, except you'll probably be passed around because you defied your husband-to-be."

"What if we—"

"We're engaged, Li. We'll make it look good. We're not telling anyone this is fake. Not Michael. Not your mom. *Nobody*."

"Why not?"

"The more people we let in on the secret, the more potential leaks."

"Vinn, this will *never* work. You may have bought me a month—maybe two—and then it'll be obvious I'm not pregnant."

I couldn't dwell on it. "One crisis at a time."

"Tell him it was a false positive."

"*No*," I ground out. "The only reason Nico backed off was because he thinks you're pregnant. No man wants a woman who's carrying another guy's kid."

Her mouth twisted. "Well, that's a lousy attitude."

"Sorry. I live in the real world."

"Faking a pregnancy is too much." She slid off the couch, shaking her head. "It's despicable. I can't do it."

I marveled at her ability to blaze past the actual problem.

"You think I want this? I have to tell my best friend I knocked up his sister." Christ, just imagining it made me sick. "You're the hapless victim. I'm the bastard who ruined you."

She flinched. "We don't have to do any of this!"

"Unfortunately, we do. He's not letting this go." I mimed a pistol and tapped my temple. "I had a fucking gun to my head. So did your brother. I saved us by the skin of my teeth."

"Ohmigod. Are you okay?"

The tenderness in her gaze was ill-fitting for the heat stirring in my chest.

"I'm fine. Let's discuss what we're telling Michael."

She shook her head, pained. "No, Vinn."

"Trust me. I don't like it, either."

"He'll never forgive us."

"Yeah, but he'll be *alive.* As long as he's breathing, he can hate me all he wants. Mike sucks at hiding his feelings. One look at him, and Nico will know I lied..." I trailed off, my stomach hardening. "You don't want me dead. Do you?"

She was stricken. "Of course not."

"Good. There's hope for us."

"Vinn, there is no *us*."

"You better adjust your attitude quick, because he's coming over. He'll expect us to act like a couple." I strolled to the couch, and she joined me, fidgeting with the pillow. "Understand?"

Liana swallowed hard. "All right."

"*Okay.*"

I steeled myself for the disaster. It'd be unpleasant. He'd despise me, but he wouldn't kill me outright. I patted my lap.

"Climb on, Li."

She touched her throat. "What?"

"Don't make a big deal out of it. He should find us together." I waited, but Liana stiffened as though I demanded a blowjob. "You shoved your tongue in my mouth not too long ago."

"This is different," she whispered. "It's more intimate."

"That makes no sense."

Liana said nothing, her hands balled at her sides.

"*Get on me.*"

Finally, she obeyed. Liana acted like my clothes were soiled. Halfway between her awkward shuffle over my legs, I grabbed her waist and yanked. Her ass hit my thighs with a satisfying thump. She rolled on me, stiffening when I pulled her into an embrace.

Liana burrowed deeper, her curves rubbing my groin. She plastered her face to my neck, her breath misting me. When she wound her arms around me, I understood what she meant. This was disturbingly intimate. My one-night stands were hollow by comparison, because even with my dick inside them I'd never felt so close to someone.

Her bra strap slipped down. I pushed it over her shoulder, a mistake, because Liana's softer-than-silk skin made me wonder about the rest of her body. I had a fantastic view of her cleavage, the hem of her tank blocking everything I ached to explore. I played with that loose strap as my cock begged me to rip it off.

Liana seemed to sense the change in temperature. She fiddled with my buttons, sliding them in and out of their holes, teasing my chest. The temptation to kiss her overwhelmed me. Ignoring it wrenched at me. It felt wrong, like smothering a kitten. I wanted it to grow, but Michael was due any second.

I couldn't summon the energy to ask her to stop. She grazed my abdomen, her fingers like little fire wands. She trailed them over my pecs, stroking my head, her touch massaging.

My frown lines disappeared. I melted into her, lost in a tide of relief.

Her lips brushed my ear.

A fist hammered the door, yanking me from the moment.

Liana dug her nails into me as Michael's greeting drifted inside.

Fuck off, Michael. "Let yourself in!"

He murmured something. A key scraped the lock, and the door opened and slammed. His shoes clipped the floor, the echo growing louder. The anticipation shot my veins with adrenaline.

I adopted a somber expression.

Michael strolled in, talking a mile a minute. "Sorry I'm late. I had to rush home and console my very upset wife. Took ages to leave, and then I hit traffic in the Pike. You know how it—goes."

Michael gaped at us. His eyes bugged out at Liana, who still sat on my lap. "What are you *doing*?"

Liana's arms slipped from my neck, but she kept them on me. Heat tingled my skin as her frosty blues swept over me and stabbed in Michael's direction.

"Nothing."

"That's not an answer." Michael pivoted at me, his voice rising. "*Vinn*. What the fuck?"

My mouth went dry.

Out with it. "So, we've been dating for a while."

He rolled his eyes. "Jesus, relax. I know you were only doing it for Nico's benefit."

"No, Michael. It's the truth."

He wet his mouth. "Wait, so you're actually dating?"

"Yeah."

Michael's chest swelled, but he didn't explode. His hands clenched and released, as though practicing his death grip.

"It's been a few months," I clarified, as Michael turned the shade of a tomato. "I never asked because I knew you wouldn't approve."

"I'll deal with you later." Michael ripped his gaze from me, addressing Liana like an outraged father scolding a child. "Get off him. *Now*."

"You don't tell me what to do anymore."

"Oh, *really*?" he snarled. "You can kiss your rent goodbye—"

"Fine. I'm not going back there, anyway." Liana faced me, beaming with a smile that raced my pulse. "I'm moving in with Vinn."

"*You're what*?"

"We're together." A joy I'd never seen before shone in her eyes and bubbled in her rushed words. "And there's nothing you can say to stop it."

My heart hammered. The pit of my stomach churned.

Why did that sound real?

I wiped the shock from my face and squeezed Liana's shoulder. "Your brother and I need a talk."

Judging by the nails piercing my skin, she objected to leaving me alone.

I fixed her a glare. "Just do it, hon."

Liana let out the smallest scoff and slid from my lap. Then she patted Michael's arm. "Don't hurt him."

Michael seemed unable to speak. He was like a robot, his head jerking toward me. He didn't utter a sound until she disappeared into my room.

"You mother*fucker*." Darkness rippled from Michael as his fist unclenched, the key fob dropping to the floor. "Behind my fucking back."

The hurt bled through his voice, trembling in the air like electricity in a lightning storm.

I stood. "I knew you wouldn't approve."

"You never asked!"

I crossed my arms. "I tried. Whenever we touch the subject, you always make your opinion of me very clear."

"Now I get it." He slammed his palm into my chest, shoving me backward. "Leo DiMaggio was in your way."

Yes, he was. "She was mine, and you were throwing men at her."

"Fuck you. You're juggling six women at any given time."

"Judge me if you want, but—"

"You're supposed to be my best friend. Jesus Christ, you were the one guy I thought I could count on!" Spittle flew from Michael's mouth as he let loose. "I'll kill you."

This was going well.

He'd never looked at me with that demented bloodlust. I retreated as he advanced, determined not to injure him. A lot of his rage was probably leftover fuel from Nico's betrayal, which I factored into my response.

"Mike, I'm not done explaining."

"You've been fucking my sister," he bellowed like a wounded animal. "How dare you?"

Heat stung my cheeks.

I couldn't deny that, could I? "I didn't mean to disrespect you."

"You're a coward and a *liar*, and I'm kicking your ass."

Michael vaulted over the sofa and lunged at me. His right hook crashed into my cheek, the unexpected force smashing my head against the wall. I ripped away from him, the agony radiating into my teeth.

Fuck. It hurt.

"Yes, I've been dating her. In secret," I snarled, rubbing my jaw. "Because I knew your reaction would be over the top."

"Don't act like you're a gentleman," he shouted, making violent moves toward me. "You were with another chick last week."

Damn it. "We weren't exclusive."

He took that even worse.

"Oh, so you're only dipping in my sister while you

bang your mistresses. You piece of shit," he screamed, the veins standing out on his neck. "I'll rip your nuts off."

He swung.

I hurled a table between us, jamming the edge under his ribs. "Michael, I asked her to marry me. At the gala."

The lie stuck in my throat as Michael's face drained of color.

"Is this a sick joke?"

"It's past time for me to settle down." I wished I had a handle of whiskey to drown in. "Get married. Have kids."

"Oh, God. Don't tell me you really knocked her up, too."

My stomach throbbed. I drew a deep breath and raked my hair.

"Yeah, I did."

Michael went rigid. He stared at me in openmouthed disgust. Devastation shattered his eyes. Then his expression grew hard. "You've ruined her life."

"Michael, I'll do right by her."

"You better, you fuck-up."

That gouged at me. "I asked her to marry me. She said yes."

"Like she had a choice, with you as the father." Michael's cold tone somehow hit me harder than his red-faced fury. "I swear to God, Vinn. This better not be fake. If you're not really marrying her—"

"I am."

"Shut up." He fisted my shirt, growling. "You saved our lives. That's the only reason you're not on the floor, bleeding. Put a ring on her. A real one, Vinn."

"I will."

He unclenched his grip and wiped his suit, as though I'd contaminated him. He stepped back, radiating contempt. "I don't care who you are or what's in my way. Marry her, or I'll kill you."

THIRTEEN
LIANA

I had to escape.

I could've handled faking a relationship, but pretending to be his *expecting* bride-to-be?

My worst nightmare. Braving the war-torn streets was more appealing than spending weeks attached to Vinn's arm, belonging to him but not *really*.

I ran into a room with charcoal walls and ebony furniture, shutting the door. Questions stuck in my throat as I took in the desaturated landscape photos—his *bedroom*. It was overwhelmingly masculine. My gaze landed on the pile of sweats and T-shirts in a basket, the walk-in closet packed with muted colors, and the bed.

The few times I'd visited with Michael, he'd caught me wandering Vinn's penthouse, but I'd never had the guts to snoop in here. Now my hands itched to look through his things. My brother's distant shouts faded to a dull murmur as I glimpsed a familiar picture.

It can't be.

I squeezed my eyes shut and opened them again.

It sat on his nightstand, wrapped in an ugly, red-and-white frame. I seized my Christmas gift to him from years ago as the disastrous party at The Black Cat washed over me. My mouth dried as I fingered the cheap wood.

I'd assumed he'd thrown it away.

He kept it.

My thoughts went blank with that simple truth. Not only that, but he also displayed the thing. Put it where he'd see it every morning. I had no measure of time as I sat, cradling the photo, and then the door creaked.

Vinn's thick build edged through, his presence filling the bedroom like a heavy mist. The angry mark flushing his cheek and his wild hair suggested he and Michael had exchanged blows.

"Oh my God. I didn't hear you fighting. Are you all right?"

"Yeah." He smiled, and it softened his expression. "What are you doing?"

I grabbed the picture. "I was just hanging out, and I saw this. I never thought you'd keep it."

"I keep everything you give me."

I met his gaze, and a javelin-like shock ran through me.

Really?

I didn't believe it—I *couldn't*. I gawked at him, expecting Vinn's deadpan to break into laughter. It jumbled my insides to watch him carefully replace it on the nightstand.

"Your brother's gone."

I stepped back, swallowing. "I'm staying?"

"I guess we're roommates, Li."

A warning whispered in my ear. This was temporary.

"Which is my room?"

"Here."

Alarm rippled down my spine. "Where will *you* sleep?"

"With you. I don't have guest rooms."

I scooted away, my anxiety deepening to a white-hot panic. "Why not?"

Vinn shrugged. "I hate having people over. Why give them an opportunity to stay the night?"

"I can't share a bed with you!"

Vinn rolled his eyes like I was a drama queen. He didn't understand what this forced intimacy would do to me.

Pretending to be his girlfriend felt just as dangerous as marrying a stranger. He had no idea how much I'd suffered over the years. How could I tell him that without confessing *everything*?

No.

Never.

He couldn't find out I'd held a torch for him my whole life. He didn't feel the same. It didn't matter, anyway. He'd changed from the gentle giant who chased me on the beach.

But he came for you.

He lied for you.

A swell of hope kicked up inside me, but I shoved it aside. We needed strict boundaries. Otherwise I wouldn't survive a fake engagement with Vinn. If I walked into this with my heart open, I'd be crushed.

That twisted in my stomach.

"Why do we have to live under the same roof?" I demanded. "You could set me up in an apartment across the hall."

"I could, but why would I want you out of my sight?"

His seductive tone blistered my cheeks, but I clung to denial like a raft in an ocean.

"Don't you trust me?"

"No. You're quite the liability, Li. I haven't forgiven you. You might pull a stunt like you did with James, and I can't have my fiancée embarrassing me in front of my friends and business partners."

"You're the one who needs to be watched."

He raised his chin, his eyes stony. "I dial it way back for you."

"I wasn't under the impression you did anything for me."

A ring of fire seized my ankle, and I flew across the sheets. He clawed my leg, pulling me to the edge, where he sat.

"Stop!"

"I'm done treating you like a princess." He glided up my calf, anchoring under my knee. "From now on, you're just another girl."

"Does that mean you'll break off our *relationship* in two weeks?"

His mocking smile taunted me. "Still angry about the other women who aren't in my life?"

"Not at all," I ground out. "I'm identifying the facts. That behavior won't fly with my family."

"I think I'll manage."

"Can you *pretend* to be decent?"

Vinn's gaze roamed down my neckline. "With the right motivation, anything's possible."

Meaning what?

A hot ache grew in my throat. My body screamed *yes*, even though it was like hitting a self-destruct button. Intimacy with Vinn would be the beginning of my end.

He released my leg. He tugged at his shoes, flinging the Oxfords from him in a careless swing. Then he tore off his shirt, his fingers unsnapping the buttons so fast my cheeks warmed. I averted my eyes, but he lurched off and moved into my vision. Shirtless. Gorgeous.

The sight of him half-naked rooted me to the spot. He was a living work of art, beautifully proportioned, his muscles carved in merciless lines. My gaze traveled across his broad shoulders and the round muscle rippling into his bicep. I sucked in my breath at the V of his muscled frame tapering to a trim waist. He still had a soldier's body. I imagined him thumbing his black briefs and stepping out of them.

The air thinned as he undid his belt.

God, yes. Take it off.

He paused. His head turned as though he'd heard the comment, his eyes sweeping over me in a passionless glance. Then his lips curled into a devastating grin. My heart thumped as he approached, his waist at eye-level. He curved a finger around my chin. I drifted on a cloud at the softness gliding my cheek.

His other hand strayed to his crotch.

"Thought I'd make it easier for you to watch."

Am I dreaming?

Riveted, I stared at the fingers playing with his slacks. He unbuttoned them with a rough snap as his other hand cupped my face, lighting me on fire. He traced my neck, jolts tingling my skin. My mouth burned as he seized the zipper. He moved it down.

Lightheadedness swept through me.

"Li, want me to keep going?"

My thighs clenched as his thumb skimmed my lips. A feverish wave began at my pussy, claiming my body. My senses spun from the aquatic scent surrounding me.

He zipped back up.

"Yes," I blurted.

His fingers threaded my hair as he lowered the zipper once again. A gasp escaped me as he rode the waistline of his pants. He pulled them. They clung to his thick legs, revealing an athletic waist, and a mouthwatering bulge stretching his black briefs. His hardness electrified me.

My heart hammered. "We shouldn't."

"Why not? You're my *fiancée*."

Boundaries.

We needed them, stat.

Truth was, I could come up with many reasons to avoid Vinn. None of them mattered to the heat flushing around my nipples or the hot ache growing between my legs.

Vinn's grip tightened. "Touch me."

His demanding tone sent a current through me.

"I-I can't."

"You had no problem following orders last time. Seems like you'll have a hard time with this arrangement," he taunted. "Can't get off. Can't mouth off to me."

"What makes you think that'll stop?"

His thumb pulled my lip, showering me with jolts. "Keep at it, and I'll give you what you deserve."

"Watch yourself, Vinn."

"Or you'll what? Make good on your promise to ruin me?"

"I could do a lot of damage." My nails stabbed into my palm as I turned away from his welcoming warmth. "But I'll settle for quietly making your life a living hell."

"A few hours alone with me will have you purring like a kitten."

"You're blinded by arrogance." I mastered my shaking voice. "I know you. I could really mess with you."

"You don't have it in you."

My nipples tingled against my tank top, betraying every thought that condemned Vinn. One glance at him and my heart lurched. Even the sound of my name on his lips made me smile. I'd spent so long waiting for him to want me. Now that he did, my thoughts whirled in a thousand different directions.

I needed to *resist*.

"You don't want to test me, Vinn." I cleared my throat and shoved backward. "I'll tell Michael the engagement is a farce."

"Then I'll force you down the aisle for *real*, and put this whole thing to bed." He slid over the mattress as he pursued me, and I fought the ripple of excitement. "Speaking of, I never made good on my promise to fuck your mouth. I meant to do it, but never followed through. I got distracted by a kiss."

My pulse fluttered as he backed me against the headboard, his hand skimming my knee. Sparks jumped across my thigh, his presence so galvanizing it sent a tremor through me.

"I haven't stopped thinking about it, Li."

Me either.

Despite my fear, an awful joy swept through me. My stomach churned, half anticipation, half dread.

"Why did you have to cross the line?"

"I should've done it a long time ago." He hooked a strand behind my ear. "I had no idea you and me could happen. I never knew, Liana."

My troubled spirits quieted.

His hands dove into my hair, and his mouth covered mine. A shock jolted my lips as he pressed into me. He angled his head, his gentle strokes burning me. The kiss sang through my veins, urging me to respond. His feather-light kisses scorched my jaw before he returned to my mouth, claiming me with a savage intensity.

I gasped.

He left my mouth to mark my body with wet kisses. Shivers of ecstasy followed as he pulled the tank top. An ache balled in my throat as he nuzzled my neck and breathed a kiss there.

My heart stalled when he pulled my tank top over my breasts. Softly, his hand outlined their curves, my skin blazing with the intimacy. I arched into his palm, and his lips crashed on mine. He claimed me with a demanding mastery, thrusting his tongue, sucking, *biting*.

I moaned, locked in his embrace. I relished in the feel of him, his vitality, the burn consuming my body. The instinct to surrender. I was only a virgin in the strictest sense, but kissing Vinn made me breathless and confused, like an eighteen-year-old girl. I had no idea how to handle a man. I tasted him with a flick of my tongue.

His tormented groan invited more, so I caressed the strong tendons in his neck and the broad panes of his back.

My emotions whirled as his hard body slid over mine, my breasts tingling with his hair-roughened chest. He caged me with his arms as he descended, devouring my mouth. My calm shattered with the hunger of his kisses.

He lit up with a carnal grin that pressed into my throat and traced my breasts' curves. My belly twitched as he descended, claiming my nipple with a wet stroke.

A lightning bolt of desire struck me.

I'd felt nothing like it before.

My fingers dove into his thick hair as he licked, sucking me into his mouth. Arousal slicked me as if his mouth was between my legs, and then his legs moved over mine. His lips teased my nipples into hardened points. His hands roamed my breasts, squeezing.

My thoughts spun. This was amazing, but way too fast.

Stop.

Shock wedged the word in my throat.

His hand slid from my breast to my taut stomach, where he fingered the button on my jeans. If I let him continue, I wouldn't be able to put on the brakes.

"*Vinn.*"

His gaze flicked at me. Then he pushed himself closer, cupping my face with his giant palm. "What is it?"

"Too fast."

Vinn smoldered. Then he shifted the straps of the tank top over my shoulders, the rosy glow in his cheeks the only sign he was affected.

I readjusted my necklace, burning.

Vinn frowned, as though it had stopped him from getting off. "No more other men, Liana."

I flinched. "What are you talking about?"

"You know what I mean. You have somebody you're stuck on." His glare dipped, boring into the necklace.

"The other Vincent—whoever he is—he's gone. He's *dead*."

Did he not remember?

I let out a choked laugh. "Vinn—"

"I'm not joking, Li."

His interruption cut off the truth—*he'd* given me the damned seashell. I'd made it into a necklace. Vinn's jealousy might've been hilarious in a different light, but the wicked irony sliced open the healing wound.

He really didn't remember.

My resentment of him swelled into a tidal wave. Horrible thoughts consumed me as I spiraled into a bleak pit. I'd clung to that day on the beach for years. He'd given me the shell before he was deployed. How could he forget? A desperate ache surfaced like old rot.

I gazed at Vinn in despair, my vision clouded with tears. I ached to tell him the truth, but selfishness made me retreat. Hearing him admit he didn't recall the moment that defined me would rip me in half.

I wasn't ready.

I couldn't let him go.

His expression turned grim as his eyes flicked over my face and clenched hands. "He better not be in your life, Liana."

As usual, he'd drawn the wrong conclusion.

A hot tear rolled down my cheek.

"He's not," I ground out. "And never will be."

"Remember who you belong to," he said, his tone chilling. "I won't show mercy to anyone who touches what's mine."

I flinched at the callousness.

Then he left, slamming the door.

FOURTEEN
LIANA

I MOVED into Vinn's place.

This was a bizarre dystopian nightmare, ripped straight from my most angst-ridden teenage years. I spent days in total isolation, wandering the empty halls between planning our engagement party. After quitting my job and internship, there wasn't much to do but explore Vinn's monochrome house.

Vinn's chef came once a day to cook dinner, but we ate in separate rooms. The only signs of his presence were the echoes of his gym equipment. When he wasn't bolting down protein shakes or fixing egg-white scrambles, he pumped iron. He worked out as often as possible, probably because it was the only room I had no interest in checking out. He'd abandoned his other hobbies. He never cracked the photography books sprawled over his coffee table, or touched the antique cameras shoved in his closet. Video games stacked his shelf, but he didn't play them.

He was avoiding me.

All clues pointed to jealousy. Whenever his gaze landed on my necklace, he darkened like it'd done him a personal wrong. If he'd have admitted his feelings, I would've told him the truth, but he had to make the first step.

He had to *remember*.

I curled up under his thick comforter and flicked through my cell, researching the LSAT. One more year at Bourton, and then I'd finish my undergraduate degree in English. I still had to pick my classes and tooled with taking a leave of absence to think about law school.

Vinn kept the thermostat set to *snow*, so I spent a lot of time hiding under blankets. It didn't help that his bed was ridiculously comfortable.

The door yawned.

Warmth slipped into my belly as heavy footsteps thumped closer. He made a sound of pure frustration and ripped the sheets off.

Bruise-like shadows smudged under his narrowed eyes. He apparently resented that I hogged his room, but it wasn't my fault he was too stubborn to buy a futon.

He peered at my phone. "Are you watching porn?"

I shoved myself upright. "*No.*"

"That was a defensive no." He wrenched it from my grip and swiped through my screens.

"Hey!" I bounced off, lunging at him. "Give it back!"

Vinn lifted it out of reach, glaring as he thumbed through my messages. "Who the hell is Adrian?"

"None of your fucking business!"

Vinn dodged my violent swings and scrolled through texts. "Why do you have so many guys on your contacts list?"

That was rich.

He had an encyclopedia of women at his disposal, but if I texted five men, including my brother, that was a *problem*.

I opened my mouth to hurl an insult and counted to ten. I couldn't lose my shit in front of Vinn. "It's twenty-freaking-twenty. I'm allowed to have male friends."

He smoldered at the screen, ignoring me.

I raised on tiptoe to read the string of texts.

James: Liana, want to hang out?

Me: No thanks. Just got in bed.

James: I could come over...wreck your tight pussy. Do you like eye contact while I'm eating you out?

Me: Error #4352 Message could not be sent because this user thinks you're a disgusting asshole.

Rage hardened Vinn's granite-like face. It struck me

how disheveled he looked with the beard clinging to his jaw, the evidence of sleepless nights, and the dark curls begging for a comb. They painted a strange picture.

I'd seen him angry, but never *upset*.

Before I could ask what was wrong, he stabbed the button to block James's number. Alarm zipped down my spine.

I choked out a laugh. "Vinn, you can't do that."

"I just did."

I gritted my teeth. James could get run over by a train. I didn't care about him. It was the principle of Vinn blocking people with impunity that mattered.

"You're overstepping boundaries," I said with a desperate firmness. "And it won't work anyway because I can *unblock* him."

Vinn rounded on me, his nostrils flaring. "You are never talking to this *jamook* again."

My nails bit into my palms. "I can handle inappropriate jerks. I'm doing it *right now*."

"This is revolting," he hissed. "Why do you tolerate his shit?"

"I don't," I ground out. "I shut him down every time."

"Why haven't you blocked him?"

I shrugged, annoyed with the inquisition. I believed in keeping my enemies close. The occasional lewd comment paled compared to his behavior, which I'd suffered through because I wouldn't bring drama to our social circle.

I was sick of men white-knighting me. "Stay out of my private life."

"That no longer belongs to just *you*."

"Then give me your phone!" My shouting pierced my ears, but Vinn never flinched. "I want to see your mistresses deleted from your contacts list."

His left eyebrow rose a fraction. "Why should I do that?"

The silken thread of warning hit my gut like a sledgehammer. Despair tore at my heart at the idea of him giving them any of his attention.

I hated him, and I loathed my vulnerability to him.

"We're together. You can't."

"Our relationship is *fake*," he mocked, a dark smile carving into his face. "The one I have with them isn't."

My cheeks blistered.

I lifted my chin, meeting his hostility head-on. "You don't have relationships. You have flings. Stupid, meaningless, one-night stands you don't even enjoy."

"How the hell would you know?"

"Looking into your eyes is like staring into a black hole. Any guy who needs that many women to feel fulfilled has a problem."

He tossed my phone on the bed, yelling. "I like

fucking random women just as much as you love pissing me off!"

Too far.

My misery was a steel weight. I bit my lip until it throbbed like my heartbeat.

Vinn's gaze searched me, and the aggression dropped from his face.

"Li?" His velvet tone was almost an apology.

Fuck him.

I smothered a sob, grabbing his phone from the nightstand. Then I disappeared into the bathroom and slammed the lock shut.

"Goddamn it, Liana." He groped the handle and twisted. "*Open up.*"

"Nope," I shouted, disguising my shaking voice. "I'm going through your contacts."

"You better fucking not!"

"Oops. Too late." My pulse skyrocketed as he wrenched at the doorknob. "Oh, look at that. Girl B sent you a naked photo. You didn't reciprocate. You are a gentleman and a scholar."

"I never claimed to be decent."

"Yeah. I should be happy you respond to my texts, unlike Girl C, who you ghosted months ago."

He pounded the door. "Stop reading my shit!"

"Oh, you don't like it? I'm so sorry!"

Vinn smacked the wall. "Open up, smartass."

"Not yet. After I block them. Wow, you have a lot of mistresses. I wonder, what happens when you reach Girl Z? Will you use a number system?" I snorted, pretending to mull it over. "That'll be challenging for them. I wouldn't want to be Girl One Thousand Seventy-Three."

"Can you have a meltdown over my sex life *somewhere else*?"

"I'm not having a meltdown," I said, the lie burning my chest. "I'm giving you a taste of your own medicine, and I'm setting these poor girls free."

Vinn huffed. "I never heard any complaints."

"Yeah, well. You might after I block them."

"*What are you doing?*" He thumped and banged, rattling the doorknob. "Liana, do not fuck with my phone."

"You should lock your cell."

"Liana, open this door."

"I'll let you in soon. I'm sending them all a little message. I'll read it out loud."

Vinn: I apologize for being an asshole. You deserve better.

Vinn: P.S. I'm engaged. Don't contact me again.

I hit Send.

Then I blocked them, one by one.

Vinn's laughter boomed from outside, curdling my

stomach. "They'll never believe that's from me."

"Why's that?"

"Because I don't owe them an explanation. They're not girlfriends. They're women I use to get off. When I cut ties, I stop responding."

"That's cold."

And yet, it made me smile.

"They're using me, too. I don't see the big deal." His body slid along the wall, vibrating with another laugh. "You're just fucking jealous."

I kicked the door. "I'm not."

"Keep repeating it, sweetheart."

"I'm angry at how callous you've gotten. You don't care about anybody's feelings." I stared at the door, boiling. "As long as they're not threatening your ego or your bottom line, they can go to hell."

"What about everything I've done for you?"

"Forcing me to be yours is *not* doing me a favor." Pain swelled in my throat. "You don't understand how much it hurts to be around you. I trusted you! I would've shifted the moon for you, and you stabbed me in the back."

"*What did I do?*"

Pure frustration leaked from his tone, and that sent me in a frenzy. "How can you not know?"

"Jesus Christ, Liana. Just tell me."

He jammed something into the doorknob, and the

lock popped. The door swung. He staggered inside and ran his fingers through his ebony locks. He was beautiful, but it echoed in me hollowly. It was like looking at a stranger. I no longer recognized him.

I hated him for that, too.

He'd ruined what helped me see past the darkness.

"You killed Daniel."

Vinn's gaze scanned me, taking in my state like a soldier assessing the situation. "Ignacio did it, not me, but *yes*. I signed off on his murder."

Tears blinded me, his presence tormenting me. He seized his phone and pocketed it. Then he grabbed a tissue box, held it to his waist, and released.

It thudded near my feet.

"I couldn't have stopped him from dying any more than you could've prevented gravity from making that fall."

"Is that a joke?"

"Daniel was a rat. We kill rats." Vinn backed against the counter, crossing his arms. "And I loathed him. I have no problem admitting I never liked him and wished him dead, many times."

I balled my fists, reliving the pain of Daniel in the hospital, shutting off life support, and his coffin sinking into the ground.

"What did he ever do to you?"

"Nothing," he admitted, softening. "It was what he did to you and Michael."

"Like *what*?" I could barely hold back the venom. "Keep us safe? Feed us?"

"You have a very selective memory."

His glare pierced my chest. As I approached him, his olive-black eyes dimmed to a soft smolder.

"What do you mean?"

"Come on, Liana. The man was sick."

My cheeks blistered. "What are you talking about?"

"He hit you both, especially Michael. You were so young. You used to cry when he walked into the room." Vinn's burning gaze stripped me bare. "You don't remember?"

My head throbbed with a dull ache as echoes from the past resurfaced—my skull bashing into a wall, my body thrown into rooms, stewing in my bedroom with a raw cheek.

"I-I remember some things."

"He was fucked up. He stabbed Michael once."

"That's a lie!"

"Ask him if you don't believe me. I was eight. I saw the whole thing." The gravel in his voice disappeared into a hush I'd never heard before. "Michael bled all over the kitchen tiles. He almost died."

I turned away from Vinn, shaking.

No. It must've been an accident. Daniel wasn't a

maniac. Sure, he'd been rough. At times, too harsh. Most men in the life had issues.

Right?

"I didn't know you were that upset." Vinn's hand rolled over my shoulder, its weight reassuring. "I never wanted to hurt you."

Are you kidding me?

I gaped at him, wondering if this was a bad joke. "That's the problem. You have so little self-awareness. You hurt people all the time, and you don't even realize it."

"As long as you're safe, hate me all you want."

The same words he'd given me about Michael.

My mind worked overtime to parse that out.

He squeezed my chin and dropped a small felt box on the counter. "We leave for our engagement party in a few hours. Be ready."

For what?

Why am I doing this?

FIFTEEN
LIANA

I COULD GET ENGAGED with the devil I knew, or walk the aisle with the one I didn't. When approaching it logically, the choice was simple.

Emotionally?

I was a wreck.

My throat tightened as I took in the beautiful setting —the deep mauve tablecloth stretched over a long table framed with a sheer-white canopy, draping in elegant arches. Chandeliers cast a magical glow over the silverware and the purple bouquet in the middle. It was perfect, and utterly confusing.

The mind-blowing confrontation with Vinn threw everything into doubt. He'd done extreme things in the name of protecting me, but he wasn't an unfeeling, cold monster. If that were true, he wouldn't let me stay at his house. My Christmas gift from *two years ago* wouldn't be perched on his nightstand. He wouldn't have a magpie-like tendency for all of my stupid presents. I'd snooped through his closet and found a shoebox filled with my letters to Iraq—they were in all great condition—except one with the signature ripped off.

The discovery had squeezed my heart.

"I'm happy for you, sweetie." Mom grabbed my hand, beaming. "Vinny is such a good boy. He'll take care of you."

"Thank you, Mama."

Mom had accepted the news of my engagement with open arms and a big smile, which seemed to annoy Michael. He shot Vinn a look of profound disgust and shook his head whenever I met his gaze.

I could hear the *poor girl* on loop in his thoughts. Michael believed his best friend had knocked me up, but he didn't buy the fairytale romance. He'd already pulled me aside to demand I tell him the truth, *twice*.

"If he's good, I'm the fucking Dalai Lama," Michael muttered when Mom excused herself for the bathroom. "If somebody did that to my daughter, they'd get a one-way ticket to the Quabbin Reservoir."

Daniel used that euphemism for years before I realized it didn't mean a camping trip.

My fork slipped, scraping the ceramic plate with an ungodly shriek. I bit my lip to keep from screaming. Michael had been a moody asshole all night. Vinn would've told him to shut up, but he'd drifted aside to chat with relatives.

"I can't stand him," Michael continued, his nostrils flaring. "Pretending not to hate the sight of him is taking every ounce of self-control—"

"Can you give it a rest?" I hissed.

Michael sipped his wine and looked away. Then he swung to me, his expression no longer livid. "You got what you wanted, but I don't think you realize what you've signed up for."

My pulse skittered. I was uneasy under his scrutiny. "I've always loved him."

"I know, hon. That's why I pity you."

"Michael," snapped Carmela. "*Enough.*"

Michael shot her a quelling look before swinging his attention back to me. "You have no idea what you're in for."

I was weary of him. "Which is?"

"You're stuck with a man who doesn't connect with people and hates children. He's said it over and over."

I sighed, loudly.

Michael's wife, a stunning brunette in a black, ruffled dress, smiled. "They *all* say that, Liana. Men have no idea what's good for them. They need to be guided."

"Really?" Michael murmured. "I seem to remember asking you out dozens of times. You were the one digging in your heels. A year later, we're married with kids. Who has the better foresight?"

Carmela's eyes flattened.

Michael needled her with a few hushed comments until he dropped his tone and whispered a husky, "I love you." Carmela melted and kissed his cheek. He looked at her with a puppy-dog-like adoration that soured as a solid warmth sank into the seat next to mine.

"Hey, Mike."

Michael turned a shade of puce. "Don't *hey* me."

"What am I supposed to say?"

"How about—'I'm a fucking jackass.'" Michael ignored his wife's attempts to shut him up, leaning across the table. "'I'm a disrespectful, lying, *coward*.'"

"How the fuck am I a coward?"

Michael opened his mouth. I shook the table with a fist, rattling the silverware and glasses. Conversation halted as I met my brother's vengeance head-on.

"Michael, this isn't about *you*. Just stop."

"She's right, honey." Carmela seized his hand and tugged until he staggered upright. "You need to stay out of their business."

Michael tore his gaze from me. "But she's my *sister*..."

Their voices faded as Carmela coaxed him away.

A sick yearning assaulted me as Vinn wrapped his arm around me. His expression didn't mirror the relaxed faces surrounding us.

"Forget Michael. We have other things to worry about."

I nodded, sipping my sparkling cider.

"We have to visit *Nico*."

I pulled a face, and Vinn frowned. "What? I'm not thrilled about sucking up to the guy who's dying to pawn me off."

My senses leaped to life as his touch found my thigh. His fingers traced a circle on my leg, the warmth inside me building.

"While you're with me, you don't have to suck up to anyone."

"Except you?"

Vinn made a dissenting noise. "You can please me in other ways."

A delicious shudder ran through me.

"How?"

"Take that beautiful mouth of yours...and shut it." As his grip tightened, his attitude grew more serious. "Or better yet, put it to work on my cock."

A ribbon of heat scorched my chest, and I inhaled sharply. "You're in rare form tonight."

"I need you to behave, Liana."

His command made the knot rise in my throat.

It'd been a long time since we'd kissed, and although we'd exchanged chaste pecks all night, the fleeting excitement was nothing compared to submitting to him. Too many times, I'd imagined him bursting into the bedroom, ripping off the sheets, tearing my pajamas' elastic band in his haste to fuck me.

He smirked as though he watched the pornographic reel in my mind. "This isn't a game. If you screw this up, I won't be around to bend you over the bed."

"What makes you think I want that?"

"The way you're looking at me."

My cheeks burned, and then the photographer approached us. "Mr. Costa? Are you ready?"

"Oh, I completely blanked." I rose, yanking Vinn's arm. "Sorry."

Vinn turned at the waist, gawking at him. "You hired a photographer?"

"Yeah, of course," I whispered into his ear. "It would be weird if we didn't. It'll be done in half an hour."

And I secretly wanted the photos.

His stare drilled into me, and my determination to hide faltered. I couldn't pretend this event wasn't a monument to the greatest love I'd ever known, even if he'd changed.

A secretive smile softened his lips.

He enveloped me in his burly embrace. As the photographer gave us direction, I fussed with his shirt, too intimidated to stroke the broad planes of his chest until Vinn took my hands and did it for me. Then he scooped my face and kissed me. My stomach did somersaults at the sensual strokes.

I slipped my arms in his jacket. I tipped my head and pressed my mouth into his. He melted into me, the touch of his lips like a whisper. My knees weakened as he descended on me, demanding. His palm roved my dress to skim my hips and thighs.

Once the photographer finished, Vinn's eyes cut at me. "Let's talk to Nico."

"Okay."

He pulled, and I followed. We wandered the outdoor patio strung with golden lights, casting a dreamy glow over the lawn where there'd been catered food. We approached Nico and his other relatives, elbow deep in cheese and drink.

Nico seemed to be channeling his son, based on the empty bottles surrounding him and the two girls perched on his lap. I didn't know Anthony well. He was my brother's age, so we'd never hung out, but he was always high or drunk whenever I'd run into him.

Nico had taken his son's kidnapping badly. Judging by the brand new sports car parked outside, he was trying to fill the Anthony-shaped hole in his heart. My sympathy for him was limited. The man had sold me to a biker.

"Geez. He's a midlife crisis on steroids."

"Yes, he is." Vinn stared at a guy sitting beside Nico,

who was micromanaging my uncle's alcohol. "Oh boy. He's got Alessio filling in for his son. Not good."

"What?" I peered at the sour-faced man beside Nico.

"Don't worry about it."

"Has that phrase has *ever* worked for anyone with anxiety?"

He patted my hip, urging us forward. "Remember, don't speak unless spoken to."

"I've been around him before."

"Not when he's like this."

Nico shot upright, his bulk upsetting the table. Alessio caught Nico's glass and dumped its contents while Nico barreled toward Vinn, arms outstretched.

Vinn winced as his uncle trapped him in a giant hug, discomfort written all over his face.

"This asshole is getting married. Alessio. Where's Alessio?" Nico blinked as he disengaged from Vinn. "Ah, there you are."

"What is it?" said the harassed-looking man, who seemed to hate this party and everyone.

"Alessio, what do you think of Vinn becoming a father?"

"Can't believe it." A faint sneer curled his lip as he stared daggers at Vinn. "Michael's sister, no less. Quite the scandal. I've never seen Michael that pissed."

Vinn shrugged. "Well, the baby's coming regardless of his approval."

"How are you handling that?" Nico pounded Vinn's back, the blows heavy enough for Vinn to grit his teeth. "You ready to be a dad?"

"I don't think anyone's ready."

"I was," Alessio quipped. "Have you read any books?"

Vinn shook his head. "Nah. I'll be fine."

I wished I had his confidence. "I'll be reading everything, and so will you."

"You all right, sweetie?" Nico asked, his attention swaying toward me. "Can I get you anything? Something to settle your stomach?"

"I'm okay, thank you. The first trimester has been smooth sailing. Luckily, I've had very little nausea."

"My wife had it bad." Nico seemed to forget his mistresses, who hovered in the background, sulking. "The pregnancy was so hard on her. She couldn't have another kid after Anthony."

I'd wondered when his name would crop up.

Alessio's eyes glazed over, and he stared into his wine. Vinn betrayed zero emotion, his face a stone mask. Nico's accusatory glare bored into Vinn, and then me.

"We should toast to the baby," Nico deadpanned, glancing around. "Hey, you. Get champagne—no, *dumbass*—I want a bottle."

"Nico, I don't drink."

Nico waved Vinn off as a waiter brought Dom

Perignon along with a half dozen flutes. He shouted, banging his spoon on the giant bottle, making a big spectacle. Nico was a shark circling the waters, closing in on Vinn, and I didn't like it.

He popped the cork and poured, sloshing alcohol over the tray. He handed dripping glasses to guests, shoving one in Vinn's protesting hands.

My insides revolted.

"No thanks."

"Drink," Nico shouted. "Don't be a pussy."

Is he fucking crazy?

Vinn's fingers whitened on the stem as Nico led the entire table into a chant. Before long, everyone had a glass.

I clutched Vinn's elbow. "You don't have to."

"Yeah, I do. But it doesn't matter, Li. It'll take a lot more than one stupid drink to break me."

Vinn tossed the flute back, his eyes closed. A battle seemed to rage within him as he swallowed. Then he set down the glass, refusing a second pour. When Nico ignored him and started pouring, Vinn stalked away.

Nico watched him go, smirking.

"Vinn, wait!"

A fierce glow of pride warmed my chest. I wanted to say that I admired him. The strength to leave was greater than giving in like the idiots surrounding Nico.

He disappeared into the men's room before I reached him, leaving me to stew about Nico.

I stomped across the restaurant, brooded at the bar, and almost ordered Prosecco—*oops*—forgot I was "pregnant." I stayed there, fuming in my thigh-length dress.

"Congratulations," said a dry voice lifting from the darkness. "On your very sudden engagement."

I jumped.

The wily Legion president cleaned up nicely. He'd buzzed his scruff and tamed his hair, and wore a plain white T-shirt under the leather cut and fitted jeans.

I tensed. "What the hell are you doing here?"

"Relax. I was invited. I'm only here to make nice with your...fiancé." Killian sat, sighing.

"Killian, I'm not interested—"

"You know what I find curious about this romance between you and Costa?" He pulled out a cigarette, stuck it between his lips, and fired the tip.

My heart thundered as he took a long drag.

"The fact you never mentioned him." He blew the smoke to the side, flicking ashes to the ground. "We must've been there for ten minutes, fifteen maybe. Flirting."

"*You* were. I was trying to figure out why you showed up in my café."

"Well, there was plenty of opportunity to tell me you were taken. It's not like I held a gun to your head."

Killian rolled to his side with catlike grace, smiling. "Which tells me two things. One, you're miserable. You didn't bring him up because you want an out."

"That's—that's not true."

"You're hiding here instead of clinging to your future husband's arm, so I'm not far off the mark."

"I'm just overwhelmed."

"Because you're scared. I don't blame you. He scares me, too." He gave me a friendly nudge and smile, but the levity disappeared like the rising smoke. "So you're either looking for an out, or you're not a couple, and this is a sham."

"You don't know us."

"I'm not an idiot. You two make no fucking sense." He dashed the cig into an ashtray. "You're as sweet as pie. You belong with someone with a heart. He is…a *block*. A giant, frozen block."

That twisted a knife in my chest because it wasn't true. He wouldn't have been so adamant about protecting me if it were.

"Anybody with eyes can see you're unhappy, and I hate that I've been cheated out of a great girl. I won't forget it." Killian squeezed my shoulder, his touch lingering like warm feathers. "And I won't forget you."

My stomach churned. "I'm engaged."

"An engagement means *nothing*. Couples break up, and I have a feeling you and Mussolini won't last."

I hated that nickname. "Don't call him that!"

Killian winked and slid off the stool, just as my fake fiancé stormed in. "Congratulations again. A baby. *Wow*."

Judging by the flush hitting Vinn's cheeks, he'd heard the sarcasm, too.

Nobody but Michael had believed us.

SIXTEEN

VINN

A boss is never at the mercy of his emotions.

He dominates them.

I used to take that advice seriously. Now I wanted to lay waste to every Nico supporter, blowtorch the fuckers who'd antagonized me at my engagement party, and rebuild the Family with an emphasis on loyalty.

He disrespected me. *Twice.*

A man is defined by his actions, and Nico had proven to be an untrustworthy cunt. Inviting Killian was the last fucking straw, a passive-aggressive threat, a sign of things to come.

Nico was pushing me out.

I would get ahead of this. Countless men had been in my position, and I'd watched them fall. I wouldn't be one of them. I needed to rally the troops and attack.

Immediately.

So I called Michael and Alessio to my house. Involving Alessio gave me pause because I'd wronged him, but Nico was grinding his nose to the floor. He expected Alessio to pick up the reins, but the guy had obviously been miserable.

We sprawled in my living room. I sat in the leather recliner while they lounged on the couch. Alessio helped himself to the prosciutto di parma that Liana had rolled around fat gobs of goat cheese while Michael ground ice in his mouth, the sound so obnoxious I could've slapped him.

"Where's my sister?" Michael shot out.

"Shopping for baby stuff."

Dark amusement flickered on Alessio's face. "Never thought I'd see the day."

"Miracles happen."

"That's the right attitude." Alessio elbowed Michael, who went rigid. "He's taking care of her, isn't he?"

"I don't approve," Michael snapped.

Confusion rippled over Alessio's forehead as he glanced from me to Michael. "Now you clowns are fighting?"

"He's the one with the problem—"

"No shit, you philandering dickhead."

My back straightened. "I called you here to discuss strategy, not my personal life. We used to be a team. We worked well together. Hell, we were friends."

"For someone so concerned about friendship, you do your damnedest to fuck us over." Alessio banged his tumbler over my coffee table, crossing his arms.

"I've made mistakes. So have you." I glared at him, and then Michael. "And you."

Michael bristled. "I won't work under you."

"So you're okay with Nico calling the shots? Bearing in mind, he hasn't been *present* lately?" I sighed hard when Alessio's eyes darkened. "You can't be happy with how he's using you."

"I'm not," Alessio muttered. "I had my run at boss, and it's not for me. Fuck the responsibility, the pressure, all of it. I'm content with running the Labor Council."

"Michael?"

"I was fine with being your advisor until you banged my sister." Some of the fire dimmed from Michael's gaze. "That said, I don't appreciate being demoted to captain. I don't like that he keeps shoving that piece of shit Killian in my sister's face."

"We know what we have to do." I drummed my knee, steeling myself. "We need to get rid of Nico."

They digested that differently—Michael with a flicker of fear, and Alessio with a swig of whiskey, all arrogance.

"That's a little overboard. He's pissed, but he won't kill off his leadership."

"Uncle Nico has lost his marbles. The moment

Anthony went missing, he's been making stupid decisions. Bribing half the police force. Getting involved in the biker wars." I stared at Michael, whose brow pinched. "We'll die trying to save his son, and if we don't...we're all fucked."

Alessio massaged his temples, frowning. "What you want to do is suicide. It'll blow up in our faces."

"Set your feelings aside and use your head. He's already undermining me. If he doesn't give a damn about the fallout, neither should we."

"No," Alessio snapped. "Killing the boss will invite a free-for-all. Nico has a lot of friends, V. What's your plan when they turn on you?"

"I'll take them out, one by one."

"You don't have enough support," Alessio reminded me. "You won't be able to live in Boston after this, so I hope you're happy with a lifetime of running. Good luck doing that with a baby on the way."

"My sister will stay here."

I wheeled at Michael, blood pounding in my ears. "She goes where I go."

Michael rose to his feet, plunging his fists into his slacks. "Are we done here?"

"One day, you'll leave Nico's mansion and get shot in the driveway," I said as he swigged more of his drink. "If I'm at risk, so are you."

"I'd rather face one enemy than the dozens I'll gain

by offing Nico." Alessio dragged his arm across his shining forehead. "Do whatever you want. But if you attack a boss, I'm taking off. I can't have my family anywhere near this catastrophe."

With that parting shot, Alessio stood and left. Michael followed wordlessly, the door swinging behind their backs.

Message received.

I'm on my own.

Assassinating the boss would be a pain in the ass. It would involve hiring the Bratva. Street bosses would probably come after me. Killing Nico could be the catalyst for inevitable disaster.

The front door opened and slammed. I lunged out of the recliner, my heart hammering, but it was only a pale-faced Liana weighed with shopping bags. I still wasn't used to someone coming and going in my house. The seashell necklace bouncing on her chest dug at my veins. Rage gushed out, swallowing me.

She loved someone else.

A frat boy, no doubt, like that asshole who kept smirking with that patented I've-tapped-that look. *James*. I pictured his stupid face and shook my head. She didn't give a shit about James.

Who was the other man?

I'D COMBED through her emails and texts, finding no evidence of another man. It drove me nuts because she was growing on me. *Literally*. She took over my shit with impunity. I chewed her out every time I stepped on a wet towel in the bathroom, but Liana was committed to being a slob. Her latest baking disaster charred scones to a cookie sheet, which she'd dumped in the sink. I picked at it for a good twenty minutes before tossing it.

Her annoying 80's ballads blasted into every room. Once, I caught her slow dancing to "Time after Time." I endured it for a few seconds before hijacking the Wi-Fi to play The Police, which was a way better choice than Cyndi-fucking-Lauper.

Despite her abysmal taste in music, my stomach turned at the idea of her leaving. I liked coming home to her. She made the place feel lived-in. She was so tiny, but her warmth was big, and it filled the apartment.

My head pounded as I paced the living room, sweating. Liana had complained about the cold, so I'd dialed up the thermostat to sixty-seven. It was hot as balls, and I couldn't concentrate on the things that mattered—like the ongoing crisis with the biker wars, the fuck-heads undermining me, and Nico.

Stuffing pillows under her shirt wouldn't work forever.

Goddamn it.

Giving up, I shoved my phone into my pocket and

blazed into my bedroom. Boxes were stacked everywhere. Liana had refused to unpack for days, but I wouldn't let her move into a guest room. Her bras and panties covered my bed. She'd emptied my drawers, and the disorder shot fire down my spine.

Liana had changed into a pink camisole and pajama shorts. She dug into an opened box, cramming her clothes into the drawer. It was surreal to witness. I'd never had anyone take over my life. She grabbed a frame from my closet—my boot camp graduation photo—and stared at it.

"What are you doing?"

"Nothing." Liana jumped and thrust the picture onto the shelf. "*God*. Stop that."

"You don't need to go through my stuff."

"I'm not trying to snoop, but you have a lot crammed away, and I have to make room."

Liana was as harmful as a butterfly, but I didn't like her digging through my shit. My annoyance faded as she straightened, pushing out her tits. Her nipples peaked the sheer cotton, the dark circles stiffening my cock.

Blood coursed through me like an awakened river. My mouth went dry as she flopped onto the bed.

"Sorry about the mess," she murmured, thumbing her phone. "I'll clean it up soon. I'm just taking a break."

I didn't understand why she and her entire generation had their heads buried in their phones. I sat on the only clear space on the mattress.

She ripped off her socks and threw them on the floor. "So, what are you going to do about Nico?"

My hands twitched. "What?"

"I overheard you guys. I came in early while you weren't paying attention, and then I doubled back and walked through the door."

Fuck.

I kept forgetting I had a goddamned roommate. I raked my hair, my skin tingling from her stare. "You shouldn't have heard that."

"Vinn, what's your plan?"

"Don't worry about it, honey."

"But I might be able to help."

The room echoed with my chuckle. "Stick to what you're good at, Liana, school and charring kitchenware."

Her eyes narrowed. She swung her legs off the bed and charged toward me, hands on her hips. "I'm sick of you being an asshole."

"Pointing out that you ruin my shit is being an asshole?"

"You underestimate me. You think I'm useless!"

It amused me how similar she was to Michael. Like him, she was prone to be offended over the dumbest things.

"You're a college student. You have a lot of life to live

before telling me what to do, honey."

"I can help with Killian!"

"You have nothing to offer him but your body." I lurched upright as Liana crossed her arms, her cheeks blossoming with pink. "I'm sorry, but it's the truth. This isn't one of your classes, Li. You can't debate him."

I brushed the skin over her knitting brows.

She flinched, stepping aside. "What about Anthony? If he came home, this would go away. *Right?*"

I wished it were that simple.

"He's unreachable."

"So what do we do? I can't just sit tight while you're dealing with all this." A faint thread of hysteria wove in her voice. "Tell me how I can help."

I'd never hold a meeting at my house again.

"Take a breath, sweetheart." I took her shoulders, massaging her delicate frame. "Breathe. There you go. Everything will be fine—"

She launched into my chest.

I closed my eyes and drifted on a cloud. Something in her manner soothed me. Liana expected me to be her anchor, and it'd unleashed a fever inside me.

I craved this.

Whatever it was, I needed it like oxygen.

My heart jolted and my pulse pounded. I fought the wave of discomfort as I pulled her close, focusing on her tits squashing against me. I spread my hand over her back. The thin satin glowed with her warmth, and I slipped underneath.

A wicked heat stroked my cock. It throbbed as Liana jammed her head under my chin, totally oblivious to my growing hard-on. She tipped her face, beaming with a sweet smile.

"Oh, I forgot to tell you. We have brunch with my friends today."

Not happening. "I'm not hanging with your college buddies."

"Why not?"

"I like you, but I draw the line at social functions with idiot kids."

"They're my friends." Her arms dropped from my sides. "You're part of my life now, or pretending to be. So you're coming."

"I'd rather swim through shark-infested waters. The answer is *no*."

"If you keep acting like a dictator, I'll run to Michael."

"*I'll run to Michael*," I mocked as her nostrils flared. "Yeah, good luck with that."

She shoved my chest and stepped around me, speeding toward the door. She paused at the threshold, scowling.

"*Asshole.*"

I blew her a kiss before she ran out.

SEVENTEEN
LIANA

I wasn't a damsel.

My brother Michael used to tell me, *don't wake up planning to be mediocre*. That attitude had served me well in life. It got me into a great university, and it made me smash the girls' high school swim meet records. My accomplishments might've been small compared to Vinn's, but I wasn't as helpless as the idiot believed.

After our argument, I'd fled to the laundry room. My chest burning, I'd yanked open the dryer. A bundle of clothes had tumbled into the basket. I'd separated the green apron from a shirt, and a business card fluttered out. The name printed on top had sucked in my breath.

Killian

Call me. Anytime.

My heart pounded with a reckless impulse. I wanted to dial the number right there, but I needed to think it through. Once Vinn left the house, I researched for hours and came up with a plan.

Then I arranged a meeting.

I sat in a booth far from the windows and tempting sunshine. The dive was in my old neighborhood, close to the café where Killian had almost abducted me, and packed with college students.

Before long, a guttural roar shook the floor. Killian arrived in a flash of chrome. He descended from the bike and lifted the helmet from his head, easily the most exotic thing in this bar with the leather, his golden beard, and wild hair. Girls turned their heads as he strolled inside. He bantered with the bartender before taking his drink. Then he joined me, sliding over the vinyl.

I forced a grin. "Thanks for coming."

"Of course." Killian stirred his cocktail. "Couldn't resist when I heard your voice."

Here we go.

My smile flickered. "This isn't a date."

He gave me a black look. "So you've mentioned."

"Let's be very clear. I'm not here to cheat on Vinn or do anything he'd consider a betrayal."

"Like ditch the bodyguards to meet me in secret?" Killian's blue gaze twinkled as he revolved his straw. "You're in denial, babe."

I gritted my teeth.

During the phone call, I was firm. I was *not* interested in Killian, but his demeanor made it obvious those words had gone in one ear and out the other.

He touched my elbow. "You're that desperate to leave him?"

I pulled out of reach. "This isn't about my relationship with Vinn. This isn't even about me. I want to negotiate Anthony's safe return."

The only thing that'd make all of this disappear was Anthony. If he returned, Nico would stop endangering Vinn's life, and we could go our separate ways. We wouldn't have to keep up a charade that was slowly killing me.

"I see." He plucked the cherry from his drink, squeezing the bright red flesh. "You think all your problems will go away once he's back. Right?"

Yup.

I clenched the table. "Will you do it?"

"Sure. Break up with Vinn."

"I'm not doing that."

"Why? Because he's so warm and fuzzy?" Killian snapped his fingers at the black-haired waitress in cutoff jeans and pointed at my empty glass.

"Why are you so stuck on me?"

"Because I've watched you for a long time."

You mean stalked.

I waved at the ladies sitting at the bar. "Take a look around. Plenty of college girls to choose from."

"What do they have to offer me besides a mountain of student loan debt?" He snorted as the waitress slid another vodka tonic over the table. "You're worth five million of them. You're leverage, the start of a new alliance, and pretty decent arm candy."

I supposed that was a compliment.

He seized my cup and sipped.

I glared at him, resenting how he took without asking. "What if I did something for you?"

His gaze dipped to my cleavage. "Like?"

"There's a warrant out for your arrest on a felony arson charge. You missed your arraignment on the twenty-third. You also have a court date for next week for a pesky armed robbery."

He smiled. "That case is built on probable cause. I'll get it thrown out."

"I'm not sure you will. Judge Gilstrap is a friend of ours. You know what he hates? Violence against women."

He raised a brow. "I haven't done anything to you."

Yet, his tone implied.

"You kidnapped me in front of witnesses. You dragged me to your bike, took off, and I barely escaped with my life."

"That isn't what happened."

"That's your side of the story."

"Are you threatening me?"

"I'm glad you've caught on," I sneered, yanking my

drink. "Isn't Massachusetts a three-strikes state? It'd suck if I filed a police report. Who knows what Judge Gilstrap will make of that information? He'll probably deny you bail, which means you'll be stuck in jail until your trial. There's a pretty big backlog these days, so it'll get pushed back. Considering your extensive rap sheet, the judge might feel compelled to give you the maximum sentence."

Killian's mouth curled into a devious smirk as he tapped the table. "You're a crazy cunt."

"Not as crazy as I'll be if you don't do what I want. I could make your life difficult, or I could put in a word for you with the judge."

His stare drilled into me. "I'll kill Gilstrap, and then I'll come after you."

"No, you won't."

"*You* won't. Doing this puts you in the crosshairs of every biker in Boston." He chewed a chunk of ice, his voice hardening. "We're done here."

He inclined his sleek head and kissed the air between us.

I grabbed his wrist. "I'll do it."

He glanced at my hand. Then he wrenched my arm and yanked. I collided with him, close enough to smell his leather cut.

"Negotiating is one thing, but threatening me? You're playing a dangerous game."

Beads of sweat formed on my lip. "I can help you."

"You can get on your knees."

I tore from his grasp, stumbling from the booth.

He caught me to stop me from falling but didn't pull me toward him. The words stuck in my throat as he released me. He winked before striding out.

I didn't breathe until he'd climbed on his bike, and then my shoulders curled forward.

Fuck.

Now what?

I rubbed the marks he'd left on me. Going to Killian had been a risk. I'd hoped he'd take me seriously, but he didn't think I'd follow through. I wouldn't immediately run to the police. Retaliation was a big concern, but it wasn't like Vinn had many moves remaining.

Lugging my bag from the booth, I nudged through the college crowd and burst into the sunshine. Then I twisted my hair into a knot, shoved a baseball cap over my head, and slid on my backpack. I bowed my head, strolling to the subway as rush-hour traffic breezed along.

A man in a suit slipped from a car. He stepped onto the sidewalk and froze, his frame blocking the way.

I walked around him until a strong, jacketed arm circled my waist. My body recognized Vinn's touch before a deep growl erupted from his chest. He dragged me, fingers biting into my flesh.

Flames blasted from Vinn, overwhelming the

summer day's heat. Veins popped from his forehead, his demeanor so threatening that passersby scattered.

"*Fuck's sake*, Liana. You better have broken it off with him." His terrible voice shot fire down my spine.

I gaped at him. "Who?"

Vinn clenched his teeth so hard that a muscle jumped in his jaw. "The man you met behind my fucking back."

Wow.

"I wasn't—"

"Get in the damned car."

Stunned, I allowed him to pull me inside the parked Lexus. I sank into the backseat as Vinn slammed the partition.

"How did you find me?"

"You are not good at covering your tracks." His tone rolled with cold contempt. "Plus, the bartender called me. I have eyes everywhere, especially when it concerns my fiancée."

Great.

He seized my backpack and ripped out my phone. He thumbed through my texts, and when he found nothing, he swiped to Recent Calls.

Oh shit.

"A five-minute conversation right before you left the house," Vinn taunted. "This is the guy."

Fire shot up my throat.

"Who is he, some frat boy? He still in there?" He tapped the window, mouth curling. "I'll drag you in there and make you point him out."

"You don't want me to do that."

"Now I'm really curious."

His thumb hovered over the screen.

"Vinn, *don't*."

"Afraid of what I'll do? You should be."

I'm scared for you. "Do not press that button."

He stabbed the number.

I lunged for the cell, but Vinn lifted it out of reach. The call connected, and Killian's purr filled the car.

"*Ready to dump Costa? Or are you offering me a blowie?*"

A bleak silence settled between us.

"*Liana, you there?*"

I cringed, hands on my ears, staring at the floor as though looking for a hole to swallow me.

"*Need me to come back—?*"

Vinn ended the call, cutting off Killian's drawl.

Then I finally summoned the courage to lift my head.

Vinn stared at the phone like it was a diseased organ. His lips whitened. He slipped my cell into his pants, slamming his fist into the partition.

The car lurched forward.

Oh my God.

My pulse raced. "Vinn, it's not what you think."

"Shut up, Liana."

I white-knuckled the armrest.

Vinn clenched his jaw the whole way home, no doubt imagining ridiculous scenarios with Killian. Once we reached his building, Vinn yanked me out of the car, guiding me by the wrist like an errant child. We left the elevator, and he shoved me inside the apartment.

"You think Anthony's been on a fifteen-month vacation?" he screamed as he slammed the door. "They'll do the same with you. They'll auction you, sell you into slavery, and force you to fuck disgusting men. Is that what you want? *Tell me*. I'll tie you up and show you what you're in for."

A dark thrill rippled through me.

"Vinn, calm down. You don't even know why I was there."

"Because I refused brunch with you," he snarled.

"My God, Vinn. As if I'd be that petty."

Words failed me as he flung my cell on the marble. The screen smashed. He stomped on the case until it resembled a hunk of shattered glass. Then he fished out the SIM card and crushed that, too.

"*Hey!*"

He stabbed the air with a finger. "From now on, I vet everyone in your life. I can't trust you. You're a liability."

"I was just trying to help you!"

"Give me a break. You went behind my back and met with Killian." He kicked aside the trashed phone and headed for his walk-in closet. He palmed a false wall, yanking a gun from the hiding space.

A sliver of panic darted through my heart.

"Where do you think you're going?"

He packed a box of shells in his jacket, suiting up like he was invading Poland.

"Don't do this." I clutched his shirt, my eyes hot. "Don't risk your life over a stupid misunderstanding."

"That piece of shit knows *exactly* what he's doing."

He shoved a knife into his ankle strap and stormed at the door.

I stared at Vinn's retreating back, my body consumed with fire. It was all I could do not to fall apart. I caught up to him and seized his arm.

"Vinn, stay."

"He's taking you from me."

The force of his words crumbled a wall inside me.

"I belong to you, not him."

A flicker of heat flashed through his ice.

I flew into his chest and grabbed his neck, the pressure on my lungs excruciating. I threaded my fingers through his hair. I buried my burning face in his shoulder and kissed him. I yanked at his dress shirt, desperate to prove my feelings. I'd have to give him a reason not to go —a piece of my pride to soothe his. I tugged until he yielded an inch. I pressed my mouth against his, sucking his lower lip.

His breathing quickened, but he didn't reciprocate. Usually, Vinn didn't hesitate to take control of me. He'd crush me in his embrace and rip off my clothes if I let him, but suddenly he refused to yield.

"Vinn, I only went there to help you. I've had a crush on you since I was *four*."

"That's touching."

"It's the truth!"

A dark smile carved into his cheek as he straightened, his imperial frame towering over mine. "You are such a liar."

My spark of hope vanished.

"I'm not lying."

"I caught you trying to leave."

His palm lifted to my face and stroked me. He was like marble pressing into me, the coolness sinking into my chin. Normally, his touch warmed me like the sun, but cold shivered down my spine instead of excitement. I was wet for him because his attention was on me, but my desire was toxic.

Ill-fated.

I clenched my jaw to kill the shaking. "I don't want to leave you."

"*Shut the hell up.*"

"Why would I lie?"

He lowered, hissing into my ear. "Because you're in love with another man."

Shit.

It was my fault he believed that in the first place. I'd only provoked him out of a selfish need for vengeance. My stupid lie had gone way too far.

He cupped my face and leaned in, brushing his lips across mine. His whisper breezed my mouth.

"Stay. *Here.*"

"Vinny—"

His fingers tightened, catching my breath before it escaped. "Don't call me that ever again."

The pulsing knot inside me demanded me to argue.

How many times had I visited him in the hospital and rehab? I cared about him. How did he not know that in his marrow?

I had to prove it.

Witnessing him in this state twisted my guts. I'd jabbed a knife between his ribs, and he'd bleed to death if he went outside. If I let him go, there was a good chance he'd do something reckless. He would die like Daniel, who was ruled by his emotions. Daniel did whatever he felt like, and that attitude had gotten him killed.

A horrific image of Vinn in a coffin burned me like acid. Desperation clawed my throat as I dug into his back. I sank my nails into him, determined to stop him.

"Vinn, let's talk." I shoved myself in between him and the door. "Vinn, *wait*."

"Out of the way."

"Let me prove it!"

"What?"

I detached from the wall, sliding my arms around his waist. I tried to squeeze ten years' worth of affection into his stiffening body.

It was a one-sided hug, but Vinn's smoldering gaze didn't make me feel unwanted. Something of the boy he was flashed through his ebony pools. I anchored my hands on his shoulders. My lips pressed into his cold cheek.

"You want to convince me?" he said gruffly.

"Yes."

Vinn considered me, eyes slanting. "Kneel."

"W-what?"

"Get on the fucking floor and kneel."

His tone froze me like the ocean in winter.

"*Vinny*."

"I'm *not* your Vinny."

EIGHTEEN

LIANA

I kneeled.

Heat stole into my face as my legs struck the marble. I lowered my gaze, unable to stomach the cruel twist of his mouth. I didn't want to degrade myself, but the alternative was letting him go.

I'd cried all the tears when my brother called a year ago with the horrible news that Vinn had been shot. I couldn't swallow my sobbing fast enough to breathe. His shooting had detonated me. If he walked out the door, the same thing might happen.

He couldn't leave.

His jacket and keys hit the tile. I was the third inanimate object he'd discarded. A dull ache pulsed in my skull as he curled a finger around my chin, the gesture unbearable in its tenderness.

"Good girl," he praised. "Now beg me to fuck you."

I looked up from the floor pinching my flesh, his slacks, over the bulge that jolted me with hope.

"W-what?"

"Beg me to fuck you."

I fingered my throat, the burn from my cheeks spreading like a head-to-toe bath. Fantasizing about sex with Vinn wasn't the same as committing to the act.

"You want me? Right now?"

He nodded, his expression marked with loathing.

I'd pictured my first time like a sweet montage in a romantic comedy, sparkling conversation over a dinner table and then stumbling to bed, not this intoxicating submission. Spirals of heat stroked my nipples as he clenched his fists. His jaw ticked with a savage tempo as his possessive gaze zeroed on me. He could've strangled me just as soon as fucked me.

"Beg me, or I'm gone."

Panic gnawed at my confidence.

Then he stepped away, heading for the door.

"Take me. Fuck me." I sucked in breath as he stopped, wreathed in darkness. "Do what you want with my body."

His stare impaled me. "Are you sure?"

"Yes."

Desperation swelled beneath my ribs, but the same sick longing seemed to grasp Vinn. He approached, sweeping his knuckles over my cheek.

"I'm not using a condom."

A thrill of anticipation touched my nipples. "Vinn, I'm not on birth control."

"Is that a no?"

"I-I won't stop you."

A war raged in his eyes. "You should."

"You were going to keep me, but never fuck me?"

"I would've been nice. I've always held back around you." His fingers knotted my hair. "You drive me crazy, Liana."

He affected me, too.

My ragged breaths cut the air as he restrained me, so intoxicated by him that I wavered.

"Do anything you want."

"You shouldn't say that. You're handing over power, giving me the tools to manipulate you."

"You won't do that."

"Yes, I will." Vinn tightened his hold, his chest pulsing. "Killian would eat you alive."

"He doesn't have my trust. You do."

I turned, grazing my lips on his leg. I kissed him through the fabric. My hands smoothed over hard muscle before sweeping up his thigh. My fingers brushed his blazing-hot bulge. I closed my fist over him.

His cock jumped. As I stroked him, he released a low hiss. He anchored behind my head, shoving my face into his groin. He rubbed his stiff cock over my cheek, his body melting me through the cotton.

It should've been degrading, but it wasn't.

"Liana, this is your last fucking chance." He backed away, still gripping my hair. "Otherwise you will be wrecked, possessed, owned, and fucked."

I had no other choice.

Even if my panties weren't soaked, I would've let him take me. I'd rather be fucked within an inch of my life than put Vinn in harm's way, so I signed on the dotted line.

I leaned forward. My lips teased his length, tracing his mushroom-shaped head.

His eyelids flickered, and he smirked. "Get up. Kiss me like you kissed *Vincent*."

I shot upright and stumbled toward him. I took his waist, leaning into him. My clumsy kiss landed on his chin before Vinn stooped, allowing me to crush his rigid lips. They parted with a breeze of heat.

"That's it? No wonder you're not together."

I seized his dress shirt and slammed my mouth into his. My tongue slashed into him, his mint taste flashing an image of the beach. I pretended we rolled on the sand while waves lapped our feet. I saw him in the military haircut, wearing the uniform. In my dreams, it wasn't a scandal to kiss him.

He ravished me. He sucked on my lower lip, stifling

my moans with his consuming kisses. I raked his hair, hissing when we bumped into a wall. He marked my neck with tiny stings. He nipped down, stopping just before my breast. His touch sailed up my thigh and grabbed my ass, kneading me. We tore at each other until he kicked open a door.

Vinn dragged me into his bedroom. He pushed me into a chair, his face still glued to mine. He cradled my cheek, which shouldn't have lit my being on fire. He used to pinch my jaw and smile. It made me feel special, but he kept doing it, and when I got older, the burn spread to naughty places.

"That's better," he whispered, kissing me softly. "Much better."

I licked my mouth. "What will you do to me?"

His breath cut my skin as I stared into a remorseless gaze. "You won't move. No matter what I do, your legs stay open."

I nodded, my breathing shallow.

Suddenly, he left the cradle of my arms. His shirt collar revealed the deep red flushing his chest.

I ached to drag him close and explore his body. It took everything I had not to fall into his embrace.

His rough fingers rolled up my sleeves. He leaned on the chair, and then his lips touched mine, soft and gentle. His tongue slid under my pout and sucked. The heat lashed me with bliss. A glow throbbed in my pussy as he played with me, the pull at my navel so strong I cupped his face.

"No touching."

My hands flew to the chair, and my legs clenched. The darkness in his tone *affected* me.

"Why am I sitting?"

"I'm asking the questions. They'll be very personal." His silky voice carried a challenge. "Refuse to answer or lie, and I'll whip your ass."

I nodded.

His smile flickered. "What's your name?"

"L-Liana."

"How old are you?"

I gaped at Vinn. "You know that."

"I will start fucking your mouth unless it's a response to my question."

That titillating image blasted my thighs with steam.

He tapped me. "How old?"

"Twenty-one."

"Where did you grow up?"

"Boston," I said, bewildered.

Vinn disappeared as he stepped around, sweeping the hair from my shoulders. He tickled my neck.

"Where do you go to school?"

I arched into his touch before remembering the order —*Don't move*. I stilled, gripping the arms. "B-Bourton University."

Vinn sank into the chair beside mine, sleeves rolled up his tattooed biceps. "Do you meet a lot of guys at college?"

"Uh—sure."

"Tell me about your boyfriends."

I wetted my lips. "Boyfriends?"

"How many have you had?"

My palms slipped. "I—what?"

He nipped the shell of my ear. "How many boyfriends?"

"*None.*"

His tone darkened. "The truth, Liana. *Now.*"

"I've never been in a relationship."

My half-hearted attempts to move on always ended in disaster. I'd never stopped loving him—even my hate was coated in so much love.

His brows flickered as he digested that. He blinked, losing his thread a little. "How many men have you been with?"

He slowly ripped open my blouse. Buttons snapped as they popped off, tickling my stomach. His raking gaze stroked my body as he pulled the shirt off my curves. His finger slid along my bra, making my breath hitch.

"I want their names, Liana."

"Let-let me think." I'd fumbled with a few in high school and college, but none had progressed very far. "There-there was Ben. James and Dennis. Then y-you."

"Three boys and me. That's it?"

"Yes." I licked my lips. "Yes, I think so."

"Do you think or know?" Vinn trailed his grip up my arm.

My heart seized. "I definitely know."

"Good. Tell me about the first boy."

"He went to a different school. We met through friends, and he took me to the movies."

"You fucked him?"

If Michael ever caught him talking like this, he'd slit his best friend's throat without hesitation.

I flinched. "No, I didn't. It-it was innocent. We made out in the movie theater."

"Did he touch your tits?"

I nodded, burning at the memory.

A smile staggered across Vinn's face. "Did he go under your bra?"

"Sometimes, but I usually—" I stopped as he cupped me through the fabric, his thumbs stroking where my nipples ached. "*Oh.*"

"You usually what?"

Vinn's voice softened, but it didn't disguise his intentions. He drew circles, torturing me through the thick cups. Heat tingled my nipples as they stiffened into points. I bit my lip against the inferno claiming my pussy.

"Liana, if I have to ask *again*—"

"I'd push him off me. Back then, I didn't like doing it in a public place."

Vinn snorted. Then he eased the bra over my breasts.

I shuddered, releasing a low hiss. Arousal pooled between my thighs as Vinn followed the band, loosening the straps. His stare dipped to my cleavage, and when it swung to my eyes, he twisted the clasp.

The bra tumbled to my belly.

His warm hand swallowed my breast. He rolled my nipple. My blood surged at the teasing intimacy. My teeth ground together as he tweezed me, the gentle friction shooting sparks. My breathing labored as he gave the same attention to my other breast.

God, he was amazing.

But why was he doing this?

Vinn offered me no answers as he kneaded me, his gaze snapping to my face as though to gauge my response. He gathered both nipples. Then he pinched.

I gasped.

"What else did you do with him?" he demanded. "Did his mouth touch your tits?"

I couldn't say a word. His skillful hands had robbed me of breath.

He squeezed harder.

The unexpected bolt of pleasure made me gasp. "N-no."

"Never fucked you with his fingers?"

My cheeks heated. *"Vinny."*

"I'm not your Vinny." He leaned forward, his words tickling my skin. "Answer me."

"No—*oh, God.*"

His mouth smothered my nipple. He suckled me, tantalizing the buds that'd already swollen to their fullest. Wet heat lashed the hardened point, and a spurt of desire spiraled within me, centering on Vinn's flicking tongue. My whole being flooded with lust. A moan slipped from my lips, and I buried my hands in his hair.

"Oh, I want more. *Vinn.*"

He bit me.

I yelped and returned to the chair.

He tore away, leaving me with a red mark and a throbbing ache. "Tell me about the other guys."

I sucked in harshly and tried not to rub my thighs together.

"I met Dennis in Anthro 101. I—um—I blew him a few times."

"Did he finish in your mouth?"

I nodded, too mortified to speak.

"Did he get you off?"

"No," I whispered

"He didn't even get you off?"

My face boiled at his warm laugh. "I didn't want a boyfriend. I just wanted—"

"To suck dick without anything in return?"

"It was *consensual*, and I liked it. He'd text me. I'd meet him on campus. We'd find a spot where I could do it. It only lasted a few weeks, but it was hot as hell. I don't regret it."

I'd enjoyed how impersonal it was while still fulfilling a depraved fantasy.

Vinn's glare heated. "Tell me about the others."

"There's only one, James. I bumped into him at a party. I made out with him, and I got drunk. I woke up on the couch. My jeans were down, and his finger was on my clit."

Vinn's calm expression shattered. A severity rippled over his brows. "The same James at the bar."

"Yes."

"And he *fucked* you?"

"No, no. I pushed him off and left."

He smoldered for a few moments. "What about the man who gave you the necklace?"

"What necklace?"

"You wear it almost every day."

"Uh—we never even kissed." A fierce blaze claimed my cheeks. "I loved him, but it was unrequited. That's all."

"He never touched you?"

Not until now.

I pressed my lips together and shook my head.

He forced air through gritted teeth. "What was your first time like?"

"I'm a virgin."

He snorted.

"It's the truth."

Vinn looked at me for a while. "You should've told me."

"Would you have treated me differently?"

"I guess not." He flipped my skirt over my waist, his palm stroking the inside of my thigh. "How many sex toys do you have?"

"A few."

"*Like?* Don't get shy on me."

I mumbled a response.

"*Liana.*"

"A few dildos and...butt plugs."

A grin split his face. "You want to be taken in the ass?"

"I-I'd like to try."

"Good to know."

He slipped under my skirt, teasing my thighs before he tugged. Vinn taking off my clothes was magic, like the sweet kisses he planted under my jaw. I burned as the fabric rolled off, exposing the pink triangle of my panties. I shuddered as the skirt glided down, and then he ripped it from my ankles.

He nudged my knees apart. His hands explored me, canvassing my legs, tracing my bikini.

I groaned. "Let me touch you."

"Not yet."

He smiled into my neck, nipping me. He sucked hard until a patch of skin burned, and then he lowered to my nipple to raise another mark. He cupped my ass, his fingers riding my seam. He pushed into me, still on the outside of my underwear.

I moaned, and then he slid my bikini to the side, sliding into my wetness. He massaged my clit. He descended to my wet mound, slipping in the river of my arousal.

I shut my thighs.

Vinn slapped my knee. "Open."

I obeyed, and he resumed the slow stroking. A flat pressure curled over my pussy. His hand curved into my folds, testing my entrance. One finger sank into me.

Desperate sounds ripped from me.

"You could be telling the truth. Maybe you clench your thighs every time I touch you. Do you put your hand between your legs and wish it was my cock?"

My mouth parted. "*Yes.*"

He tore me from the chair. My knees hit the desk before he forced me to bow. My belly pressed into the wood. My toes skimmed the floor. Then he gathered my wrists.

Shit.

He snapped his palm over my butt. The bite of it seeped into my flesh. He spanked me again. A yell burst from my closed lips. He stroked the burn. He touched where I clenched madly on emptiness. Then he fucked me with a finger.

I drowned in a pool of silky pleasure as I sealed around the hardness, aching for longer. Thicker. I pushed against him.

"Oh, Vinn. That's so good."

"Want more?"

"Yes, I do. I *really* do."

He slapped the fullest part of my ass.

It seared with a blooming pain. The sting of his blows radiated to my pussy, throwing gasoline on an already raging fire. His fingers plunged inside me, the wet sounds filling the room. He pulled out of me and whacked my ass. He rubbed my clit hard.

Holy fuck.

A searing wave twitched my hips. My orgasm smashed into me and left me reeling. Rich groans erupted from my mouth. I was a discarded marionette, but the relief I sought never came. My pussy still contracted. I groaned with a sharp frustration as Vinn yanked me from the desk.

His eyes sparkled as he cradled my heaving body. He watched me with a wicked smile as he ran a finger down my side, as though he loved how I shuddered. There was laughter in his gaze clouded with suspicion.

He tossed me onto the bed.

I slashed at his shirt, clawing it off in my haste. He threw it aside, and I grabbed the bulge straining his slacks. He sucked in when I squeezed him and broke from my grip to remove his pants, and suddenly his weight settled over me.

I gasped at the sensation of being held against a naked man. I expected him to throw me onto the mattress and rut me, but Vinn explored my curves, easing my thighs apart with a tap. He closed the distance. His heartbeat hammered my chest.

"You really want this. With me."

I bit my lip, fighting the grin. "Yes."

Vinn said nothing for a while. He stroked my hair, front to back, his fingers tingling my shoulders as they skated down.

"I trust you."

He nodded, and he drew me into a soft kiss.

A hardness nudged my pussy, dropping into my wetness. He inched forward. He was so hot and thick, like a fist wedging me open.

I grimaced.

Vinn paused. "You okay?"

"Yeah. Just—are you all the way inside?"

"Not even close, baby."

Baby.

My heart sang as he claimed my mouth, his hips rocking slowly. I'd played around with so many toys that it wasn't torture, but he was big enough to make me wince. He rained kisses on me as he pulsed, his strokes deepening into thrusts that stole my breath. His ragged breathing hitched with an anchoring thrust. The full length of him pushed into me.

A sharp agony split me in two. I fought to inhale, my palms slipping off his neck.

"That's all of me. Li, breathe."

"Trying."

He pulled back, relieving the pressure. He caught my leg, sliding his touch to my knee, which he marked with a love bite. Eyes shut, he rolled his hips.

The fullness from this position ripped a groan from me. I hissed as the pain melted into sweetness. The more he fucked me, the less it hurt. My thighs relaxed, and we settled into a comfortable rhythm. God, I needed our mouths touching—not having anything but the sheets to grasp made this unbearable.

Vinn had plenty of me. He gripped my hip, then he shifted to my waist and belly, cupping my breast. He punched forward with deeper thrusts. Ecstasy glowed through me like warm honey.

I tangled my fingers with his. I dragged him to my cheek and kissed his knuckles, my breath hitching. My nails dug into his hand. It was much better now, so easy. Lying under him while he worked up a sweat while fucking me was the best thing ever.

Amazing.

Every sensation heightened my arousal—his strained grunts, the obscene, wet slapping, the sharp scent of male.

His arm buckled, and he fell as though weakened. He seized my hips, and he pounded me with an unhinged rhythm. It was like he shoved his cock into my stomach.

I gasped as my breasts crushed against his pecs. I explored the planes of his back as he caged me in his arms. I melted, my world filled with him. His hard body sailed in my hands. He clutched my hair and mashed his kiss into me. His tongue forced my lips to part, and I succumbed to his domination. I burned for more. He showered kisses over my mouth and jaw. My emotions and thoughts whirled and skidded. All I could do was take the rolls of his hips.

He kissed my nipples, rousing a melting warmth. He picked up a lock of my hair and inhaled. The raw passion lifted me to blissful clouds. I soared. My blood sang with the tempo of our bodies. I raked his shoulders.

Then I shattered into a million glowing stars. Ecstasy flooded my whole being as his cock anchored deep. A tremor heated my thighs as a gust of pleasure swept me away.

Vinn arched. His face squeezed, and he let out a delicious groan. Liquid heat jetted from his cock, filling me with wetness. I quivered with the sensation. I couldn't speak. I did nothing but savor him.

His pulse hammered my breast. He panted, forehead touching mine. A bead of his sweat trickled to my cheek. His eyes crashed into mine, no longer pools of pitch-black but burning with a feral possessiveness.

My giddiness popped like bubbles from soda, exploding with Vinn's growing smile. He looked at me under his lashes with an arrogance that demolished his sweetness.

I moved to free myself. Bitterness cut my chest when he resisted, eye-fucking me.

He kissed my cheek.

That one kiss sparked a fierce ache.

He pulled out, hands sliding over my body like furniture. He tapped my leg and slid off the bed. Then he disappeared into the bathroom to clean himself.

My stomach gaped hollowly. I'd saved myself for him only for it to be met with his indifference. This moment was supposed to mean something, and now it was ruined.

I trembled. My throat burned with a silent scream. I shoved off the bed and picked up my clothes, eager to put every moment of this night behind me, until I kicked something round and hard. The necklace he'd ripped off me dug into my foot.

I grabbed it.

I was a volcano on the verge of erupting, all my bottled feelings slamming into my chest. Years' worth of anguish clawed at my throat as I met his puzzled gaze.

Vinn stood in his carpeted walk-in closet, pulling on slacks. He pulled on his jacket, but I laced my hands with his, stopping him from buttoning.

He resisted. "I have to go."

"Stay with me."

My eyes pinched shut against the rejection that would come. A sick yearning assaulted me. My throat tightened. I was tired of this. I couldn't bear the sight of his coldness without breaking down.

I can't do this.

He pulled me off him and pinched my chin. His lips curled with a small grin, as though he found me begging him to stay amusing. "I had fun, but I'm still very pissed. I'll be back. Tomorrow."

The stone wall within me crumbled.

My palm opened around the seashell clutched in my fist. My thoughts careened as I slowly untangled the chain and draped it over my neck.

Vinn ripped away from me and roughly tugged on his jacket. His stiff outrage was my only victory. The only power I held over Vinn was the pendant dangling on my neck.

He would never love me.

I had to shove him away.

He gave my throat a bitter glare, and left the room.

NINETEEN
VINN

Fuck, she'd been a great lay.

The best I'd ever had. I couldn't get it out of my head, how her soft curves had molded into my body. She might've been a virgin, but she got my blood pumping like nothing else when she arched her back, ripped at my clothes, and slashed my mouth with her tongue. She should be held responsible for turning me into a maniac.

Thirty years, and I'd never made the stupid decision to fuck a woman bareback. I'd taken note of men like Michael, who'd ruined his life by knocking up a stripper, and kept my dick wrapped up. If a girl hinted at having stronger feelings, my ass was out the door. And yet, I'd broken every rule tonight, and I wanted to do it again. I might've gotten her pregnant. A sick part of me hoped I had.

I could keep her forever.

The reckless thought consumed me with a flame before I shoved it away. Jesus, I'd lost my mind. I'd officially gone off the deep end, if I was that desperate.

The shot of whiskey trembled in my grip. I'd headed straight for Sunset Tavern, and I'd stared at the glass for the last fifteen minutes. Hanging out in bars was terrible for my sobriety, but if I didn't drown myself in alcohol, I would do something *insane*.

A body bumped into my chair. Only one motherfucker would be so cavalier with my personal space, and I had no interest in listening to his snide comments all night.

Michael leaned against the counter, his teeth flashing with a fake smile. "Let me guess. You're in the doghouse for being a prick."

"We're not fighting."

"Then why are you at the place where you find all your hookups?" A deadly edge crept into his voice.

"*I don't want anyone else.*"

I swallowed the drink as the truth burned in my chest. Liana was mine, wedged so far inside my chest I couldn't breathe without a sharp ache.

Was it the same for her?

No.

She couldn't go a day without pining after the other man, regardless of her "crush" on me.

I hurled the glass at the wall. It shattered, raining on the peanut-shell-covered floor.

Michael gave me a vicious side-eye. "What the hell happened?"

"None of your business."

"She's still my sister," he warned in a deep growl. "And I'm waiting on your wedding invitation. Don't think I haven't noticed, *asshole*."

"There will be a wedding."

And hopefully, a baby.

God, I was fucking nuts.

"When?" Michael pressed, shoving a tumbler of seltzer in my hands. "She'll be showing soon. There's nothing tackier than a bride with a baby bump."

"Within a month."

"Then you need to get with the program."

He was absolutely right.

"Thanks for the pep talk." I patted his shoulder, and he flinched. "Later."

I grabbed my coat and slid off the stool, leaving the bar.

My mood was black.

My hatred for the man who gave her the necklace clogged my lungs like toxic smoke. I couldn't breathe without the sting of a thousand tiny knives. This was unlike me. I didn't become a fuming wreck when they wore another man's jewelry. I didn't stalk their exes.

Exes.

The frat bro's round face swam in my mind, poisoning my stomach. James had signed his own death warrant. He'd touched parts of Liana I considered mine. He'd almost raped her.

Unforgivable.

I PARKED my car in a blackout area.

Then I strolled into the sports dive doubling as a miniature golf course that advertised half-off pints. The male, early twenties crowd packed every available spot. Pitchers of beer stood precariously on steel tabletops. It would've been easy to swipe one, but I honestly had no interest in the cheap bilge they were drinking.

I'd come here for something else.

Or rather, someone.

I had so much shit on my plate, but this was personal.

I entered a room filled with pool tables. I bellied up to the counter, finding the pasty-faced bastard ignoring the queue of customers to chat with a girl. James teased a finger around her hair and tugged. She laughed and swiped his hand away.

He winked at her as she headed for the bathrooms, and then he grabbed her half-empty mug. He adjusted his fingers, slipping powder over the rim. The small, white grains vanished as he refilled her drink.

Well, that sealed it.

James was a dead man.

It hadn't taken long to find him. Poking around Liana's social media gave me all the information I'd needed. After she'd casually mentioned her near-rape with the frat bro, I'd made it my mission to erase him from Liana's life. Judging by what I'd witnessed, I was doing the female population at Bourton University a solid.

I knocked over her glass.

The roofied beer splashed him in a wide arc. He jumped back and groaned.

"What the fuck, man? Damn, it's all over me." He mopped himself, the wet stain on his crotch growing. His sour gaze landed on me. "You're that guy. Liana's bodyguard."

"*Fiancé.*"

"Oh yeah, Queenie told me." He seized a dripping rag and cleaned under the taps. "Congrats. That's cool. Super happy for you guys."

The *jamook* must've finally Googled me. I liked him better when he had a pair of balls, although his creep-factor suggested he never possessed any.

"Crazy to run into you here." He wrung the towel,

tossing it in the sink. "Didn't think this place would be your scene."

"I'm all about cheap beer and low expectations."

He flushed. "Look, I haven't touched her. I did what you said. I don't exist to her anymore."

Not yet.

I smiled. "I know."

He nodded, tensing. "You here with Li?"

God, I hated her name on his lips.

I shook my head. "I was in the neighborhood and spotted you inside. Thought I'd say hello."

A fracture snapped through James's thin veneer of calm. His cheeks blazed red.

What I wouldn't have exchanged for two hours with him and my Ka-Bar knife.

"W-what would you like? IPA?"

"Give me what you gave that girl."

His wide eyes locked on mine.

I could practically hear his thoughts. No doubt, he imagined his coveted internship, his enrollment at a prestigious Ivy League, and his shiny, bright future vanishing in a puff of smoke.

And it would.

He filled a glass and banged it on the counter. "On the house."

I peered into the crowd. "That chick is headed this way. I'll leave you alone. Thanks for the beer."

"You're—you're welcome."

I winked at him and left the bar, waiting for him outside.

Minutes later, he used the service exit, hoodie drawn tight, hands deep in his pockets.

I peeled from the wall and grabbed him.

He flailed as I cupped his mouth. My bicep slid over his throat. As I compressed his neck, he clawed at my forearm, slapping me with pathetic, meaty thuds before he passed out with barely a whimper. Jesus, Liana fought me with more violence than this little bitch. It ended so quickly that my heartbeat never picked up the pace.

I bound him with zip ties and threw him in the trunk. Then I wound tape around his skinny ankles and mouth. I could've made his death quick and painless by bagging his head, but that was too bloodless. Too easy. And I wanted him to think he had a chance.

He deserved to suffer.

I pulled over once to stab him in the thigh. When I reached the Quabbin Reservoir, my car reeked of piss and blood. Thankfully, the liner caught everything.

I dragged him out. He smashed into the hard-packed ground, his cheeks streaming with tears. I ripped the tape from his lips. He screamed as though I'd stabbed him again. Then I seized his arm and strolled through the thicket of trees. When I dumped him into the freshly dug grave, he lost his shit.

"O-oh God! Please don't kill me, man!" He gritted his teeth, blubbering. "I won't—I won't tell anybody what you did. I'll—I'll never, *ever ta*lk to your fiancée. I swear."

I drew my gun.

"No, no, no!" He shoved himself against the grave, his high-pitched pleas digging into my ear. "I didn't do anything!"

He sounded like he really believed that.

"You took advantage of her."

His eyes widened, and the color drained from his skin. Men like him were always shocked at the order of the universe turning against them. They were oblivious to the destruction they caused, the shattered lives and the broken women.

Crimson blanketed my vision.

I shot him.

Blood burst from his stomach, his abdomen, his chest, *everywhere*. His head rolled back, the tension in his muscles gone. I emptied the whole clip. I wiped the gun, dumping it beside his body. Then I shoveled dirt over James's slack-jawed face.

Next, Killian.

TWENTY

LIANA

Something was off.

The hairs on my neck rose when Vinn walked through the door, hair mussed, *smiling*. He immediately dumped his shirt and pants in the washer, which set my alarms on red-alert. My mind dove into the worst-case scenario as Vinn jumped in the shower.

I almost stormed into the bathroom to ask where the hell he'd gone. Instead I clenched my teeth and glowered at the TV show I was supposed to be absorbing. He'd been out all night and for the better part of the morning. The clothes in the wash and his aura of giddiness pitted me with dread.

Was I not enough?

I dismissed the insecurity and crushed it under my heel. It was time to wake up. I'd loved a cardboard cutout of Prince Charming that had never existed. I'd never known Vinn at all.

I switched off the TV and flung the remote onto the table, the void in my stomach growing.

I shuffled to the blinding kitchen for a coffee. Vinn, freshly washed, stood at the stove, pouring egg whites on a plate. He wore gym shorts and nothing else. The sight of his naked back brought home the ache in my pussy, my sore breasts, and my tingling mouth.

The knot in my gut pulsed.

"I got you a phone," he announced, gesturing at the counter. "I already synced it with your laptop."

I folded my arms across my chest, ignoring the cell beside its packaging. My head pounded with the effort of not calling him a dozen expletives.

"What, no catty remark? Your contacts are all on there, except the asshole."

"Along with a million security apps to track my every movement and keystroke."

He winked as he sat, tucking into his food. "Smart girl."

The taunt lashed my cheeks. It wasn't enough that he'd humiliated me. He had to be a jerk about my privacy, too.

"Shove it up your ass, Vinn."

I slid the cell over the marble.

Vinn caught it, frowning.

I shot from the kitchen.

A potent rage seared my spine. The skin on my face strained. My hands clenched and unclenched. I bulldozed into Vinn's bedroom and threw open the closet. I seized a bag and shoved articles of clothing inside, packing so quickly I barely paid attention.

"What are you doing?" Vinn's baritone was like a clap of lightning.

"I'll be at Michael's."

He gave me a black look layered with confusion, and then he set his chin into an unyielding line. Every muscle in his body spoke defiance, right down to the one twitching in his jaw.

"You're not going anywhere."

I shouldered the backpack, standing. "I'll return in a few days. I'll tell Michael we're in a fight over wedding venue locations, so he doesn't murder you."

His expression hardened like someone who'd been slapped. He grabbed me as I headed out. He palmed my back, and then he scooped me into his arms.

"Li, what's the matter?"

The gentle touch shattered me.

"It was supposed to be special." I screwed up my face, battling the rising lump in my throat. "I never wanted to have sex with anyone but the man I married. It's stupid and outdated, but I'd saved myself for this. It meant a lot to me, but it wasn't anything to you."

"You don't know that."

"You took off right after!"

Vinn dropped his gaze as a red flush claimed his cheeks. "I needed time alone."

I swung, almost hitting him with the bag. "Time alone? Or time with *someone else*?"

Vinn seemed to resent the accusation. He ground his teeth before letting out a long, harsh sigh.

"I went to Sunset Tavern. Michael was there. We talked, and then I left to buy your phone. I ran another errand at a construction site, and my footing wasn't balanced, and I fell into the dirt. Then I came home. The *end*. Call Michael if you don't believe me."

I bit the inside of my cheek.

"There's no other woman. You deleted them all from my phone, remember?" He slipped the pack from my shoulder and grasped my arm, his grip white-hot. "Besides, I have my hands full with you."

He tugged me onto the bed, sandwiching us together.

I didn't know what to believe.

Maybe expecting an emotionally distant man like Vinn to be sensitive to my needs had been foolishly optimistic.

Vinn's touch skimmed my waist and anchored me to his side. "How are you feeling?"

A suggestion lingered in the question. It was less concern, and more—*Are you ready for more?* The heat spiraling my body made me want to answer with a resounding *yes*.

"I'm a bit sore."

He brushed a kiss across my forehead. "There's Advil in the kitchen."

A chime from Vinn's pocket shattered the silence. Vinn handed over my phone. I glanced at the screen.

Queenie.

I answered. "Hey, babe. How are you?"

The tiniest sob crackled the speaker.

"Have you seen James?"

JAMES HAD GONE MISSING.

He'd skipped two work shifts, and nobody could reach him.

An inconsolable Queenie sat on my couch. Tissues scattered the coffee table. She'd poured out her heart about her longtime crush on James. I would've set her straight, but speaking ill of him now seemed like bad form.

"They've filed a missing persons report," she sniffed, clutching the gray afghan. "It's a nightmare."

My pulse raced at the grim reminder that we no longer lived in a safe city.

"Maybe he took a weekend trip without telling anyone."

Queenie blotted her tear-stained face, shaking. "He needs his job to pay his rent. He wouldn't just leave."

I squeezed her shoulder, wishing for the words to comfort her. "Walk me through what happened."

"He went to Flatstick Pub on Saturday." Queenie's voice steadied as she launched into the story, as though reexamining it for the fifth time might offer new insight. "He mentioned he had a volunteer shift at the—oh, wow!"

Vinn had strolled into the room. He slid a cutting board topped with crusty Italian bread, thinly sliced soppressata, and hard cheese over the table. He handed the flabbergasted Queenie a plate and loaded another with snacks before pressing it into my hands.

A jolt hit my stomach as our fingers touched.

"Thanks, Vinn. That's sweet." Queenie beamed at him as she made a sandwich. "I love a guy who brings me food without asking."

I grumbled an affirmative.

Queenie bit into the bread, moaning. "So good."

Vinn's thigh brushed mine as he sank into the couch. "Glad you like it."

"By the way, I'm impressed. I assumed she'd need at least a few weeks before she said yes." Queenie winked at him. "Smooth moves."

"Took a couple tries, but I got there. Right?"

He elbowed me, and I glowered.

Queenie gasped. "You said no?"

Vinn's knuckle caressed my cheek. "Honey, you didn't tell your friend?"

His chastising tone raked my skin.

"Vinn. We're supposed to w—"

"She's pregnant," he told Queenie.

I groaned.

"*What?*" Queenie gaped at him, her shriek piercing the air. "You're pregnant?"

Thanks a lot, Vinn.

My face went up in flames. "I was going to mention it—"

"Oh my God, you guys are nuts." She threw a pillow at me, knocking the cheese from my hand. "You let me blab about my problems this whole time!"

"Let's not make a big deal of it."

"I called it!" Queenie shrieked, covering her mouth. "I knew this would happen. What did I say? You'll be married and pregnant by the end of the year."

Vinn's grin twitched as though on the edge of laughter.

Queenie leaned over and shook my knee, grinning. "You must be so excited. I'm thrilled! I'll be godmother. Your brother has *three* kids of his own. He'll never prioritize your baby. I will."

Vinn straightened, flashing her a polite smile that said *no-fucking-way*.

I poked at his bicep. "Thanks for the food, but you're interrupting our girl time."

"Yeah, leave us alone so we can talk about you!"

Vinn's granite-like features softened. He pinched my chin and stood. As soon as he rounded the corner, Queenie clutched her chest and fell into the couch.

"You two are so cute it breaks me. The way he looks at you makes me melt." She flattened her dark curls and burst with a nervous giggle. "You're having a *kid*. Are you freaking out?"

"A little." I would be if it were real. "It's so far ahead I'm putting it on the back burner. Maybe there's something I can do about James. My brother's professional network is robust. Hell, I'll ask Vinn."

Queenie lifted her head, bleary-eyed. Her mouth twitched. "Well, I should get going."

"You sure?"

She nodded. "We're searching the parks today. Just in case, you know."

I pulled her into a hug. "Keep a positive attitude. No sense driving yourself crazy until he's found."

"I'm trying," she whimpered. "Thanks for listening."

"Of course."

We exchanged goodbyes, and she headed out the door. I'd decided before I'd slid the deadbolt. I didn't like asking Vinn for favors, but I'd put my pride aside for Queenie.

Vinn was working out in the gym. He'd changed into shorts and a tank top. He stood in front of a wall-to-wall mirror, lifting an Olympic barbell. His features were so perfect and symmetrical that any more would've made him too beautiful for a man. Dark hair stuck to his handsome, square face. He jerked it to his shoulders and swung down, releasing the bar. He picked it off the ground and repeated the exercise.

The plates banged into the rubber mat.

Vinn cupped his shoulder and let out a raw hiss, massaging the muscle surrounding the gunshot wound from a year ago.

My feet smacked the floor as I rushed toward him. "You okay?"

Vinn gave me a narrowed glance. "I'm fine."

His frosty tone should've sent me running. Something disturbing had replaced his smolder, and it cautioned me to stay away, but I hated leaving him alone.

I approached, lungs filling with the scent of iron and his heady musk. "I didn't realize it still hurt you."

"It doesn't."

Like hell.

Sweat glistened on his forehead. His nostrils flared as a timer beeped from his phone. He closed it and wiped his rippling brow.

"You don't have to pretend. You can be vulnerable with me." I joined him on the bench, fidgeting with my shirt. "I'm always here to listen."

"Not the talkative type."

He patted my knee and lurched upright, then snapped the safety clips off the barbell. He eased the Olympic plates while lifting the bar. His bicep trembled, and a bang erupted through the room as it landed.

"*Fuck.*"

I stood. "I'll get ice."

"Don't bother." Vinn sighed, dropping onto the mat. "Fuck."

"Would a massage help?"

He stared into the mirror, silent. His arm fell in his lap as he rested against exercise equipment, his eyes shut.

I rolled my hand over his shoulder. He tensed but didn't throw me off. I slowly dug in. Vinn released a ragged hiss.

I paused, my heart pounding.

"Don't stop," he whispered. "Harder."

I did my best to work out the rock-hard knot, but it was like massaging stone. I sank into him. His mouth twisted, beads of sweat rolling down his neck.

"Am I hurting you?"

"No, it's good." Vinn leaned into me, sighing. "I used to have a physical therapist do this, but I got sick of a dude touching me every week."

"You're ridiculous." I took a deep breath and held it in. "So when you declared yourself healed six months after the shooting, that was total bullshit?"

"I keep everyone in the dark and oblivious."

"Why?"

"I see no point in letting people in."

"You should've texted me," I growled. "I could've helped you."

Vinn's broad face split with a smile that tickled my cheeks. "Hey, Li. Want to come to my place? I could use a back rub. Your brother would've loved that."

"Like I'd tell him."

He made a deep sound. "Tempting, but I'm nobody's dirty secret, and neither are you."

"I would've done anything for you."

My insides clenched at the blunder. I was doing it *again*. Pouring out my feelings would get me hurt. I throttled the current zipping through me.

Vinn's gaze riveted on my face. My skin tingled as he searched my eyes. He turned, hand cupping my cheek. Warmth bloomed inside me, betraying my resolve. My attraction to Vinn had nothing to do with logic. It screamed for me to take the leap.

Our lips touched.

He melted into me with gentle strokes. I slackened as he lulled me into a trance. Ecstasy swirled in my body. He traced my lip with a swipe of his tongue, and a hot ache grew in my throat. His nails grazed my head.

I was a furnace. He'd captured me at a young age with his magnetic presence, but this dreamy intimacy had signed my heart over forever. His light touch blossomed with sharp aches in my skin.

I pressed my open lips to his, but he didn't crush me. He held me hostage with his slow, drugging kisses. I drifted on clouds. His uneven breathing caressed my neck as he broke away, dragging me to the rubber floor.

Vinn's heavy palm weighted my head.

My knees buckled.

I faced his groin. Not in any hurry, Vinn thumbed his shorts and pushed, grabbing his cock from a bed of trimmed hair. It swelled, the head shining with a bead of precum. He held it to my mouth. I licked my lips, stroking Vinn in the process.

"I can't stop thinking about the other night." Vinn's heartbeat pulsed through the taut skin as he stared down. "I hate every man who touched you. Hate. Them. Especially the guy whose cock you sucked on demand."

A sensual quality quivered through Vinn's voice that made me slowly spread my legs. "And?"

"It should've been me."

He fisted my hair. His head nudged my lips, and my mouth parted. He worked in his thumb, hooking it on my cheek. His cock slid inside, filling me with a rock hardness I barely breathed around.

I choked.

He groaned as he buried himself, and my body clenched as though he'd satisfied the ache between my legs. His hold on my hair slackened. His fingers trailed my jaw. Everything was more sensitive. His light touch *hurt*. The pain lingered like a smoldering kiss. He fucked me, his eyes glazed as he chased his pleasure. He rolled his hips with quick, abrupt jerks, his grip hardening.

His need stirred me like a finger teasing my clit. The hot, iron-like pressure thrust mercilessly as he gripped my head, making a mess of my hair. He sped up. He released a long, tortured groan, pushing himself deeper, holding me still.

I leaned into him, meeting his thrusts. Saliva dribbled onto my chin as he pounded faster, hissing. He slammed home and made a desperate sound, and thick, salty warmth filled my mouth. Vinn's cock jumped in my throat.

"Swallow," he ordered.

I flicked my tongue along his shaft, relishing in his possession.

"Swallow, or I'm not taking it out."

I swallowed, a thrill touching my nipples when his cum slid down.

"Open and show me."

I obeyed, heart pounding.

"Good girl," he said, his tone soothing. "Now I want you on your back. Legs spread wide."

I flattened on the rubber mat as Vinn ripped off my pants. He removed my panties and settled between my thighs. He fisted the necklace as he smashed his mouth into mine. It was a brutal, possessive kiss. His tongue swiped in and claimed me as his blunt head fitted to my pussy.

I writhed.

He shoved inside, stretching my walls. He gave no time to adjust. He slipped out and rammed in, trailing kisses over my body. Muscles within me contracted. I raked his back and sank my nails into his steel ass.

Vinn reeled up, hovering above like a sculpted god. He was a blur of muscle. His whole body tensed with the force of fucking me. He was an unhinged animal crashing against gates.

My defenses weakened as he cupped my breasts. I welcomed this fierce possession, even the painful thrusting because it proved that he wasn't a master of himself. He couldn't control himself around me, either.

He staggered his thrust, back arched in a harsh climax. He dropped and crushed me with his weight, kissing me. He sucked my lip, biting, the cruel ravishment the final push over the edge.

I gasped with the sweet agony. I vibrated with liquid heat. Long, surrendering moans burst from my chest.

We lay there for a while. Then he carried me to bed, and I curled into the rigid contours of his body. I was a glowing fire of affection and love, and he let me hold him.

And he stayed.

It was like a beautiful dream.

TWENTY-ONE

VINN

I fucked her again.

Again.

And *again*.

My plans became a distant memory dissolved in a night of wild sex. I took her standing up, in the bathroom, against the mirror, and in the shower because shoving her against the glass turned me on. I checked off a list of every depraved fantasy. My last recollection was nuzzling her perfect tits before falling into an exhausted sleep.

Until she woke me with a blowjob.

Liquid heat surrounded my semi. My cheeks burned with a rousing steam. Liana's head bobbed as she made the sloppiest sounds. My fingers dove into a tangle of hair. Liana gagged before I dragged her to my chest.

I cupped her face and growled into her mouth. Liana

slammed her lips into mine, refusing to let me breathe. My head buzzed from the lack of oxygen.

She was burning me up. Her lips pressed into my jaw. Her thighs glided over my hips. She fisted my cock and rolled over my body, gorgeous with her tits marked with my lust.

Her pussy wrapped me in silk. Before her, I'd never ridden bareback. Incredible. So fucking warm and wet. I slid into her like butter. She teased me, inch by inch.

No condom. I couldn't believe we were doing this.

Michael's sister.

Insane.

I patted her ass. "Did you have fun last night?"

"Oh, yes."

"Good. So did I." I palmed her breasts as she rode me. "You're beautiful. So goddamned perfect."

I squeezed her nipples.

Her stomach tensed, and she hissed. Her velvet skin tempted, and I couldn't stop touching her.

"I want to do so many degrading things to you."

"Like what?"

My imagination ran wild.

I groaned, rolling over her curves. Her natural, plump tits filled my hands. I played with them. I turned my head and licked her nipple.

Liana let out tormented groans, squirming beneath me. I explored the perky breasts budding with pink and stroked the wide hips that opened for me. She arched. Wet and wanting. I rubbed her clit.

I curled her leg over my thigh and kissed the base of her neck. I sucked my way down her breast.

Then I fingered her.

She made a delicious sound, thrusting her body into my chest. Fuck, that was hot. She clenched her thighs on me. I slapped her thick ass. Then I pulled out and stuck my hand in her mouth. Her rosebud lips fastened on me.

Crimson stained her cheeks as I moved between her legs. Blood throbbed in my cock, the skin tight and aching. I pushed into her pussy and moaned. Silky heat gloved my dick, squeezing. Fucking her raw intoxicated me better than any whiskey. Her touch blazed me with lust.

I caressed the gorgeous hollow of her back and gripped her ass. I lifted her and rammed home. A brightness sprang into her gaze as I filled her.

She clawed at me, whining.

I pounded her, muffling her whimpers with a finger in her mouth. I dragged it out before lowering and kissing her.

Liana broke from me, panting. "I want to be on top."

I rolled onto my back and enjoyed the ride.

She straddled me. So eager—I loved it—so many girls expected me to do everything. Liana plunged up and down as I teased her taut nipples. I caressed her silken belly before grabbing her hips, guiding her movements with quick, upward jerks.

A red-hot tide raged though me as she abandoned herself. She let out a loud cry, fisting my hair. My thighs trembled. The release came in a flood of melting opium as I fucked her with cum. Her body quivered with my two hard thrusts.

I sank into a peaceful pool, eyes half-closed.

She collapsed over my legs, breathing heavily. Her sighs blew across my groin. She grabbed my wet cock. Then she put her mouth to my shaft.

The pleasant shock of her tongue jolted me upright. "What are you doing?"

Liana paused, her hand wrapping me. "The guy I fooled around with said men liked being cleaned after sex."

I laughed, torn between rage at that son of a bitch and admiration. "You don't have to do that."

"You don't like it?"

"I didn't say that. I think it's sexy." I traced the line of her jaw. "But you don't have to."

"I *want* to."

My cock twitched with the lurch of excitement.

Was she doing this out of a twisted sense of obligation?

"Li, you were great. You know that, right? I'm more than satisfied. You're amazing."

"It's—it's not that."

Liana's cheeks flooded with pink.

Clearly, she had a filthy side. In that case, we'd get along just fine.

I gestured to myself. "Have at it, honey."

A tentative smile carved into her cheek as she popped me into her mouth.

A groan ripped from me as she stimulated where I throbbed with a post-orgasmic glow. I seized her hair as her tongue swirled the sensitive skin. God, it was so wrong of me to encourage this, but she was liquid silk. My body tingled as she sucked me clean, gliding down my painfully hard dick to lave my balls. She was getting all up in there—Jesus. She licked the base of my cock and glided to the head.

I lurched upright. We moved to the edge of the mattress. She kneeled, lips wrapping me. Watching her take me on the floor zapped me with a lightning bolt of desire.

I stood.

She wrapped her arms around me when I drew out to give her a break. She wanted it rough—all right. I fisted her hair and went to town. She made delicious moaning sounds.

I pulled out and threw her on the bed.

Then I stroked my shaft, aiming over her glistening pussy. Milky ropes shot from my cock. I drenched her in cum. I gathered it all and shoved it inside her. Then I slammed it home.

Liana's tortured moans told me she was close. She came with a tremor of her thighs and a crushing, long kiss.

A shudder passed through me. I savored the satisfaction I'd left inside her, but a longing tugged at my ribs. I wanted *more*.

Of what, I had no idea.

Minutes later, we finally stumbled out of bed.

Liana melted as I enveloped her in a button-up shirt. "Thank you."

"For what?"

"Giving me the best night I've ever had."

Warmth spread over my chest. "I had fun, too."

She grinned coyly. "We should've done this when I turned eighteen."

A cold shock gripped me as I pictured her at that age. A teenage Liana lusting after me seemed so outrageous, but she hadn't faked any of this.

"I've no idea how I would've reacted if you hit on me."

"I *did*. Plenty of times."

I shook my head, smiling. "You needed to be more blunt."

Liana snorted. "I don't know how much more obvious I could've been without jumping on your lap."

I made a sound of disbelief.

Was I fucking clueless, or what?

I thought back to every interaction with Liana. She'd always hung around me, clinging to my arm, seeking me out at family events, texting, calling. She visited me while I recovered in the hospital, and I'd never seen her beyond Michael's little sister with an abnormal attachment to me.

It'd always confused me because I'd done nothing to deserve her affection.

A burn raked my throat, clawing me from the inside out. "You want pancakes?"

"Sure."

Liana's smile was as intimate as a kiss. The glow of it warmed me. I dressed in boxers and strolled into the kitchen, where I grabbed ingredients from the pantry as she rifled through my cupboards. I mixed everything and set a timer for fifteen minutes.

I opened the fridge. "Damn. I don't have any blueberries."

Liana settled into the counter stool, sipping orange juice. "I haven't had blueberry pancakes since I was a kid."

I closed the door, raking my hair. "Right."

"You're cute when you don't know what to do with yourself."

I couldn't stop admiring the red marks dotting her

skin. "Honestly, I've never gone through the morning-after."

"Really?"

I pulled a skillet over the stove. "They're out after an hour or two. I don't let them stay."

My mind spun. This was like an out-of-body experience.

The phone beeped, and I spooned a dollop onto the hot pan. It sizzled, and I flipped the blackening pancake. I finished cooking and dropped the stack of steaming cakes in front of her. I ate eggs as Liana feasted on carbs, her plate a pool of syrup.

"Wow. This is good. Letting them rise makes a difference." Liana stared at me, her eyes sparkling. "Who taught you to cook? Your mom?"

"She wasn't around much. I learned on my own. Trial and error. Lots of failed dinners." My insides pulsed with a seething rage. "She gave me nothing but a roof over my head."

I'd never told anyone how bad my situation had been. I could never risk losing Mike and my *zia*, the only people who'd made me feel safe and wanted. Even though my *zia* took care of me when I came over, I couldn't tell her there wasn't enough to eat at home.

What if CPS placed me out of Boston?

What if I never saw them again?

Liana gripped my bicep, her voice tentative.

"Michael said before how he used to pack two school lunches. One for him and the other for you."

"Yeah." I nodded, the bitterness boiling in my gut. "My earliest memory is ripping open a bag of flour and eating until I vomited. I was three. She'd shove me into a closet, lock it, and leave for hours. Sometimes while she was with a man, the heroin dealer. My father."

Liana squeezed me, but I looked anywhere but at her. I couldn't bear her pity. I should've just shut up, but something inside needed to purge.

"When I was fourteen, he tried to take me away. I didn't want to go. He lived in New York, and I hated him. He woke me up with his hand on my thigh. I grabbed the stun gun from under my pillow and shoved it in his neck. Then I stabbed him seven times. He died right there. My mom was nodding off in another room, so I called my uncle. Nico cleaned it up for me."

Her fork clattered to the plate and banged the floor, but she paid it no mind. She gazed at me.

"And after that?"

I shrugged. "I went home."

Was she disgusted? I couldn't gauge her reaction, and it set me on fire. The uncertainty clawed at my insides like a rabid animal.

Liana's eyes gleamed. "Why tell me this?"

"Because you deserve to know why I'm this way. I'm

done pretending, Li. I want to be with you, really be with you."

Her knuckle brushed my cheek. One finger became two, and then she cupped my face.

"Why?"

My stomach tightened, and I dragged her into my arms. "You stopped calling me. Texting. Showing up at my door. *Everything*. You did so many things. I didn't realize how much they mattered. I never knew how bad it'd feel when they vanished. I missed you. I needed you, so...I took you."

I kissed the top of her head and held on tight.

Owning her wasn't enough.

I would make her fucking love me.

TWENTY-TWO

LIANA

What was that?

An ambrosial aroma beckoned me from sleep. My cheek unstuck from the pillow as I inhaled mouth-watering, savory deliciousness. I dropped out of bed and padded toward the scent of crackling bacon.

A banquet of cheese, cold cuts, pastries, fruit, eggs, and meat was spread over the kitchen counter. Folded napkins were perched on gilded trays. A bouquet of calla lilies burst from a glass vase. Standing beside this image of perfection was Vinn.

He was decked in a black tux I'd never seen before. He stood tall and straight, as though he prided himself on his good looks. The sharp outline of his muscles strained against the suit. His ebony hair swept back over his head. A wide smile broke on his handsome face.

"Morning."

"Wow, look at you." I slipped my hands inside his jacket, my heart flipping. "Am I dreaming?"

His steady gaze bored into me. "Am I in your dreams?"

"Only the best ones."

My hands glided up his chest to anchor on his shoulders. I grazed his smooth neck and shaven chin, kissing the dimple under his lip. A need to touch him everywhere consumed me as his aquatic scent wrapped me like a warm cloud.

"Take me before you leave."

His eyes met mine, sending a jolt through my body. "But I'm not going anywhere. Not without you, at least."

I beamed at him. "Isn't today my lucky day."

"Baby, you have no idea." He pulled away from me. "Sit. Eat."

When I hesitated, he grabbed a handful of my ass and guided me into a chair. The harsh line that defined his eyebrows softened as he loaded a plate of food and slid it in front of me.

I picked up my fork. "Did you make all this?"

"Hell no. I had a chef come in early."

I'd barely dug into my eggs before he poured me coffee, serving it just how I liked, and then he slid a flute of orange juice beside me. My stomach burst with warmth. I'd dreamed of being doted on like this, but it was bizarre coming from Vinn.

"You're very nice today."

Vinn shrugged. "I have my reasons."

"Which are?"

He swiped a thumb under his freshly shaved jaw. "You'll see."

Well, that's ominous. "Did you eat anything?"

"A little."

I moaned as I bit into airy waffles drenched in bourbon maple syrup. The strawberries soaked up the excess sugar. I grabbed one. Vinn moved my wrist aside before I touched the berry to his mouth.

I laughed. "Seriously, what's with the suit?"

"Eat your breakfast."

"I'm not hungry for food. I want to sit on your lap and let you do things to me."

Vinn's smoldering expression made my body ache. His hand rubbed the back of my neck. "I'll do you dirty in a few hours."

"Promise?"

"Oh yeah."

My pulse thundered as he dragged the T-shirt over my head, locking my arms together. My world darkened as the cotton shielded my gaze. There was nothing but the distant hum of the air conditioning.

Then wetness stroked my nipple.

My thighs clenched as the wicked heat scorched a line straight to my pussy. A sharp pang nipped the sensitive skin, and then his hands cupped my ass, pushing me down the hall.

"What are you doing—*oh*."

He ripped off the shirt, and suddenly I stood in a wedding boutique. Racks of familiar Vera Wang dresses filled the room.

I fingered the lace of one, heart pounding. "What is this?"

"We're getting married."

My laughter rippled through the air as I whirled, facing him. "I never knew you to be a practical joker. That's Michael's thing."

"I'm not joking."

Vinn leaned against the doorway, his posture nonthreatening, but the no-nonsense tone indicated I wasn't leaving until I wore something white. I gaped at him, my belly fluttering. I'd imagined my wedding to Vinn a hundred thousand times. Not once did this scenario cross my mind.

"I made an appointment at City Hall." His voice was kind but firm. "Pick a dress. We leave in two hours."

A high-pitched sound broke from my lips. *"What?"*

Is he crazy?

Shock wedged the protest in my throat. I fought the bizarre impulse to laugh. This was absurd.

He didn't want to marry me.

"Why? Is this because of Nico?"

"This is for me," he said.

I blustered through a half-assed protest as Vinn crossed the room and kissed my cheek. Blood rushed to the spot where he touched me.

"I need this, and I need it *now*. Not in two weeks or five months." Vinn didn't soften, but he lightened the gravel in his voice. "Honestly, Li. What did you expect would happen after I took your virginity?"

"I-I thought we'd take it slow!"

"*Slow* isn't in my vocabulary."

My throat tightened. "Vinn, this is insane."

"I don't do casual with my best friend's sister. It's all or nothing, and we're past the point of no return."

It was light-years from the proposal I'd wanted, but he gave me a sudden, arresting smile.

My stomach churned with doubt.

"But I want a *real* ceremony."

It wasn't frivolous to complain about being marched into a courthouse. There was no romance in rushing a wedding. He hadn't even asked me to marry him.

"I always pictured my friends and family there. It's important to me."

"If you want another wedding, then we'll have one. But we're getting married today."

"*Vinny.*"

"I'm not caving."

My mouth dropped open. "Are you sure you want this?"

"Yeah, I really do." He swept the hair from my shoulders. "Get ready."

I squeezed my eyes shut and reopened them. Vinn still stood in front of me, which ruled out the possibility of a dream. I had no idea who he was anymore.

Two hours later, Vinn dragged me up the brick steps of City Hall. I followed in my A-line dress, hesitating as Vitale, Vinn's soldier, opened the doors. Vinn palmed my back, nodding at him. I'd worn the seashell necklace in a last act of defiance that was more silly than anything, considering I was marrying the man who'd given it to me.

Vinn hadn't pitched a fit. It was as though the knowledge I'd soon be forever his had quieted his soul. I bounced my knee while we waited and swallowed a lump of nerves as we approached the judge.

"We're seriously doing this?"

"I already applied for marriage licenses and paid off the judge." Vinn pressed his lips to my ear, triggering a wild swirl in my stomach. "I made up my mind weeks ago. Nobody else will be your husband."

My future husband was a damned enigma.

Little of the ceremony branded into my memory except for those words, and his brimstone gaze, blazing with hellfire as he promised to love and cherish me. He slid the wedding band onto my finger. His eyes seemed to glitter with savage laughter as he held my face and crushed his mouth into mine.

My heart flip-flopped like a fish on dry land.

It was *possession*, not love.

TWENTY-THREE
LIANA

I'd married Vinn.

The shock and disbelief wore off quickly, and a boundless joy exploded within me like garish Christmas lights. The man of my dreams was my *husband*. I wished I could send a letter to my teenage self, and tell her one thing:

One day, he will marry you.

The lack of splendor didn't bother me as much as I thought it might after he swept me in his arms and threw me onto the bed.

Vinn dragged me to the edge of the mattress. He wedged my thighs apart, and steam tingled my clit. I inhaled sharply at the contact. His tongue stroked my seam before his mouth covered me hungrily. The engulfing warmth shot electricity to my aching nipples.

His hands locked around my hips, rocking me back and forth.

Shivers ran down my spine. The pit of my stomach churned. I writhed with the tight, heated circles of his tongue. A burning desire screamed for more to fill the void, but his lips feathered me, teasing, balancing me over the precipice. Faster and faster, he swirled and sucked, and then I shattered into a million bolts of light. Then a broad head fitted to my pussy.

Vinn slammed into me, shoving me headlong into a second wave of pleasure. I seized his hair, mashing our lips together. He tasted sweet and clean, his lips wet with me, and I could've climbed on him again. He came with a tense arch of his body, eyes shut. Vinn's breathless kisses faded to a peck on my cheek.

I snuggled against him, our legs intertwined.

"I'm taking you to Paris for our honeymoon."

My heart squealed. "When?"

"As soon as we roll out of bed."

Easier said than done. The high of marrying my dream-man wrapped me in a stupefying bliss that had no interest in doing anything but him. Eventually, we had to eat, so we wandered into the kitchen and finished the breakfast leftovers. Then Vinn dragged me into the walk-in closet.

He crammed his suitcase with shorts and T-shirts until I made him check in a suit, so he retaliated by grabbing a scantily clad number from my wardrobe. Laughing, we rolled our bags outside and whisked to the airport. During the eight-hour plane ride, I read Vinn's dog-eared travel book. It tickled me that he'd already marked it up with notes. I killed the rest of the time by sleeping—I really needed to catch up on z's—and woke up at the flight attendant's voice crackling on the speaker.

I plastered my face to the window as the gray sprawl of Paris broke through clouds. His heavy weight leaned into me. Heat burst through my chest. I hugged him, kissing him hard.

Vinn granite lips curved. "You act like you've never been abroad."

"It's different with you."

I love you.

The words fought for freedom as he patted my arm, pink in the cheeks.

After we landed, the cab took us to a small apartment over a cobblestoned street in the Marais. Vinn stopped at a grocery store for cold cuts, cheese, and a baguette. Then he took our suitcases up the narrow staircase into a dingy flat.

"I know it's not a five-star hotel, but this is the better way to travel. Trust me." He slid the bread over the kitchen table and washed his hands. "You want lunch?"

I grasped him from behind and held him for a solid

minute, refusing to release when he gently pulled at my arms.

Vinn tensed. "You letting me go anytime this century?"

"Nope."

"All right then."

He guided us into the bedroom with me trailing him. I laughed as we faced the tiniest double bed.

"That can fit one of my ass cheeks, maybe."

"We'll make it work." He yanked me on the mattress.

"Have you been to Paris before?"

He nodded. "A few times."

"Did you go with someone?"

"With a girl, you mean?" Vinn's mouth curled as heat stole over my face. "No. Never wanted to."

My pulse pounded. "Why not?"

"Nico gave me advice once. About marriage. I took it to heart, I guess." Vinn's fingers trailed my temple. "If you find a woman you think is the one, travel the world with her. Visit places that are hard to get to. And when you come back to Boston, if you're still speaking to her, marry her at the airport."

"But you did everything backwards."

"I figured the fake engagement thing was close enough. Stress either pushes couples apart, or it binds them closer. You and I have that covered. Don't we?"

We did.

My stomach knotted. "Have you ever been in love?"

He hesitated. "No. You?"

I pictured Vinn as a younger man, that beaming smile, his hand closing mine over the shell. Then I thought about his murder confession and all the things I'd done in the name of love.

I met Vinn's soft eyes, hesitating.

I couldn't lie to him.

"Yes."

"Love seems to make people miserable as hell." He darkened as his gaze dipped to my throat, at the seashell hanging there.

"Sometimes it really hurts." I gripped his hand, flipping it over to admire the gold band. "It's like drowning and breathing the sweetest air at the same time. It's the best thing that ever happened to me."

I smiled at him, but Vinn glowered.

He grabbed my neck. He hovered an inch from me, bristling. "*I'm* the best thing that ever happened to you. Don't you forget it."

Of course you are, you idiot.

I love you.

TELL HIM. *You're married.*

It made no sense to keep the truth from my husband,

except for the violent fear jangling my nerves whenever I opened my mouth. I'd already said *I-love-you* in so many ways. I'd skipped classes during midterms so he wouldn't be alone while he recovered in the hospital. I should've confessed, but the past decade had thoroughly jaded me.

He would never love me.

Maybe it was beyond him.

I needed to live with that and stop forcing him into a box, but my heart broke at the idea of never being loved. What if I told him, and he patted my shoulder like I'd paid him a nice compliment?

The battle waged within me as we spent the day sightseeing. We visited art museums, kissed under the Eiffel Tower, and ate brunch. I had a bounce in my step, but what I looked forward to most was wrapping up the evening in bed.

We retired to the flat after dinner to "rest," which was code for "fuck" because he pressed me against the wall the second we closed the door.

My pack hit the floor.

His elbow bumped the switch, bathing us in semi-darkness. Outdoor lights slid across Vinn's face as he gripped my arms. His punishing hold sent a warning shiver through me. I angled my head. He stiffened when I went for the kiss.

Great. He was in a mood.

"What's got you all bothered?"

He glowered at me, his voice filled with reproach. "Every Frenchman in this city thinks it's all right to ogle my wife."

A fierce breeze swept the wings of my butterflies.

I rolled my eyes. "Nobody's ogling me."

"You haven't noticed, but they are."

"Better not take me to Italy. You know how the men behave over *there*."

"Do I ever."

"Or the South of France. Topless beaches."

"Don't tempt me." Vinn's hands glided to my waist as he guided us toward the living room. "I'll have us there in an afternoon just so I could admire the light from the water bouncing off your tits."

I laughed. "Then everyone else could see me."

"They would have my permission."

I gaped at him. "Really?"

"There's a big difference when *I* invite others to watch what they will never be allowed to..." he broke off, his fingers brushing my breasts, "*touch*."

My blood pounded like an awakened river. He fondled one globe, his thumb teasing my nipple to hardness. I went limp. All day, we'd exchanged chaste kisses because Vinn wasn't a fan of PDA. My body sang as he slipped under my bra. His warmth enveloped my tits, and he squeezed, dragging a moan from me. Then he ripped the shirt over my head. My seashell dangled on my neck.

He gripped the chain. "I will fuck him out of you."

Good luck with that.

Holding the necklace like a leash, he yanked down.

My knees hit the floor.

His fist balled my hair and the golden string. His expression was tight with strain, as though he'd held off on dominating me, and it had cost him. He smiled, but it was without humor, and the tension grew between us, stretched beyond endurance.

"Who do you belong to?"

My pulse beat erratically. "You. Always."

"Show me."

A hot tide surged into my thighs. I stared at him, amazed by the enthusiasm his command gave me. I unzipped his jeans and tugged them down my husband's gorgeous legs. I stopped to stroke the slab of thigh muscle before splaying over the bulge straining against the fabric.

He was so hard. His briefs didn't want to come down. I pulled the elastic, and the heavy weight of him dropped into my hand. I leaned forward, hands braced on him. My tongue traced the head throbbing with his heartbeat, and then he tightened his hold. I cringed at the hair-pulling as much as I relished his possession.

He slid inside my mouth, velvet wrapped around

steel. He didn't give me time to adjust. Vinn took his pleasure first. A sensual flame ignited in my pussy. Slick arousal pooled into my panties as he sawed my tongue. It was a relief for him to seize control so he could fuck me however he pleased, to submit to this burning ecstasy. We might've not known what to do with our words, but our bodies communicated just fine.

Vinn tapped my cheek. "Do you want them to see?"

I looked at the half-open window, tempting a breeze. We weren't that high above street level. Anybody could glance up and see Vinn taking my mouth.

I reeled back, gasping.

"I didn't tell you to take my cock out," he chastised, forcing me to swallow him. "Answer my question."

I murmured a yes, but all that came out was an unintelligible gurgle.

Vinn rolled his hips, stabbing deep. "Sorry?"

My cheeks burned as I nodded.

"Good girl."

The compliment stroked me with feathers. Then he dragged me toward the window.

He gripped my head and pushed inside me. His hips pulsed, fucking me until my throat was raw. His tortured groans radiated to my pussy.

As if I were drugged, my senses slowed. Shivers of wanting rippled through my body, the look in his eyes so stimulating that the window disappeared. He claimed me, testing my boundaries until he'd anchored himself.

He gritted his teeth, holding me there.

My lungs screamed for air. I dug into his legs, and he drew out and jerked me upright. I breathed deeply as he placed my palms over the windowsill.

"Bend over."

I obeyed, distracted by the ache clenching on air.

He unzipped my skirt, sliding off my panties. Then he hooked his head over my shoulder.

"Stay."

My nipples tingled as he left the room to rummage through a suitcase. He returned, his body warming my back.

"Guess what I brought from home?" He revealed a small butt plug in his fist. "I just bought it. Yours were a bit too adventurous for the first time."

Oh my God.

He stuck it in my mouth. "Get it nice and wet."

My heartbeat skyrocketed as I lapped around it, shivering from the magic of his touch. His big hand held my face as he pulsed the toy between my lips.

I murmured something.

He took it out. "What's that?"

"I said, aren't you going to use your cock?"

"Hold your horses. You need to be eased into it." He

replaced the plug and nipped my ear. "Hands on the wall. Keep sucking."

He moved behind me. A moan shivered through my clenched teeth as his thighs pressed into mine. A blunt edge glided in the river of my arousal before he shoved inside.

No condom.

Jesus, we were playing fast and loose with the condoms, but I stopped caring after the third thrust like always. He fit so perfectly that it was sacrilege to erect a barrier between us. We were two incomplete wholes, shoving into each other. It was divine ecstasy.

I gasped.

"Keep sucking."

I obeyed as he plowed into me, but Vinn's steady, brutal thrusts made it hard to concentrate on anything else. My senses reeled as though short-circuited as he stroked my belly and hips. He tapped my clit, showering my body with sparks. He plunged deep, knocking the breath from my lungs.

I almost dropped the toy.

He yanked my hair, forcing me to arch. Then he took the plug from my mouth. A coolness slipped down my skin. The rubber skimmed my ass, circling to a forbidden spot. He teased the opening as he fucked me, and I bit my lip against the groan.

"Somebody's looking."

I choked, my eyes flying open. "Really?"

"Yeah, some guy."

Sure enough, a man in a parka stood in the middle of the street, head angled toward us. He was too far to read his expression.

My breath quickened, and my cheeks warmed. My burning shame rushed down, claiming my neck, shoulders, and breasts. The thrill of being watched flooded me with unexpected heat. So wrong. Why did it make me want to widen my legs?

Vinn traced my breasts and impaled me with jerks of his hips. He worked the toy inside, and, as he did, my walls protested. It was a giant invasion, but the overwhelming fullness tingled my pussy.

This was incredible. Dirty. So goddamned hot.

"I'm going to finish inside you, and then I'm fucking your ass. What do you think? You want that?"

"Yes, I—*oh*."

The room split with my moan. Vinn chuckled softly, and then he fucked me in earnest. For a solid minute, I was nothing but a body to make Vinn come. His tempo increased. I came apart from the merciless pounding, and then he made a desperate sound that clenched inside me. I came as sweet warmth pulsed from his cock. My thighs shuddered, and a peace entered my being.

He eased the toy out, the delicious fullness ripped away. I ached with the void. Then he squirted lube all over me, shoving it inside with his fingers. Slowly, he pushed. I gasped at the blunt edge warring with my body, which wanted to tighten.

"Relax," he said hoarsely, stroking my back. "This part hurts the most. Once my head is inside, it'll feel better."

My mouth gaped as the slick pressure widened me. God, it was so naughty, so against what I'd been led to believe that I was supposed to enjoy. My pussy contracted against the ache not quite rubbing in the right spot. He went slow, and then a buzz hit the air and suddenly—electricity shot into my clit.

He massaged it before shoving another toy in my pussy. It anchored over my clit. I'd never been filled like this. My body shattered and melted as he picked up speed. He rubbed in lazy circles.

Everything was hazy except for the blinding pleasure in my pussy. I might've screamed as I came, shuddering and crying. I was thrown into a tsunami that yanked me deep into the undertow, the sensation violent, like water flooding my lungs.

His cock pulsed, filling me with seed. He pulled out and dragged me into his arms, taking me to bed. He balled me into his chest, soothing me from the shock of shattering that last barrier.

He wiped the tears tracking my face and ghosted kisses to my neck until he reached my ear.

"You're the best I've ever had."

That swelled behind my ribs, pleasing and disappointing me.

I fulfilled his desire, but sex with him tore apart my *soul*.

He cradled me until I almost drifted off, when a loud shriek jerked me into alertness. Vinn disengaged from me, the floorboards creaking as he sat upright.

He answered the phone. "What is it?"

He sucked in air, the irritation smoothed from his face as a voice blasted from the speaker.

"Nico was shot. He's dead."

TWENTY-FOUR
VINN

COSTA FAMILY DON KILLED BY LEGION MC.

Headlines everywhere blazed with the lie. The killer had strolled through Nico's gated community and shot him while he picked up the newspaper. Authorities found him in his bathrobe, sprawled on the pavement. A tip from the police department informed me that there hadn't been signs of forced entry, so the killer had access to Mob Row, Nico's coveted cul-de-sac of connected gangsters. Within hours, leaked photos of his corpse flashed over the dark web, posted by a biker claiming responsibility for the murder.

A robust PR campaign rolled over social media, blasting Legion MC. Somebody with lots of cash tied up the crime in a fucking bow.

We sat outside in folded chairs under a troubled sky.

The cemetery echoed with the quiet sobbing of his mistress, a girl about Liana's age. She was probably upset that she'd get jack shit from his dead ass. No way he'd have left her any money. Michael stared daggers at me as his five-year-old son yanked on his tie. He'd finally noticed the rings on our fingers, and he wasn't happy we'd eloped.

Deal with it, buddy.

Liana palmed my chest. "Vinny, you okay?"

Her hair glistened like polished wood, and it tumbled down her back. Soft color slicked her mouth. The black velvet of her dress highlighted her firm tits.

Damn, she was beautiful. It stirred something inside me.

"I'm still recovering from my botched honeymoon, but I'll be fine."

She glared at me.

"What? Am I not allowed to mope at a funeral?"

"Not about *yourself*."

I buried the smile fighting for release as pink patches burned high on her cheeks. I couldn't help but feel light. If our brief trip was any indication, I'd have my hands full satisfying my kinky wife.

I counted down the minutes to Nico's service, which ended with an anticlimactic thud. As his coffin lowered into the ground, his mistress let out a hysterical cry, and I fought not to roll my eyes.

Alessio lingered the longest. His mouth twisted as he stormed off, kicking over empty seats. Michael barely glanced at the grave. He paid his respects and zoomed to his car with his family—thank god he hadn't asked about my wedding ring.

As the cemetery emptied of people, I stayed put. I was replacing a man I'd admired my whole life. Heaviness weighed my chest as I mused on a memory of Uncle Nico loading up my backpack with Anthony's old toys.

Li rubbed warmth into my hands as the sun dipped behind clouds, throwing us into a chill. The sky had darkened to a dim blue when a man in a suit trudged up the hill. My gaze skipped over him, but not the two bikers flanking him.

"Rage Machine," I growled, reaching for my gun.

"What the hell are they doing here?"

"No idea."

I dragged Li upright, heart pounding. My soldiers headed off the group. Vitale halted mid-stride, gaping at the man. "Tony?"

Liana staggered. "Is that *Anthony*?"

No fucking way. He couldn't be here.

Anthony Costa was thousands of miles away, shackled to a wall, trapped in servitude, not strolling to his father's grave. The man in slacks and a black sweater passed me without a flicker of recognition and stopped at the hole in the ground.

It *was* him.

Anthony had packed on what seemed like thirty pounds of muscle since his disappearance. He had tanned to a rich bronze. He might've just immigrated from Sicily. His demeanor had changed, too. Anthony had a magnetic personality when he wasn't loaded on drugs, but the healthy complexion hinted otherwise. This grim-faced Anthony imposter could've blended in a subway of people.

I approached him, my skin tingling. "Hey."

He stared at the grave as though he wanted to fall inside. He blinked, stepped back, and raked his hair.

"Hey, Vinn."

My mind reeled. "Sorry for your loss."

Anthony didn't respond, but gloom stoked in his gaze. Something spoke to me from his eyes. They seemed tortured, enraged, and calm, shifting from one extreme to the next. A deep fracture had split him open. He was like a poorly healed wound. His nodded at Liana.

"You and Michael's sister," he commented mildly. "Never saw that coming. Congrats."

"Anthony, what's going on? How did you get here?"

Anthony fished a cigarette from his pocket, the flame eating the darkness. Then he slowly walked down the hill.

Was he ignoring me?

Liana's moonlike face reflected my bewilderment.

I followed him. "Anthony, wait. We need to talk."

"Let's do this another time."

What the hell?

The abrupt dismissal almost pulled my lips into a smile. "Anthony, you were missing for fifteen months. You can't expect me to let it go."

"Thirteen. I've been home for a while."

My guts clenched. "I don't understand."

Anthony stopped his descent. "It's a long story."

I waited, but he never elaborated. "Where have you been?"

"In a loft downtown."

"In a loft," I echoed. "Downtown."

"That's what I said."

"Why didn't you go to your dad?" I wiped my face as he fell into silence, my temptation to strangle him rising. "You know how many people are looking for you? Do you have any idea what we've been through because of you?"

He folded his arms. "Keep telling me how bad it has been for *you*."

"Fuck you, Anthony. Your dad was riding my ass, threatening me, *aching* to kill me because he thought it was my fault you were kidnapped. You've been here for *months*?"

He stood there mutely, like a soldier at attention. "It hasn't been a picnic for me, kid."

Who the fuck was he calling *kid*?

"*What happened?*"

His hollow gaze cut at me. "Nothing I want to talk about."

"Did they make you a slave?" Liana elbowed me hard, and a twinge of remorse nagged at me. "*Sorry*."

"No, I wasn't a fucking slave." His lips pulled into a hard, cold-eyed smile. "I'm back. I'm alive. It was a learning experience. And it's also none of your goddamned business."

Liana gasped.

My insides squirmed as I wrestled with a feeling I'd never experienced with Anthony—sympathy.

I glared at the bikers standing behind him. "And you're with them because?"

Anthony motioned at his goons hanging around him. "Give us some space."

"Sure thing, Tony."

They trudged down the hill like obedient lapdogs. Rage Machine doing the bidding of Anthony, a man who couldn't get to his sobriety meetings on time, stunned me more than anything.

Suddenly, a missing puzzle piece clicked in my head.

He was working with them.

"I'm using them to kill Legion," he said, shooting me a dead-eyed look. "I've been funding the war against them. I'm killing the MCs, starting with the biggest one in Boston."

My mind exploded. "You're why Boston's a fucking war zone?"

"It's not just me," he rasped in that toneless voice. "There are others."

Was I witnessing a man's mental breakdown?

"Anthony, go to rehab—"

"I'm stone-cold sober."

I had plenty of reason to doubt him based on the thousands of times he'd repeated those words.

"Your father died," I reasoned. "Maybe you should take it easy."

"I'm done being your charity case, V. All you need to worry about is the new direction I'm taking the Family."

My insides flipped. "Since when do I follow your fucking orders?"

"You don't have a choice. Daddy left me everything. It's all in his will. I'll send you a copy. He gave me the empire, so I will do whatever the fuck I want. And I'm killing every last scumbag on a bike."

"You think you can *walk in* and take my fucking job?"

"I'm not interested in being boss." He flicked his cigarette at my shoes, the spark dying in the wet grass. "I have something much better."

TWENTY-FIVE
VINN

Anthony had no interest in being a Costa.

He blew off a homecoming party, refused to talk to anyone that wasn't me, and acted like we were strangers on phone calls, but he made good on his promise for the first time in his life. He didn't want my job.

He had an axe to grind against Legion.

So did I.

I didn't mind Anthony's directive to fuck over the MCs because frankly, I'd always loathed bikers. Killian's attitude toward my wife had cemented that view. The creep stalking Liana needed to die, and Anthony had given me the perfect opportunity.

My most pressing issue wasn't Anthony or the Family. It was the pressure tightening my throat when I went home. Liana had spent the last few weeks immersed in research. Anthony's reappearance had inspired her to "do more," or so she kept saying. I opened her laptop days ago, and a dozen different tabs related to human trafficking filled her browser. I snorted, glancing at a cover letter she'd written for an internship at a charity.

My wife, the humanitarian.

Our differences amused me to no end. I admired that she spent so much energy helping people and pushing me to do the same. I'd grudgingly agreed to volunteer for Habitat for Humanity with her, like an idiot. She'd convinced me to run a toy charity drive for needy children in Dorchester, and I'd conceded.

I had to pull back.

If this woman looked at me with her stormy blue eyes and whispered *please*, I'd do anything for her, and it pitted my stomach with dread. I should've been content with owning her, fucking her, but as long as she wore the necklace...I was miserable.

It taunted me every day, a constant reminder of who I was. Who I wasn't. More than once, I'd fantasized about taking a hammer to it. Grinding that salmon-colored monstrosity to dust. I couldn't stand the thing. She'd started shoving it in her nightstand, but I couldn't forget the other man. I couldn't let it go. I raked her social media profile to find out who the fuck it was for the twentieth time.

My office doors burst open, admitting a flustered Liana. She was terrible with boundaries, and it irked me.

I slammed my laptop shut. "Can you knock?"

Red patched burned high on Liana's cheeks. She wore a smoldering look that sometimes meant she was down to fuck.

"We need to talk."

My mood nosedived. "If you're here to rope me into another charity event, I have one word for you—*No.*"

That came out nastier than I'd intended. It'd been a bad day. Liana had a string of guys vying for her goddamn attention in her text messages, and one of them had invited her out for coffee. She turned him down, but that didn't stop me from scouring his personal information and sending Vitale to his apartment with explicit instructions. She was probably pissed about that.

I didn't care.

"Did you send Vitale to threaten my classmate?"

I smiled. "Of course."

"Why would you do that?"

Because I had no self-control with my wife. Because the idea of her sitting down with someone else boiled my blood.

I cocked my head, refusing to respond.

A thin smile staggered across her face. "You know, I thought you cared about me. I was *stupid* enough to believe you had a good side, but you've gone too far this time."

I didn't like where this was going.

She stormed to my desk, her hair flying as she slapped a piece of paper down. I glanced over the business card, and my insides ripped apart.

Flatstick Pub

Her stare impaled me. "Tell me you had nothing to do with his disappearance."

Fuck.

Liana swept around the chair, hand on my arm. "*Please,* Vinn."

Her suffocated whisper tightened my chest. I couldn't lie to her, but what would happen when I confessed? A rapid chill encased my limbs in ice. My brain froze with an image of her storming out the door. A wave of dizziness passed over me.

No.

She couldn't leave.

"Vinny."

"He's dead, Li."

Hurt lay naked in her soft eyes. She cupped her mouth, gasping.

My heart squeezed.

Fuck.

"Does human life mean that little to you?"

An inner torment gnawed at me. "Do you want honesty or are you just looking to feel better?"

"Honesty!"

I flinched. "I don't see why I should care about everyone."

"That's soulless," she hissed.

"Maybe I don't have a fucking soul, then. Is that what you want to hear?" I shouted, agony piercing my stomach when she backed away. "Wait. Honey, I'm still the same man."

She palmed her face with trembling hands, crying. "That's what scares me."

I sighed heavily. "You know what the Marines' unofficial motto is? *Get some*. We chanted it all the time. Whenever someone brags about getting laid. Whenever we fired our weapons. Whenever we killed. Especially when we killed. There was no hesitation when I took a life, and that feeling hasn't changed."

"James was not a soldier!"

"No, he was a predator."

"You think you're judge, jury, and executioner?" she screamed, and I flinched. "You can't kill people for making a—"

"Don't you call it a fucking mistake."

"I didn't want him to *die*. I might've hated him, but I'd never ask you to do that."

She wrapped her arms around herself and broke down.

A deep pain in my chest twisted and turned.

"Liana, it wasn't you," I said hoarsely. "It was all me."

"You've made me feel like I've killed someone!"

I palmed her shoulder.

She cringed as though I'd struck her. "If I had said nothing, he'd still be alive."

"Yes, he would," I deadpanned, shrugging. "I caught him sprinkling powder in a girl's drink, just like he probably did yours. I won't apologize for what I did. That asshole deserved to die. Look me in the eye, and tell me your friend isn't better off."

Liana wiped her eyes, trembling. "It wasn't for me. You didn't kill him for the safety of other women. You were such in a hurry to defend my honor that you didn't consider my feelings."

"Li, I never would've put that burden on you."

"You don't get it," she moaned. "It's a betrayal. You killed someone after I confided in you."

My first instinct to argue smoldered as that sunk in, adding fuel to the fiery gnawing. She was right.

I'd shot him because I'd despised the bastard.

My innocent wife gave me the perfect excuse. I'd traded her trust for my pride. She'd never look at me the same if she looked at me at all. And I couldn't promise I wouldn't do it again.

My cheeks burned as I grasped her hands, a violent battle wrestling in my heart. An apology hung on my lips. Then a pink-and-white piece of jewelry reminded me why I couldn't let her go.

I took her face and kissed her.

She shoved my chest. Her groans faded to whimpers as I crushed her mouth in a bruising kiss. I dragged her to the floor and made her forget how much she loathed me. Then I carried her to bed and did it again, and I would've kept going if not for her gentle breaths warming my neck.

Halfway through the night, she slipped out of my arms and tiptoed into the walk-in closet. Her frantic packing pitted my stomach with bitterness. I didn't stop her, even though it killed me.

Don't go. Please.

Liana paused, lugging a duffel bag. She seemed to look in my direction, where I pretended to sleep.

Then she ran out the door.

TWENTY-SIX

LIANA

"Hey. Can I crash here for a few days?"

Carmela's pretty face registered shock. The strap dug into my muscle, and the bag hit the ground after I staggered into the house.

Michael was out on a business trip, which was why I'd headed straight for their place. I didn't want to field a million questions about my relationship with Vinn to my overprotective brother.

Carmela gave me a searching look. "Does Michael know you're here?"

"Let's not tell him. You know how he gets."

Carmela bit her pink lip. "I won't mention it until he's back."

I shuffled defeatedly in Michael's mansion dominated by steel blues and earthy browns. It was the opposite of Vinn's stark white and black apartment. As I stepped into Michael's bright kitchen, longing wrenched at my gut.

They were a perfect family.

Carmela fed Baby Luke in a highchair, mopping the applesauce that rolled down his chin. Mariette and Matteo ate their waffles. The children screamed a greeting before I lugged the bag to a guest room.

When I returned, Carmela busied herself in the kitchen, grabbing plates as I limped to the table.

"Eggs?"

My stomach turned. "No thanks."

I had no appetite.

My guts clenched when I imagined Vinn at home, alone.

I wished I hated him.

I soul-searched as I sat there, digesting his terrible crime. I'd always known he was capable of murder. Michael had hinted at it plenty of times, but I hadn't expected him to kill a man who'd wronged me. Though a small part of me agreed with Vinn.

Queenie *was* better off.

A second later, I loathed myself.

Vinn tried to do good, in his own twisted way. Wasn't that better than the monstrous version I'd led myself to believe?

Vinn's motivations were the same as mine. Family first.

He just took that to extreme lengths.

You're making excuses.

Doubt plagued my conscience. I loved Vinn, but he scared me. He'd already compromised my soul, and now he'd added *murder* to the list.

Regret hit me hard after another day of being stuck in Michael's home, awaiting my brother's return, gently refusing Carmela's attempts to talk. I helped her fold laundry in the living room while the kids watched a movie. My fingers smoothed the Boston Bruins onesie I'd bought for Luke. A lump lodged in my throat.

It became a surge of nausea.

Carmela grasped my wrist. "Are you okay, sweetie?"

I shook my head and ran.

I dove into the bathroom, slapped the seat against the bowl, and vomited. I huddled the toilet all afternoon, purging. It was relentless, and the awful feeling festered in my stomach.

Carmela wet a rag and pressed it to my forehead. "Maybe we should call your OB/GYN."

Alarm zipped down my spine.

I forgot about the stupid fake pregnancy.

"No doctors." I wiped and rinsed my mouth, never so tired in my life. "It's probably nerves."

A distant door opened and slammed.

Michael's hearty voice echoed through the house. A pitter-patter of feet stampeded toward the foyer. My heart swam in a murky swamp of regret and longing as Michael greeted his wife with a purr.

I didn't want to be here.

I'd hoped Vinn would swing by and demand I return to him, that he'd sense my distress over the distance, drag me into his arms, tell me everything would be fine.

That he loved me.

God, I needed him to love me, but it was hopeless.

He wouldn't or couldn't remember what he'd meant to me, and waiting for him to figure it out wasted my time.

A small body hit my back. Two little hands clutched my middle. I turned around, at Matteo's sweet face beaming at me, and burst into tears. I hugged my nephew and sobbed, the hug triggering a deep agony. I might find someone else to love me, but I'd never love another man as much as *him*.

"Don't cry, Zia." Matteo patted my hair. "It's okay."

"Honey, go play with your sister."

My insides twisted as Michael appeared, peeling his son away. He shooed him away and returned in a flash of Derby shoes and a suit. He'd planted himself in front of me, his brows knitted.

"What's going on? Carmela says you've been here for *three days*."

I shook my head, sobbing. "Nothing."

"I have the right to know what that asshole did to you."

If I told him about James, he'd probably call me insane for being upset.

"Before him, you were moving on. Dating other guys. Finding yourself." He sighed heavily, slapping his thighs. "Now you're miserable. Pregnant. He's not even taking care of you."

"He doesn't love me," I choked as I finally admitted it. "I thought it wouldn't matter. I hoped he'd change."

"Didn't I warn you so many times?" A note of desperation tore his voice. "Why didn't you let me set you up with another guy?"

"Because I don't want someone else! I love him!"

Michael stooped to one knee. He dragged me into a fierce hug that melted every last ice wall as I sagged into my brother's arms.

"You don't have to be with him, Li."

Vinn didn't love me.

Vinn kept secrets from me.

Vinn gave me everything but his heart.

Wild grief consumed me, and I couldn't stop crying. I clung to Michael's shoulder as he pulled me past his shocked children.

"He has a responsibility to you," he began, his tone dropping a thousand degrees. "You're sick, and he's leaving you here. I'll kill him. I've had it!"

Michael shot upright and ripped off his jacket. My heart slammed into my chest as he grabbed his keys and headed for the door.

Carmela watched him, brows knitted. "You just got here."

"I'm going over there and giving him a piece of my mind."

"Michael." Carmela followed him, her angry tones blasting through the mansion. "Stop getting involved."

"Sweetheart, she's my sister. He knocked her up and threw her away." Michael shouted down his wife. "I love you, but stay out of this!"

Carmela staggered down the steps, yelling after him. "Don't do anything stupid!"

I ran outside as he climbed into his car.

"Fucking men." Carmela sighed hard. "I love your brother, but Jesus. He has a temper."

She didn't understand the danger.

I'll kill him.

Michael wasn't kidding.

TWENTY-SEVEN

VINN

I craved alcohol like oxygen.

When I reached for the bottle, Liana's soft *don't do this to yourself* whispered in my ear. She was my strength, but it was funny. I had no interest in eating when she wasn't around.

Life dragged. It'd only been a couple of days, but every second ticking by mocked me. I faced a bleak future without Liana. I'd never hated my existence more, not even while I was being court-martialed, or the months after, in which I abused every drug imaginable, and Michael had found me nodding off with a tube wrapping my arm.

Losing her had ruined me. It was like slow suicide. More than once, I jumped into my car to go drag her from Michael's. I still considered her mine. Nothing could change that but divorce and a restraining order. Because I fucking loved her.

I loved her.

It was the only reason I *hadn't* stormed Michael's home. She had to choose, and I hoped to hell she'd choose me. I desperately needed her. I looked for ways to keep her, and thought of her grief over Daniel. That I had no self-awareness. I hurt people.

She was right, so I spent the week performing good deeds. I sent flowers to Queenie with a nice message. If James were alive, I would've put him in jail, but since he wasn't, I called the Bourton dean and told him someone I knew was sexually assaulted at James's fraternity. The next day it was shut down. The news outlets rolled with a storm of articles condemning campus rape and the Greek system's toxicity combined with grisly stories from Bourton alumni.

Why did I want to help?

I felt closer to Liana when I was less of an asshole. It made me drive through Boston aimlessly until I stopped at Alessio's house. I hadn't been here in ages.

Heavy rain drenched my shoulders before I'd stepped through the wrought-iron gate. The red door swung open as I reached the gables.

Alessio walked out, his dark eyes narrowing as I approached. He crossed his arms.

"What the hell are you doing here?"

Honestly, I don't know. "I wanted to talk to you and Mia."

Alessio's mouth twisted. He had good reason for hating that idea. I'd kidnapped his wife a couple of years ago. I'd rationalized it by telling myself I was saving her, when in reality I'd only done it to lure him out, so I could kill him and succeed him as boss.

"I don't want you anywhere near Mia." His baritone cooled to a condescending whisper. "Jesus, you look like a fucking wreck."

The red door yawned again, and the pint-sized Mia popped under Alessio's arm, cradling their toddler daughter. A deep frown creased her forehead.

"Oh, it's you," she said, her greeting steeped in reproach. "What do you want?"

Coming here had been a desperate move.

I waved aside my hesitation and inhaled deeply. "I let you both down, and I'm sorry. I fucked up, and I'm here to make amends."

Alessio looked like Christmas had come early. He flashed me a wintry smile, sneering. "What is this, some twelve-step bullshit? You don't give a damn about us."

"Then why am I standing in the rain?"

He shook his head. "Go home, Vinn."

"I can't. I have to do something." If it would ease the weight crushing my heart, I'd do anything.

Alessio's smirk carved a dimple into his cheek. His black eyes drilled into me.

"She dumped you, didn't she?"

The fire consuming me dampened.

What if she had?

Alessio folded his arms, grinning like the cat that ate a cage of canaries. "Well, it's about time. That girl is way too good for you."

I turned away, my stomach boiling.

Mia descended the steps, ignoring her husband's warning. She bit her lip. "She left you?"

A pang hit the back of my throat. I couldn't bring myself to answer, because saying it out loud would make it permanent.

"Boy, you're really hurting." Alessio's dark gaze searched me, lapping up my misery like it was gold. "I have to say, seeing you in agony is nice."

Mia's toddler squealed, and Mia passed the baby to Alessio. His face lit up as he shifted, hoisting her. He kissed her. She beamed at him, and a sledgehammer hit my chest.

An ache pulsed inside me, new and terrifying, but real. I gritted my teeth. I raked my hair, tearing away from the infuriating sight of their wholesome happiness.

I bolted down the path.

"Wait. Vinn, hold on." Mia jogged to my side, stopping me. "Come back."

"Mia, let him go."

She frowned at her husband. "It doesn't hurt to hear him out."

Alessio released an exaggerated sigh and waved me forward.

"I'm tired of butting heads with you, so name your fucking price."

"Fine." Alessio rolled his eyes. "Make me partner in all your construction firms."

I glowered at him. "That's a big ask."

"Hey, you're the one seeking amends."

He'd thrown that out to test me, but my anguish was so acute it punctured my lungs with every breath.

I sighed. "Fuck. Fine."

His laughter grated my ears. "Seriously?"

"I'll make you a managing partner. You'll have executive powers."

"I don't care about that," he snapped. "I just want your money."

"I'll give you a twenty-percent stake."

"Thirty-five," he shot.

"Twenty-five."

Alessio shrugged and offered me a hand. "Deal."

I shook it, as an inner voice screamed. By far, the worst deal I'd ever made, but it'd be worth it if it convinced Liana I wasn't a hopeless asshole.

He held onto me, smirking. "Having a conscience gets expensive, doesn't it?"

You have no idea.

My gaze slid to his wife. "What about you?"

"Ask him for another twenty-five, honey."

Mia ignored her husband and smiled at me. "I don't need anything, Vinn. I forgive you."

Alessio tutted. "Terrible negotiator."

I stepped back, well aware I'd signed over hundreds of thousands of dollars. "So we're good?"

"Yeah," Alessio muttered after a long pause. "I think so."

"Maybe I'll have you both over some time."

Alessio quirked an eyebrow. "Let's not get ahead of ourselves."

Mia thumped his chest. "We'd love that."

"I'll see you guys later. Have a nice night."

They gaped at me like I'd said something in a foreign language. As I walked to the car, my loafers drenched, I waited for a weight to lift off my shoulders. Intense nausea and desolation swept over me.

Nothing had changed.

THE NEXT FEW hours were pure torture. It somehow topped being shot, stabbed, and dragged to a mock-execution, because at least she'd still been in my life. I couldn't inhale without a stitch in my ribs. All I'd done since I got home was stare at photos of my wife.

I missed her.

A fist hammered my door.

I tossed my phone aside and yanked it open.

Michael stood in the doorway, his shirt half-untucked, his hair askew like he'd spent the ride to my place clenching it, and darkness billowed over him like a rolling storm. He stepped in, radiating a corrosive contempt that fouled the air.

"Is Liana with you?"

I was so damned pathetic.

"Why, so you can break up with her again?"

He shoved me.

My back hit the console table, pain slicing my spine. He punched my face. Agony exploded across my jaw. My teeth ached. My world spun. Two savage blows knocked out my breath. He'd never hit me like this, even at our worst.

I collapsed, gasping.

"You sent her away, you fucking loser!" Michael's foot whirled, slamming into my stomach. "She's carrying your kid, and you give up on her?"

I rolled over, stunned. I'd never confessed to Michael about the fake pregnancy. The chaos surrounding Nico's death had driven it clean from my mind, and it'd stopped being a fake relationship weeks ago.

"I warned you." He glowered, his shoe pressing my neck. "Hurt her, and you're dead."

I gripped his ankle and shoved him off. A blow struck my head, and my vision blacked out. His knuckles bashed my skull, hitting me so hard the echo of grinding bones filled my ears. He refused to let up. His merciless punching slammed me into the ground.

If I didn't stop him, he'd kill me.

I tackled his middle, hurling him into a console table. Michael grunted at the impact. Hissing, he launched at me. I scrambled out of the way, warding him off with a chair.

"Michael, calm down. I didn't send her away."

He batted the chair. "Put it down and fight me."

"No. Let's talk about this."

I had fifty pounds on Michael, and I would murder him. If anything happened to her brother, Liana would be devastated. I couldn't have that on my conscience.

"I'm done with you, buddy."

Michael grabbed his sidearm. He pointed it at me, chest heaving.

I held up my hands. "Do you have to dial everything to eleven?"

"I warned you," he snarled. "I told you what'd happen."

"Christ, Michael. I did nothing wrong. I just—"

"I gave you a chance. You blew it!" His voice tore, the gun trembled. "You used my sister. She is the only sibling I have, and you destroyed her."

His words ripped me apart.

"What—what do you mean? Is she okay?"

"No, she's not, you fucking maniac."

A horrible dread went through me. "She's hurt?"

"Of course she's in pain. Her husband abandoned her with a baby! You kicked her out of your home!" A red flush wrapped his throat as he screamed at the top of his lungs. "You knocked her up, and you can't deal with it."

"Michael, listen to me. She is *not* pregnant—"

"You really can't handle being a father, huh?" he shouted, railroading me. "What a coward."

"Michael, I love her. I'd do anything for her." I backed into the couch as Michael advanced, his eyes flashing. "Look at me, and tell me you don't believe me."

His hazel pools bored into mine. "Then why is she at my house?"

"It's complicated."

"Explain."

I strolled into the kitchen and poured myself water. My grip shook, sloshing the contents before the glass reached my mouth. "She would've left me, anyway. She wants someone else."

"What are you talking about?"

A sick yearning yanked at my insides. "There's another guy."

Michael wiped his face, growling. "She said that to make you jealous, you idiot. She loves you. She has since she was a kid. While you were fucking around, she dreamed up names for your future children. She begged me to set you up on a date. She's loved you forever."

I dropped my gaze, startled at blood streaming from my clenched fist. I'd broken the glass. I picked a shard from my skin, but it didn't even sting.

"I don't understand."

Michael snorted. "Of course."

I stiffened as a wave of heat passed through me. Parsing through what he'd told me was like sifting sand. Then it landed on me.

Ice spread through my stomach.

"Why the fuck didn't you say so?"

"The better question is, how did you *not* notice? You're so dense, Vinn." Michael launched into a tirade that seemed years in the making. "She visited you. She brought your favorite dishes to the hospital. She wrote you letters and cried every time she saw you with other girls. What did you think that meant?"

I didn't think about it.

I'd never let my thoughts go there because she was too young, was Michael's sister, and was forbidden on every level. Now that Michael had laid it out, it was so obvious. She'd downplayed her feelings as a crush, and my dumb ass had believed her.

I was so stupid.

A needle-like feeling prickled my face. "So you've talked to her about me."

"Many times."

My heart pounded. "And what did you say?"

"That she should move on," he deadpanned. "Don't give me that look. You're nine years older. You're a dog with women. You never cared about her the way she did about you."

My insides curled up and blackened.

I picked him up by the shirt and slammed him into windows. My vision clouded with sick fantasies. I pictured him begging for his life as I hung him from the balcony. My fist smashed into his jaw. He smacked the ground and tackled my knees. I ripped him away from me. I shoved him into a photo.

Glass shattered over his head.

A second shadow crept along the wall.

"Mike." I jerked my head toward it.

He spun around.

A man's silhouette peeled onto the floor. A man in a leather cut tutted as he stepped out, pointing a gun at Michael, whose Glock lay several feet away.

"You idiots made this too easy. Door's wide open."

Killian slicked his teeth, the sound wrenching at my gut. "Considerate of you. Thanks."

Fuck.

"What are you doing here?" I kept my tone even, trying to buy us time.

"Killing you. Taking your wife." He threaded a hand through his hair. "Where is the little woman?"

"She's not here."

"That's too bad. I wanted your baby doll to see you die." Killian's slack-jawed expression glazed over. "Right before I fuck her over your corpse."

He'd shoot.

He wouldn't miss.

This was how I'd meet my end—at the hands of a two-bit psycho who'd somehow bypassed my security just because Anthony had to get revenge.

A female voice echoed in the house.

"Vinny."

The faint whisper was a desperate wish from my dying brain.

"Vinny?"

Less distant and louder.

No, no, no.

Killian's stare drifted past my shoulder, his mouth parting.

A tremor shook my arm as I slowly turned. My gaze crashed into a pair of soft, blue eyes.

Liana stood in the hallway. She wore the clothes from three days ago. The necklace gleamed on her neck, like a beacon dragging me forward. Her lips parted as though she hadn't noticed Killian.

"Vinny, I—"

"*Run.*"

Her brows furrowed. She hesitated.

She stepped toward me.

A gunshot blasted the air. Something splattered my wrists. I lunged at Killian, who'd lowered his gun. I tackled him. I grabbed his wrist and wrenched, knocking the piece away, and then I dove for it. He yelled. I shoved the barrel under his jaw. Pulled the trigger.

The deafening boom cracked like a thunderbolt.

Killian choked on the hole in his neck. He sputtered and stilled. I threw the Sig on the bloodstained floor, the ringing in my ears dimming to a dull roar punctuated by Michael's screaming.

Why was he yelling?

A small, choking sound fisted my guts.

I whirled as Liana stumbled into the wall. She slid down. A streak of red painted the white, marking her descent. She collapsed, clutching her stomach.

I sprinted to her side. My fingers shook as I dragged her arms from the darkening skirt. A hole buried in her hip filled with crimson. My hands slipped until Michael thrust a towel underneath my palms. Blood soaked through it in seconds. She was bleeding too much, too fast.

Michael dialed 911.

She grasped at my forearms, the tan rapidly drained from her body. Her gaze faded to blue slits. Tears streaked her cheeks, and she mumbled my name.

"Deep breaths, Liana. Don't close your eyes, baby. Please." My free hand cupped her pale cheek. "Stay with me."

I pushed on the wound.

She grimaced.

A sheer, black panic wrapped my chest. I couldn't stop the bleeding.

I blinked.

People stood everywhere. Police and EMS swarmed the apartment. The paramedic listened to her lungs as I screamed. She couldn't breathe. Why was nobody listening? Why—

Someone yanked me away as they loaded her onto a stretcher. She was whisked out of my sight. I rushed after her, but officers pulled me back. They asked me things I didn't understand. Over and over. The same stupid questions that made no sense. Their garbled voices sifted through my brain, like sound passing through water.

She'll be all right.

She'll make it.

A sharp edge stabbed my palm—the seashell.

A dull confusion swirled in my head. I must've ripped it from Liana's neck. As my thumb stroked the familiar surface, my stomach dropped. A gallery of images flashed through my mind.

I gave it to her.

It was me.

TWENTY-EIGHT

VINN

We love each other.
We'll be together.

I muttered the words into my closed palms, as though repeating them triggered a spell that'd make everything right. The bloody necklace wrapped my hands like a rosary. I didn't believe in God, but I fucking prayed. Anguish shattered my last sense of control.

During the hospital ride, I clutched at my hair. I screamed. I rode a wave of intense flashbacks in the waiting room. I covered my face, trembling, a deep pain gnawing at me.

We love each other.
We'll be together.

I wiped my eyes.

White surrounded me, so vivid it burned.

Michael sat a short distance away, probably

drowning in his guilt. His wife massaged his back, whispering hopeful words I clung to.

"She's been in surgery for a long time. That's a good sign, honey."

He nodded and swallowed. "Yeah."

"She'll pull through," she said, her voice thick. "She grew up with you. That means she's stubborn as hell and won't give up."

I tuned her out, unable to hear *give up* without a wrenching agony in my chest. I focused on breathing. In and out. Slow. I counted my breaths as though they might help Liana in the OR.

"Can I get you something? A clean shirt?" Carmela's hand rolled over my shoulder and squeezed. "Cup of coffee?"

I met Carmela's winged gaze.

Save her. Please.

She flinched and let go.

Michael's hot eyes cut at me, and I could've grappled with him on the floor if fighting with him hadn't gotten her hurt in the first place.

A man in blue scrubs emerged from the double doors. He ignored everyone in the waiting room, making a beeline for me.

"Are you Liana Costa's husband?"

I stood. "Yes."

He rubbed his flushed neck. "She's in recovery.

The gunshot caused multiple fractures, and it tore through a major artery, but we were able to stop the bleeding. Her vitals are stable, but she's in critical condition."

His words worked through my frozen brain.

"When can I see her?"

"Right now. One at a time."

He brought me into a maze of dark rooms and showed me to a bed where Liana lay, unrecognizable under the tubes. A suffocating sensation tightened my chest.

It'll be okay.

I gripped her ankle. The relief I'd waited for wouldn't come. I didn't want to leave her, but they made me return to the waiting room, and I sank in the same seat. Michael came and went.

My awareness faded to a dull murmur as hours ticked by. After a gentle suggestion from Carmela and a bundle of clean clothes shoved under my arm, I showered. Liana's blood spiraled the drain. I cleaned her jewelry before dressing in jeans and a T-shirt.

Numbly I headed toward her room. Michael and Carmela already sat vigil at her side. I joined them, winding the necklace around her limp hand, tucking the shell behind her fingers.

Liana's brown waves spilled over the pillowcase, her eyes shut, her body lifeless. Maybe it was the fatigue. It was easy to daydream. The hospital bed melted into a deep orange sunset over water.

"I'm sorry I forgot," I croaked, waiting for a flicker of life. "It was a long time ago, and so much has happened between then and now, but I remember everything—the seagulls, the stack of fried cod, and you begging me to stay. I'm sorry I didn't. I had so many dreams, and I was going to chase them. After a few years of service, the GI bill would've paid for college.

"You were so upset I joined. You stormed up and down the beach, screaming, crying. I couldn't calm you down, so I grabbed a shell off the sand. I pressed it into your hands and promised I'd come back. I told you to hold it when you thought of me."

Her strangled cry echoed in my head—"*I love you, Vinny!*"

"*You too, kid.*"

My eyes pinched.

"They shipped me out, and it was a disaster. I read your letters so many times. I had a major problem with my CO. He did terrible things. It's a long story, but my issues with him escalated until they kicked me out. Then they dumped me in Boston. I couldn't get a loan. I couldn't find a job."

The weight of my story seemed to stifle the air and rise, sucked through the vents.

"I never wanted to be vulnerable again, so I pushed

you away...I'm sorry I didn't catch up until I realized I'd lost you."

There was nothing more to say.

I'd purged it all.

I squeezed her hand.

Michael's chair scraped the floor before he exited. Carmela's fingers threaded my hair before she followed him, leaving me in the machines' horrible noise.

TWENTY-NINE

LIANA

A KISS WOKE me from sleep.

The patch of heat burned high on my cheek, and I smiled stupidly. Blankets weighed me down as I sought my husband's warmth, my fingers brushing a cold surface. Air hissed into my nostrils through plastic tubes that tickled. My eyes cracked open.

Too bright.

I shut them. "Vinny?"

"Right here." He clutched my heavy hand. "How are you feeling?"

The catch in his voice staggered my heart.

I took in the intense white blanketing my sheets, ceiling, and walls.

What the hell?

A violent memory clawed my head, and a knife seemed to saw into my hip. I craned my neck, but the movement pulled at sore muscles. I winced, patting the fabric constricting me. Bandages wrapped my torso.

"You were shot, honey."

A numb shock ricocheted down my spine. "I was?"

"Yeah."

"Where—why?" I blinked, sifting through blurred images. "I don't remember."

"Killian got you. He's dead."

Vinn's jaw clenched. He sat beside me in a hospital chair, wearing a wrinkled gray T-shirt and gym shorts. He seemed wound like a steel spring, his eyes glassy and distant. His hands clasped mine, which curled over something jagged. He stroked me over and over.

"Are you okay?" I coughed.

A miserable smile broke through his melancholy. "You scared me, Liana."

"I'm sorry."

He let out a deep, shuddering breath. "Now I know what it's like on the other side of the curtain."

"Vinn, it's all right. I'm alive, aren't I? It doesn't—hurt that bad."

He softened. "Li, the doctor said you're pregnant."

Shocked wedged the words in my throat. I opened and closed my mouth as a warm glow moved through me.

"Oh."

"*Oh?*"

I fidgeted with the sheets, struggling to contain my grin. "And the baby's okay?"

"So far."

A cry of relief broke from my lips. My hands tingled as though with new life.

How was he taking it?

"Michael told me a few things," he said, smiling broadly. "Like the fact you've had our kids' names picked since you were thirteen."

Nice one, Mike.

My cheeks flushed. "Of course he did."

"So, it's true."

"Josh, Chris, and Vincent."

A secretive grin staggered across his face. "Three boys, huh?"

"I didn't think we'd have any girls—why in God's name am I telling you this? It's *embarrassing*." My mind careened as I struggled to grasp a single thought.

"Your inhibitions are lowered at the moment."

"Taking advantage of a gunshot victim should be beneath you."

He said nothing, but his smirk was enough of a response. "Let's get back to my questions."

"I plead the fifth. Call my attorney."

He leaned forward. "There was never anyone else."

I nodded, sighing.

"You lied to me. Why?"

His hushed voice filled me with a wild hope.

I met his widened gaze, eyes welling.

"Because I wanted you so much. Because putting myself out there for you was terrifying. You would never, *ever* feel the same about me. You would never love me."

An understanding seemed to dawn over Vinn, blowing away the storm clouds that'd darkened his mood.

"You love me?"

"Yes," I murmured, marveling at how easy it was to tell the truth. "Since I was little. I named all my imaginary boyfriends after you. I pictured you every time I thought about dating or marriage, and it drove me crazy that you were always going to be with someone else.

"You were there when my parents died. You turned the worst day of my life into something special, and I loved you for that. I loved you before I understood what it was. I could never stay away from you or get you out of my mind."

Vinn rubbed his forehead, his frown deepening. He was the opposite of composed, red-faced, strung-out, on the verge of exploding. He nudged open my palm.

I relaxed my hand, revealing the seashell necklace. My stomach dropped with the weight of Vinn's torment, and my lips parted with a broken whisper.

"I'm so sorry. I wanted *you* to remember."

His tortured gaze pinned me to the bed. "I do now."

"I took the shell to a jeweler, and he drilled a hole

and put in a cheap string. And I never removed it. Not once. Not even in the shower. When the silver tarnished, I replaced it with gold. I was that obsessed with you."

"I get it. I didn't at first, but I think I understand." He fixed me with a potent stare. "I'm not that man anymore, honey."

"I-I know. It was stupid."

"I still love you. That never changed. Not for one second. No matter what happens, that will *never* change. I love you. I always have." He cupped my face, gliding his thumb across my cheek. "I thought that was obvious."

My throat thickened, and I lost him behind a sheen of tears. "You're not mad?"

"No. I'm the happiest asshole who's ever lived." He paused, grinning. "You're carrying my kid, so that's that. You're stuck with me."

He kissed me.

I burst into happy tears.

TWO WEEKS LATER, I limped into Vinn's car.

He squeezed my hand as I hissed through every pothole home. I shut my eyes through the abnormally long drive, gripping Vinn's palm as we snaked over roads.

A salty scent breezed inside, and then I paid attention to my surroundings. We'd arrived at a colonial house overlooking a misty beach. My jaw dropped as Vinn rolled into the driveway nowhere near Boston.

I gripped the door handle. "Where are we?"

Vinn parked the car. "Your favorite place."

"Salisbury Beach?" I laughed, ignoring the ache in my side. "You're laying it on thick."

"We're staying here for a while."

Excruciating pain had marked my hospital visit. I'd refused everything but over-the-counter meds, determined not to let an opiate touch the baby.

Michael had visited often. It appeared they'd set their feud aside in the face of my difficulties. Vinn still shouted him down when he suggested that I recuperate at his mansion. Carmela had yanked a red-faced Michael out of the room before they started World War Three across my bed.

The timeline of my pregnancy made it obvious that Vinn hadn't betrayed his best friend. Michael wasn't thrilled about being lied to, but at least he didn't hate Vinn for something he'd never done.

Vinn left the car, lugging in two enormous suitcases before he helped me across the green lawn and up the wraparound porch, into the house furnished with quaint furniture.

"I asked Carmela to decorate. I hope you don't mind." Vinn wheeled me into a cozy living room.

I dropped into the couch. "Isn't this a rental?"

"I bought it."

"*What?*"

"Yeah. The doctor was very clear. You need rest, and this is the perfect place." Vinn disappeared to the kitchen and returned with a tall glass of water.

"There are photos of us!"

Ignoring Vinn's protest, I limped toward the fireplace and grabbed the gilded frame I'd kept on my desk. My gaze swam as I fingered our cheerful faces, overcome with a swell of grief and happiness.

Vinn set the cup down, hooking his head over my shoulder. "I thought this would be a nice vacation home. For us and the kid."

My lungs tightened, and I crashed into his chest. I sank my fingers into his shirt and cried, purging every dark feeling that'd plagued me since we'd been separated.

Vinn's big hand caressed my back. He stroked my hair, but I couldn't stop crying.

It wasn't about the house.

Or the gunshot.

It had nothing to do with him, or his fight with Michael, the baby, or the fact my life had been flipped upside-down.

It was hope.

It had died and been rekindled so many times. *We'd be together one day. He would love me.* Life was so fucking cruel. I'd looked in all the wrong places. I'd suffered so needlessly when all I had to say were three words.

He would've said it back.

He loved me, too.

LIANA
FOUR YEARS LATER

Our first boy turned three just days after I graduated from law school. Josh was his father in miniature form—camera-shy, sweet, and introverted. He blew out the candles as my husband cradled our newborn, Vincent.

Josh grinned toothily as the house erupted in cheers, and I scanned the table, grinning at the people who filled my heart. Michael hugged Josh, and helped him cut slices of cake as his four-year-old, Luke, clung to his legs. Carmela passed out paper plates, beaming. Carmela's pixie-like sister clapped her hands, radiant beside her tanned husband, Alessio. Queenie and Vitale ignored the noise as they cozied up in a corner, kissing. My law school buddies clinked their champagne flutes with the few Vinn counted as his friends.

Since we married, Vinn and I had left Boston to the beach home for a month-long vacation every summer.

Then we started inviting Michael's family and his in-laws. It was too crowded, so we built extensions to fit everyone. Eventually, it became a base for barbecues, holidays, and birthdays.

A bottomless peace settled into my soul whenever I stepped inside this place. I exhaled a deep sigh as Vinn slid his arm around my waist. Warmth tingled my cheeks as he kissed the shell of my ear. His thumb stroked the round, circular scar from the gunshot wound.

The recovery had been difficult, especially with a baby on the way. A media firestorm had lit up the local news until Alessio Salvatore threw enough dollars at the CEOs, who pushed the articles out of the circuit. It'd been handled quietly. Vinn had kept the details from me, but the police investigation dropped shortly after they ruled that Killian's death was self-defense.

A faint line creased Vinn's forehead, his gaze riveted to my face before it moved over my body. My heart jolted as his fingers grazed my thigh.

"Your mom's watching the kids tonight. Let's sneak off later and fuck."

His velvety voice dipped heat in my chest.

I drank in the comfort of his closeness, the very air electrified as he nipped my skin. "You sure my brother won't walk in on us?"

I referenced the incident involving an unlocked door

and Michael drunkenly wandering in the wrong bedroom while Vinn and I were preoccupied.

Vinn laughed loudly, something he'd slowly learned to do during our marriage. The best part of my life with him was Vinn blossoming into a devoted father who hosted playdates and always managed a small, tentative smile. The kids had softened his harsh edges. He was still a *don*, but, at least in private, he was my gentle giant.

"Joshie, hold on," Vinn barked, detaching to grab our son. "You need sunscreen."

Vinn slathered the stuff on Josh's body. Michael corralled the children and ushered them outside, where the water mirrored a cloudless sky. Vinn fitted our son with a lifejacket before he brought Josh to the water. They played in the waves, and then Josh decided to build sandcastles with his cousin Luke. Michael's older kids raced the beach.

Vinn's hawklike gaze zeroed on his son as he settled in a chair. "Where's Vincent?"

"Mom has him."

He pulled me onto his lap, and a delicious shudder heated my body. Wrapped in his arms was my favorite place. My heart hammered as I scanned the coast.

"I'm not seeing a lot of places we could get away with being naked."

"Use your imagination, sweetheart." He pressed his

mouth into my ear, jolting my skin. "I've already scouted an area and left supplies."

"*Supplies?*"

"A couple towels…and toys. We'll have fun, provided nobody finds my stash."

"Oh my God, Vinny." A wicked laugh tore from my throat as I pictured two teenagers stumbling upon a bag of lube and vibrators. "You're insane."

"It's not the worst we've done."

My cheeks flared as he scooped up my hand and kissed the knuckle with the wedding ring. I'd hired a jeweler to craft a rose gold band with scalloped seashells among the diamonds.

He caressed the jagged line before finding the necklace. Guilt nagged at me when he locked eyes on it and sighed. I removed it and bundled it into his fist.

I'd released the old Vinny ages ago. It took a while to admit I'd never really known him. I'd worshipped a fantasy, not a real, flawed human being.

"I give you permission to throw it in the sea."

He chuckled. "You have no idea how often I've fantasized about that."

"Do it."

He played with it, fingers rotating the shell.

"Nah," he murmured after a long silence. "I only hated it because I thought you loved someone else. It reminds me of the man I was, the hope, the lightness in my chest before everything went dark. I don't ever want to become that asshole again."

Slowly, he slipped the chain around my head.

He tenderly traced my jaw, the fire spreading into my heart. "Keep it, Li. I like that you never gave up on me. But I think I have you beaten on the obsession front."

A ridiculous grin staggered across my face.

He winked at me, grabbing a wallet from his pocket. He opened it, retrieving a torn, yellowed piece of paper. A wrinkle ran along its edge. He stared at it for a moment and handed it to me.

I took it, recognizing my handwriting.

Love,

Liana

"What's this?" I flipped it, but there was nothing. "My signature? Where'd you get it?"

His gaze dropped as he smiled. "I tore it off one of your letters."

The ripped up letter I'd found stuffed in his shoebox swam to my mind.

I gasped, that long-ago mystery sliding into place.

"I've had it in there forever," he admitted, pink in the cheeks. "I wanted your love with me everywhere I went. Cheesy, I know."

My feelings warred. I could've socked him in the

shoulder for hiding such a sweet gesture from me, and sobbed for the teenage Liana who'd spent years writhing in angst over this man. Emotion thickened my throat. I couldn't speak, but Vinn seemed to understand.

"I love you more than you know."

"I love you, Vinny."

He wiped the tear tracking my cheek. "Take a nap. I'll look after the boys."

I yawned, nodding agreement as he shifted our positions. I watched him through heavily lidded eyes as orange sunbeams sparkled on waves. Vinn kneeled beside Josh, who'd smashed his fist through Luke's sandcastle. He redirected Josh's attention to a sleeping Michael, who lay on a towel.

"Let's bury him alive," Vinn whispered to Josh. "You start at the feet. I'll do the hands."

"Okay!"

Father and son heaped sand over my unsuspecting brother, who hadn't yet noticed the attempt on his life. Vinn upped the ante by squirting lotion into his hand. He wrote FUCK on Michael's back in big white letters, laughing when Carmela swiped through the profanity.

"What you doing, baby?" Michael stirred, jerking away from Vinn. *"What did you do?"*

"Nothing," Vinn said breezily. "Carmela ruined an amazing practical joke."

"Vinn made a joke?" Michael turned on his side,

upsetting the sand burying his ankles. "Am I in a parallel universe?"

Vinn dumped a cup of ice water on Michael's neck. *"Vaffanculo!"*

The children shrieked with laughter as Michael sprang upright. Vinn sprinted into the ocean. Michael gave chase, tackling him. Both fell with a wide splash. Vinn was far from the dreamlike perfection I'd worshipped.

And I didn't care.

I loved him, flaws and all.

# # #

ACKNOWLEDGMENTS

Writing this last book of the Costas was a huge struggle. It fell victim to the The Great Curse of 2020. I went through so many versions and iterations that I could fill two novels with extra scenes. I made a lot of choices in the previous books that made matching the tone of the other books very difficult.

Anthony was never supposed to survive. He was destined to die, just like the man he is based on, Nick Rizzuto Jr. Poor Anthony! I have a lot planned for him. :)

Kelley Harvey, as always, your editing is top-notch. Thank you, Christine LaPorte, Kevin McGrath, and my wonderful readers in the Bad Boy Addicts group.

I love you! Thank you for being so supportive. I couldn't do this without you.

ABOUT THE AUTHOR

Vanessa Waltz loves to write steamy romances. She lives in the Bay Area with two crazy cats. To be the first to know about her new releases, please join her newsletter (no spam, ever).
Vanessa's Newsletter

For more information, follow her here:
www.vanessawaltzbooks.com
info@vanessawaltzbooks.com
Bad Boy Addicts - Facebook Group

Made in the USA
Columbia, SC
07 October 2021